Pray for Us Sinners

My life, my love, I am yours!

MARILYN L.R. HALL

"Pray for Us Sinners," by Marilyn L. R. Hall. ISBN 978-1-62137-548-7 (hardcover); 978-1-62137-549-4 (softcover); 978-1-62137-550-0 (ebook).

Library of Congress Control Number: 2014912481

ACKNOWLEDGMENT

All these stories in this series are completely fictional—and were written for the writer's own creative enjoyment—the characters, incidents and towns, except for the mention of major cities are fictitious and any resemblance to real persons or places is wholly coincidental and unintentional. This has been written over a great number of years—beginning in the mid to late 1940s—when the writer was in her early teens and the story and characters are original with her and her deceased cousin.

GOD CREATED THE WORLD—AND HE SAID, "IT IS GOOD."

God did not create conformity. No two snowflakes are alike. In his divine love, he luxuriantly takes the time to create even each snowflake separately to be unique.

EACH SNOWFLAKE UNIQUE.

Why then does man in his arrogance force square pegs into round holes? Why, in his arrogance, does man demand conformity and in the process destroy the individual works of art that God himself created—and approves and encourages and loves!

Prologue

The angel left her place in choir when she heard her name called and as quick as the thought, she was in the presence of the Father. While the voices of the choirs swelled round her, the eternal light that was the Creator impressed a message upon her heart. Love poured over her, and a thrill of joy shivered her being as the words came alive in her and simultaneously on Earth in the womb of a woman during the act of love with her husband.

Praising and glorifying God, Varda sang her thanksgiving and then, wrapped in the awesome love of her Maker, was again transported in a twinkling—this time to an earthly destination. In her exquisite joy at being designated a guardian, Varda took no notice of her physical surroundings, choosing instead to focus on the woman who had conceived the child who from this moment on would be her special charge—the child she would watch over, guard, protect, and guide safely back to heaven.

The enormity of that responsibility weighed lightly upon her at this moment. For the time being, all she felt was an inexpressible thankfulness to God for the privilege she'd been granted and a tingling anticipation of the actual birth of the child. For now, there was little for her to do anyway, except to get to know the family—the environment—the history, and all that would affect the child. To be an effective guardian, Varda needed to know the baby's background. It would have simplified matters to have been able to ask the mother's own guardian all those pertinent details, but the Creator, in his wisdom had made it impossible for one guardian angel to see another while they were with their charges. Varda couldn't know if Rose Nash's angel was there with her or if she was with the Father in heaven—or taking her place in the choirs— or even, although it was unlikely, being disobedient and abandoning her charge. In any event, such an angel would answer only to the Father, and it was probably for that very reason he had made them invisible to one another on earth.

It would be several weeks before Rose Nash would know that she carried a new life in her body. Because of that, she would continue doing things pretty much as she had up to now. That would be helpful to Varda; it would give her time to get to know the young woman, to learn what kind of mother she would be. So with anxious but joyous eagerness, Varda—God's gracious gift to her daughter—hovered above Rose Sharon Nash and began her new and future existence.

It was the second week of the month of December in the year of our Lord, 1933.

December 1933

Rose awakened long before dawn that morning—jerked to awareness out of a strange dream whose message evaporated even as she struggled to remember it. She sat bolt upright, shivering with excitement and a sense of change in the air, her heart pounding. She hugged the blanket under her chin, staring wide-eyed into an eerie blue-tinged darkness. Something. What? Had reached down into the depths of slumber and jerked her straight up in bed while her flesh tingled into goose bumps. There *was* something different about this new day!

Her sister Claire Louise had always preached that such an electric experience indicated a visitation of the Holy Ghost, and Rose thought it might be considered *blasphemy* to entertain that Mighty Spirit while lying next to Jack Nash in his bed, even if he was asleep. So, cautiously as a cat stalking a bird, she worked her way to the edge of the bed and rolled off it onto the linoleum, which was cold as a chunk of ice against her naked body. Then, though she was shivering hard enough to shake the bed where her husband still slept, she crept into the kitchen. There, her heavy winter coat hung on a nail by the door; with that wrapped around and under her, she knelt in the dark and waited for something to happen.

Nothing did.

Jack would say it was just the cold made her shiver, but she knew it was something a lot more portentous than the apartment's ill-fitting sashes. Sure as Christmas, something good was gonna happen! And oh, Sweet Jesus! Wasn't it about time.

Too excited to go back to sleep, Rose returned to the bedroom to gather her clothes. Jack was lying as she left him; the blankets that covered him moved gently with his soft breathing. She had an urge to climb back beside him and snuggle close to his warm body but discarded that notion and instead grabbed her clothes from the chair where she'd tossed them the night before and high-tailed it into the bathroom.

When she emerged a little while later, she was wearing several layers of clothing and a pair of woolly socks she'd purloined from her husband's bureau drawer. Over them, instead of her shoes which were stiff from the cold, she wore a pair of old felt slippers given to her by her friend Mary Jean, who had lived in this ice-box of a city all her life and knew what to expect once summer was gone.

In the kitchen, she took her apron off the chair, pulled it over her head, and tied it around her before starting a batch of biscuits. They were baking in the oven and the water was bubbling in the coffee-pot when she lit the burner under one skillet to fry some eggs and another for milk gravy. Resentfully, she noted the feeble Chicago-winter sun was just beginning to nudge darkness from the room. Back home in Mississippi—she started thinking, but *remembering* was a foolish waste of time, and besides there wasn't anything she regretted leaving in Mississippi.

Except maybe January.

She heard Jack go into the bathroom and she sent him a merry little "Mornin' Hon," over her shoulder. He acknowledged her greeting with a surly grunt and she smiled understandingly. Jack hated these frigid winter mornings even more than she did.

The eggs sizzling in the skillet and the coffee percolating in the pot made a cozy and comforting music that set Rose's felt-covered foot to tapping and she added a beat by patting the pancake turner against the rim of the skillet. Pretty soon her hips had started to swivel and her mouth flew open, "Mammy's little baby loves shortnin', shortnin'—Mammy's little baby loves shortnin'…" Her song ended right there, though she whispered the final word "bread," just to satisfy her own sense of propriety.

"Squash blossoms!" she chided herself, all too aware of Jack's feelings on the subject.

"Dammit!" Jack's voice exploded from the bathroom. She heard some curse words plain enough and then a long stream of guttural mutterings that she couldn't make out and didn't try to, but she smiled tenderly and blew a consoling kiss in that direction. "Poor darlin'," she crooned. Jack's handsome face was lean and his cleft chin and sharply chiseled jaw with deeply etched dimple lines down both cheeks rarely allowed him to get through his morning shave without inflicting another notch or two on it, no matter how carefully he pruned his whiskers.

Rose had started her tapping and patting and swiveling again and was about ready to burst into song when she heard Jack slam out of the bathroom and stomp off into the bedroom growling and muttering and she realized the recklessness of her behavior. "Oh squash blossoms!" she swore again. On more than one occasion Jack had let her know that she embarrassed him with her "schoolgirl antics" and that he expected her to act with dignity, which wasn't all that easy for her. Sometimes, she just couldn't keep still and act like a lady her age ought to. Sometimes she just had to wiggle and shimmy and jig as if the Spirit himself had a hold of her. She felt real bad about mortifying Jack and she felt tremendous bad whenever he chewed her out over it, but every now and then she just went on and did it anyway. It was her nature to be exuberant and excitable. And sometimes she just felt so good she couldn't resist acting up. Then her grin turned smug—it wasn't like Jack didn't enjoy that side of her personality—especially when the spirit got a hold on him too.

But with Jack's temper already on simmer, she decided not to push her luck, and stiffened her spine and planted her feet and stood there rigidly facing the stove, focusing all her attention on the stirring of the milk gravy.

In a couple of minutes she heard Jack return to the bathroom and took note that he shut the door a little less irately that time. Shortly thereafter, she heard a long, drawn-out groan that shook the plumbing and echoed clear down to the basement, bringing to mind the agonized souls of the damned. It was a sound she recognized well enough after two and a half years, and after having endured it that long, had actually grown comfortable with. Now she knew it signaled that Jack had flushed the commode, was about finished with his morning routine and would soon be sitting down to breakfast.

The table was already set for the two of them and the butter was out along with a Mason jar of peach preserves she'd canned herself with a crate of fruit that got too ripe for Leo to sell in his grocery store downstairs. Hurriedly, Rose slipped the eggs out of the skillet onto a platter and poured the thick, peppery milk gravy into a small blue-rimmed crock. She took her perfectly browned biscuits out of the oven and turned them onto a tea towel in another bowl and was pouring the coffee when Jack opened the bathroom door and came out.

She looked up to meet his eyes, which were giving her a tantalizing look of lusty appreciation from where he stood just outside the bathroom and even from across the kitchen she could see the crystal blue of his eyes glinting as if lit with a fire behind them. She shivered with delight. Those erotic blue eyes showed his notion plain enough and made the blood burn in her cheeks. She had long ago understood that Jack Nash knew she liked him to look at her like that—that she thrilled to the sight of his wild and willful sky-colored eyes just about eating her alive.

Mary Jean was always telling her how she ought to feel pretty special having a man like Jack Nash still look at her that way after being married to her for five years. And truth be told, she did, and not just *special* but blessed as well.

She returned his stare boldly in spite of all the blushing and then she tossed him a coquettish smile. "Come on, Jack. Sit down and have your breakfast. The biscuits are gettin' cold."

She had just finished pouring his coffee when he came over and took his seat at the table. He flung an arm around her waist and hugged her against him, bending his head to plant a kiss right about where her tummy button was before he let her set the coffee pot down and take her place across from him.

From that vantage point, serenely content in his presence, she watched him scrape three eggs off the platter onto his plate and add three biscuits, which he split and buried under a couple ladles of gravy. He still had a scrap of tissue paper stuck to a nick on the bony jut of his jaw and that made Rose smile tenderly. His face was smooth-shaven, but his beard, like his hair, was as black as a raven's wing. So there was always a darkness, like a shadow, under his skin.

"You cut yourself," she murmured sympathetically.

He glanced at her, shrugged a smile and started eating.

Rose sipped her coffee, buttered a biscuit, and plopped a spoonful of peach preserves on it. Then she nibbled at it with little *bunny-bites* that she knew aggravated her husband but she persisted at it anyway until Jack raised his head. He stared her down with those piercing eyes of his, and his expression was fierce, wicked. She thought, with a delighted shiver, that if *Old Nick* himself were to take human form to seduce a hapless maiden, he'd like as not look exactly like Jack Nash did when he was being sassy.

Thinking that, she couldn't suppress a giggle, causing Jack to grin and utterly destroy the stern, disapproving façade he had intended to worry her with. Defeated, he snorted and took a swig of coffee while she continued to vamp him with her smug, self-satisfied smirk.

Abruptly, he changed the subject. "Sugar, I want you to get all dolled up tonight. Put on that soft blue silky thing we got you for our wedding portrait. And those high-heeled dancin' slippers! And that pair a' silk stockings—you still keep 'em in your little hope chest, don't ya?"

Surprise made Rose abandon her smirk and replace it with a wide-eyed stare. "Whatever for?"

Jack's eyes were skating all over those parts of her he could see above the table. It was a quick but thorough examination that might have unnerved a more humble soul.

"Honey! What for?" She asked again when it became plain that he intended to ignore her first query. She was about to ask a third time when he swung his eyes up to meet hers and lowered his voice provocatively.

"You are sure one hellava woman, Rose Sharon." And to reinforce his meaning he growled at her out of the corner of his mouth. "Even Mary Jean's old nightgown and my long-johns can't hide all the goodies lurkin' under them!"

"This ain't no nightgown," she frowned down at her dress and then raised her eyes to glare at him."

"Whatever it is," he grinned, "it sure as hell don't discourage me."

Rose giggled and then because her curiosity was still unappeased, she demanded he explain his earlier request.

He cocked his fine dark head at her, narrowed his beguiling blue eyes, and kept her waiting while he decided just how much he cared to divulge to her. When she'd just about given up on him, he started talking.

"I haven't said nothin' before, Rosy, because I didn't want to jinx this thing, but now…" and he paused to take a deep breath while he gave the table a sharp rap with his knuckles … "knock on wood" he said with a superstitious wink. Then confidently he continued. "I think it's a done deal now. Anyways it appears to be all set and I can't hardly keep it to myself anymore. So I think I *will* let you in on it now, Rosy-Love".

With that he tipped back his chair, clasped his hands behind his head, and crazy as it seemed to her, started looking kind of nervous. Rose couldn't recall ever seeing Jack Nash look nervous before and having it happen just now gave her a real start … even made her feel a little shaky herself.

"Oh Jack, don't drag this on so" she pleaded and he started grinning at her. Not quite as reckless and provoking as his grins tended to be on most occasions but at least it was a bona fide grin and not the trembly misbegotten lip-spreading that had preceded it.

Rose relaxed and leaned toward him with her elbows on the table in eager anticipation and he nodded at her. "I got a *real* job, Rosy," he said and his grin finally looked natural—moved up into his eyes and lit up the whole room.

"Oh Jack, is it true? A real honest-to-goodness *regular* job? No foolin'?"

He nodded again. "Sure as hell, Rosy. Anyways it's *almost* sure as hell. I'll know tonight. I got to meet this gent down at a place called The Wine Cellar. I got to be there tonight at eight-thirty sharp."

"*The Wine Cellar*?" she echoed.

"It's no speak-easy, Rose Sharon. It's a restaurant. A real fine joint, too. I'm gonna take you there once I start drawin' a regular paycheck."

"But what about the *law*?"' she argued contentiously. "I thought nobody respectable could sell alcohol. How can they call it a *wine cellar*?"

"Dammit, Rosy. I guess they can call it whatever they want. Far as I know there ain't any laws against words yet." It was plain Jack was losing his patience with her. "And anyways, Prohibition is repealed and done with. Don't you ever read the papers?"

"Just the funnies" she said with a coy, little-girl grin.

So Jack relented and returned her smile. Then he leaned forward and reached across the table to take her hands. The happiness he was feeling made him almost giddy.

"We are not even gonna think about getting disappointed this time, Rose Sharon. We are just gonna *straight out believe ...* like you're always preachin' at me. I'm just gonna believe like hell! Like I got that old devil by the tail and the crafty rascal can't do nothin' but give me my due!" He paused, and a frown flashed and disappeared. "Anyways, all I want you to do Pretty Lady, is haul that slinky garment outta your cedar chest and slither your pretty little body into it sometime before I get home tonight and then we will go out on the town and damn well celebrate our butts off! Honey, we are gonna live it up till the cows come home!" And then his eyes crinkled and the dimple lines in his cheeks deepened. "Or maybe till the milkman gets home since we're not in the boondocks any longer." He squeezed her hands tighter. "You just slip into your sexy silk stockin's, Sugar. You still got 'em, ain't you? You never did say..." When she nodded, he bounced her hands a couple of times. "And them *tall-heeled* dancin' slippers?" Rose nodded again. All the excitement was making her eyes sparkle.

"Hell! If you ain't just as glamorous as a movie star in those duds! And won't I be swaggerin' and struttin' alongside you just as proud as a peacock. Just because I haven't *seen* you all dolled up for a while don't mean I can't remember how good you look. No lie! Rosy, with you shinin' like a movie star and holdin' onto my arm and me standin' there like such a proud dude, even that swanky Wine Cellar won't be good enough for the likes of us."

Jack went back to his breakfast then and Rose poured more coffee. But her curiosity had not yet been mollified.

"What kinda job is it, Jack?"

He shrugged off her question. "Just a job. Nowadays it don't pay to be too particular and it sure don't pay to ask a lotta dumb questions."

Then suddenly, he was furious. "God almighty, Rose Sharon, for a woman whose man ain't worked steady a whole week at a time in more than three years, you got a lotta gall askin' *what kind of job is it?"*

Rose shrugged at him. "I didn't mean nothin' by askin'."

But Jack's handsome angular face had turned to stone and he finished his breakfast in silence.

Rose watched him patiently, thoughtfully. She wasn't all that much worried. He never stayed mad for long.

Finally, having sopped up the last bit of egg yolk with the last hunk of biscuit, he raised it to his mouth. But instead of going ahead and eating it, he held it hanging there, his fingers caught in time like in a photograph, just a couple of inches from his lips, and looked at her. Studied her with a most serious expression.

Rose hid her apprehension as best she was able and met his gaze without flinching while a whole bunch of time passed. At last he shoved the biscuit into his mouth, past a row of even, pearly white teeth, chewed and swallowed it, all the while holding her eyes with his. Then all of a sudden he was on his feet and pushing his chair back with the toe of his boot. He reached across the table for her and before Rose could take a good breath, he had her slithered across the room and squeezed up tight between him and the door jamb and was kissing her most ardently while his hands slid downward, past her waist, down her hips, and closed on her backside, lifting her body up and into his. A blissful sensation of helplessness weakened her knees and she began to tremble and instinctively moved against him. Then Jack raised his head and narrowed his eyes at her. "If you just weren't wearin' my long-johns!"

"Jackson! Ho! Jackson!" At that instant a powerful male voice boomed at them from the other side of the door and simultaneously a fist began to pound on it. "*Speederup*, old buddy. The morning's a-wastin'!"

Rose whimpered her disappointment and Jack swore under his breath but loosed his hold on her and bellowed back at the door. "Hold your horses, Mac." He had already slid into his bulky sheepskin-lined jacket and was pulling on knee-high rubber boots. "I'm comin', I'm comin'," he hollered while flashing Rose a shameless grin along with an irreverent wink.

Rose sighed and handed him his red plaid cap with the earflaps down and then bent to retrieve his gloves that had fallen to the floor. Because she was unwilling to let him go—she asked as she straightened up, "You really want me to get all dolled up this evenin'?"

"You betcha, Sugar!" And then his voice softened ...became almost a whisper ... and he leaned his face close to hers. "I know I ain't got a whole lot of the world's riches, Rosy," then he snickered "actually, I guess I got a whole lot less than I planned to have at this stage of my life." He paused to brush her cheek lightly with the gloves he held in his hand. "But I got just about the finest looking woman God ever blew breath into" and he took the time to pull her into him again and give her mouth a light kiss. Then he whispered the rest of his compliment directly into her ear.

After she'd giggled and nuzzled his throat, he backed off, grinning with satisfaction, and added, "I want you to get all gussied up so you can dazzle these big-city boys and show them they ain't got nothin' on this old Mississippi cotton-picker. I got the best there is and I got sense enough to know it! I just want to show you off, Rosy-Love."

The pounding on the door had resumed and Jack reached for the door knob. "Cut out that damn racket—you crazy sonofabitch!" but he was grinning. "You wanna wake the landlady?"

Then, before he opened the door more than a slit, he looked sternly at Rose. "Don't say nothing to nobody about the job." But before she could reply to that, Jack swung the door wide open.

A big man with a bushy red-orange beard was standing there. He removed his cap to reveal a mop of hair to match the beard and smiled politely at Rose. "Howdy, Missus."

Rose smiled back. "Howdy, Jess."

He nodded while pulling his cap back on and then looked at Jack again. "Sanderson's got some trucks to unload at the warehouse first thing. It's likely somethin' else will turn up afterwards."

"Ed Schmitt told me he's gonna need some men to shovel coal," Jack told him and followed the big man out the door. Then, to Rose's surprise, Jack turned back and grabbed her arm; pulled her to him. She kissed his mouth lightly and then as if it had just that moment occurred to her she put the question to him; because with Jess right there she felt safe.

"If Sister Claire should ask again about the Christmas presents, can I tell her we decided to take them and could she just drop them off downstairs?"

She watched Jack's eyes darken malevolently and knew her rashness was going to cost her.

He took a moment to motion Jess on down the stairs before he stepped back inside and shut the door. Then he jerked her up close with one hand and grabbed a handful of her hair with the other to pull her head back so he was able to glare down into her eyes and his pretty mouth was just inches above hers pinching off his words in sharp, icy chunks.

"Why'd you do that, Rosy? Why'd you ask a thing like that?" You know I won't have that Bible-spoutin' hypocrite in my house—no matter how humble it might be. No matter if it was a tent in shanty town. And if you ever shame me by askin' her favors, you just might as well pack your little suitcase and catch that ole Mississippi Cannonball because you won't ever be sleepin' in my bed again! You hear me, don't you, Rosy? You understand what I'm saying? Am I makin' my meaning plain enough for your backward little brain? It seems like I have to keep saying the same shit over and over. Why can't you get my meanin' into your head? If you don't get it straight this time, I'll walk you to the god-damn depot myself. I swear to God, Rosy!"

Rose twisted and struggled to free herself. "It's just a couple a' dumb Christmas presents! And I said I'd ask her to drop them off at the store. It don't mean we have to be friends with her—we wouldn't even have to see her—and if she wants to give us somethin', she can sure afford it. I just thought it would *feel good* to get somethin' new for a change."

"Well dammit, Rose Sharon! How many times do I have to say the same thing over again? Nothin' your sister does for us is meant to make us *feel good!* It's meant to *shame* us! To *shame me!*" He let her loose then and just stood there looking down at her with questions in his eyes. "I just can't believe how dumb you are sometimes!" And then shaking his head he sighed. "You just went and spoiled what might have been one of the best days of our life." And then with his anger mollified, he opened the door and started toward the stairs. At that moment Jess called up from the bottom urging Jack along.

But Rose's temper was just catching fire and she followed after him. "You be damned, Jack Nash!"

He stopped at the top of the stairs and turned around. "What?"

Reading his eyes and scared witless, Rose decided the only thing for her to do was fall down at his feet and plead insanity and that thought conjured up a vision of her poor sister Flora, racing round and round the kitchen table in the dreary old farmhouse of her childhood while saliva dribbled down her chin and her eyes stared terrified at something hideous that nobody else in the room could see. Instantly, all the *spoiled-little-girl* posturing and whining that Rose harassed her husband with made her blush with shame. All she wanted to do then was tell him she was sorry, but he was already more than half way down the stairs, and Jess was hollering at him to "get the lead out."

"Oh, shit," Jack muttered, glancing back at her, "I haven't got time for this crap," and he took the rest of the stairs two at a time. Then just before he disappeared from sight and without looking back he admonished her.

"Why don't you just try to recall what your saggy-assed old hypocrite of a sister told us the day we came to her door weary from that long ride out of Dobbin to ask if we might spend a night or two in one of her *hundred and one exotic bedrooms*? Why don't you just do that, Rose Sharon, and then take some time to sit and ponder on her answer for a while. Maybe then you can decide whether Sister Claire means to shame us or not!"

Rose stood there staring over the railing until she heard the door to the street open and shut, and then she raced back through the apartment to one of the windows where she could look down into the street. With her forehead pressed against the cold glass, she watched Jack tug on his gloves while he and Jess leaned into the wind and started up the sidewalk, their bodies hunkered down, bracing themselves against another bitterly raw gale. Just before they got to the corner, Jack turned around and looked up at the window. His lips spread in a wide grin and then he blew her a kiss. Seconds later, he and Jess trudged across the street and out of her sight.

And Rose's earlier jubilant optimism crumbled like dead rose petals—as ugly as the dirty brown slush under Jack's boots.

A sense of the unfairness of life smoldered in Rose's brain and manifested in a petulant thrust of her chin and a pouting of her mouth. "Squash blossoms!" She swore and her copper-colored eyes sparked ominously. "It just ain't fair, God!" She raised her eyes and noticed that the shallow sun of dawn had already been swallowed up by dark clouds. Again she pressed her forehead against the frosty pane and cried out at a leaden sky that was just beginning to spit sleet back at her, "Oh Sweet Jesus—it just ain't fair! Jack tries so hard ... he works like a *darky* at whatever work he can get—he puts in long dreary hours doing any pitiful job he can find—gettin' paid barely enough to keep us in biscuits and gravy. Freezin' in the cold and sweatin' in the heat and he never complains out loud, though I can feel his heart and his spirit cryin'."

She was almost in tears by then and had about decided to go on and vent all her frustrations with a fit of weeping when a vision came to her. It hardened her jaw and narrowed her eyes and she looked up into the somber sky seeking some kind of answer—but all that came to her was a reflection of her own bitter resentment.

"And Walter Bradley sits all day in his big fancy office," she scowled, "just rakin' in the money—and he goes home every night to sleep in a soft, warm bed in that grand ole house of his—and he gets to ride back and forth between it all in that shiny, black automobile that sits in his driveway—everybody and everything always keepin' him warm and toasty."

For the third time she shoved her forehead against the wet window pane and challenged the sleet-spitting sky, "How come Walter Bradley never even gets his nose cold?"

Rose wasted some more of the morning as Jack had suggested, thinking about Claire Louise and her merciless nature: about all those years of nagging and preaching and finding fault when there wasn't anything Rose could do to please her. Claire was hard on everybody, but Rose seemed to be the one who routinely lit her fire and who most often got burned by it. According to Claire, she was lazy, she was wild and willful, she was too rambunctious, she was too mouthy, she was just plain too sinful to be worth the time and money spent keeping her alive! Truth be told, Sister Claire had even predicted she was too dumb to ever get out of the eighth grade—much less go on to high school, which was meant to discourage her Papa from even considering that possibility.

Sister Claire Louise was the first and only Saylor family member to go to high school and that was only because she was so *strikingly brilliant* that the Grade School Master insisted she go on with her education. He even offered to pay for her books and clothes and any other expenses she might bump into. Of course, Papa wouldn't hear of that ... it smacked too much of charity ... but Mama did convince him to let her go, wearing whatever dresses she managed to make herself, which suited Claire Louise fine because she wouldn't wear a dress if the collar wasn't right up there around her chin and the sleeves better at least cover the elbows, thank you! And nobody even knew for sure that her legs went any farther than her ankles because her skirts hid everything above them.

And naturally she had managed to excel at high school too. She even got to be valedictorian of her class, which was just something else Rose wasn't good enough to be. Then a tender-hearted God sent that old angel, Walter Bradley, to sweep Claire Louise up and away from the family farm and eventually carry her off to Chicago. They'd come back on vacations in the fall or winter and around Christmas every year—mostly it was too hot for them in the summer. And when Claire Louise found out that Rose had a serious crush on Jack Nash, who by then had earned a less than noble reputation, she joined her father in a relentless self-righteous harangue to malign and disparage her little sister.

But Rose hadn't always been so abused. There was a time when *she* was the spoiled and petted darling of the Saylor clan. And she kept the memory of those early years encircled in a *sweet-clover-chain of joy*, isolated from all the abuse and violence that came later—because *remembering that* was the only thing that kept her from absolutely despising her relatives.

Rose was the fifth and last girl-child born to Art and Olivia Saylor amidst a string of tow-headed boy babies that included two sets of twins. She was petite and pretty with an innocent boldness that captivated everyone around her. Her copper-colored curls were cut short to make them easier to manage, and her eyes, large and wide-set and the color of shiny new pennies, reposed serenely behind curly dark lashes that fluttered charmingly. Her little rosebud mouth wore an engaging pout that at least in her infancy was saucily becoming. She looked so much like a big baby doll that nobody could resist picking her up and squeezing her.

In the summer of 1920, when Claire Louise and Walter Bradley caught the train that took them to Chicago, Rose Sharon was just 6 years old. She was wearing faded bib-overalls and brown high-top shoes and Claire's heart was about to break with the sadness of leaving her. Nobody could have convinced her than that those feelings of unconditional love would ever turn into something else.

Because Jack Nash was only a boy whose reputation then was as yet untarnished, and anyway, as a descendant of pre-Civil War landowners in the area, he belonged to a social class so far above that of the tenant-farmer Saylors, that to imagine any connection between him and Rose was preposterous.

But Rose Sharon had fallen in love with him.

Truth be told, though unknown to Claire or anybody else then, the first time Rose really looked at Jack Nash, she'd set her cap for him—and she was no more than four or five years old, playing house with her dolls and making mud pies in the middle of the Saylor's front yard. The yard also served as a lane past the house and the barn, where it turned onto a narrow road that led to the back of the Nash's big house. Art Saylor had a real good relationship with Toby Nash and his family back then. He share-cropped one of the Nash farms, planting and picking cotton. But he also planted corn and hay for himself and raised some pigs and chickens and a few cows. He also had two mules, Jimmy and Roy, to pull the wagon that served as the family's transportation. Sometimes in the late afternoon, Mr. Nash would ride up on his big gray gelding and come up on the porch to sit and visit with Papa. Then Mama or Grammaw Saylor, who lived with them, would bring out glasses of cool water to drink or on rare occasions there might even be a glass of apple cider. The two men would laugh together and Mr. Nash would convey all the local news and gossip, to which Art Saylor politely nodded and then later reminded his wife and children to ignore, because he didn't believe in carrying tales. On Christmas, there was always a ham and some fruit for the family and a big bag of candy and toys for the little Saylors. Back then, there was no animosity or bad feelings for anybody.

Summer 1919

On the particular day that Rose fell in love, Jack Nash had ridden up with his father. While he and Papa talked on the porch, Jack wandered aimlessly about, followed by a bunch of Rose's little brothers and big sisters, a few assorted hounds, and some cats. They checked out the chickens and the pigs and the cows and the mules and when he tired of all that, Jack ambled back up the lane. For a little distance he was walking backward, teasing and flirting with Rose's sisters. That was when he stepped into Rose's mud puddle and smashed a whole afternoon's worth of meticulously crafted mud pies. The howling that ensued brought Ollie Saylor, her belly swollen with her eleventh child, lumbering ponderously to the screen door, expecting some kind of horrendous disaster. But Flora and the twins darted up the porch steps to tattle on their sister, so their mother just hollered out to Rose Sharon to behave herself. "Just make yourself some more mud pies, honey," and returned to her work in the kitchen.

In the meantime, Jack Nash had recovered his poise and was hunkered down in front of her apologizing with sincere remorse and offering to help her replenish her stores. Even on his haunches, he towered above her and when she tilted her head to look up at him, the beauty of his intense blue eyes stunned her. Not only were they sympathetic to her plight but they were also absolutely lit with patient understanding. Rose had never before looked at a boy other than her brothers and up to that moment she considered them all pesky little creatures on the order of mosquitoes and flies. This one, who was almost a man in her eyes, and who was so beautiful he

17

made her heart twinkle and dance in her breast, and who smiled at her as if he meant it, was no ordinary run-of-the-mill, brother-type.

And that was when with absolute certainty Rose Saylor knew this was the man she would marry one day. There was no way he would ever be free of her after that moment. Their coming together was as fated by God as the Resurrection of Jesus. And he must have sensed some of her feelings because he stopped talking to reach out and pull her to her feet to stand between his knees. Now their eyes were almost on the same level and she leaned closer to stare into his. She had forgotten all about the mud pies and unknowingly, was standing right in the middle of them herself, but the only thing that mattered to her at that moment was the darkly handsome young man whose hands held her there between his knees. Impulsively she flung her arms around his neck and kissed his mouth. Jack backed away in surprise and nearly lost his balance, but then he laughed, righted himself and hugged her.

The two men on the porch chuckled, and Toby Nash shook his head and grinned at Art Saylor. "I'll wager that little beauty is going to cause you and Olivia some sleepless nights, Art," and then everybody went back to their business. Jack Nash got to his feet, and feeling he had done all that was expected of him, strode over to where his horse was tied and started rubbing her neck. And Rose, from her place in the lane, watched his every move and etched his walk and his voice and the way he cocked his head and grinned—into her mind creating an image she would keep there forever and one she would eat, sleep, and dream with as long as she lived.

And truth be told, that was exactly the way it all turned out.

When confronted with those sweet memories and her natural optimism, Rose's sense of despair was whisked away and soon she was busy washing the breakfast dishes and assuring herself out loud what a waste of time worry was. All the years she was growing up on the farm in Mississippi, her Papa read scripture to his family every evening come hell or high water, and gave all his children passages of the Bible to learn by heart while they busied themselves with their chores. So Rose always had some divine promise to cling to in the bad times, which had come often these past few years. Truth be told, they never failed to uplift her, though she rarely got up the nerve to spout them in front of Jack Nash. Those scriptures were about all her Papa had ever given her, but she had to give him credit for that, because a lot of times, they were the only things she had to hang onto when the worries got too much to bear. Claire Louise didn't think she had sense enough *to know* when to worry. "That Rose Sharon," she'd say to anybody within earshot, "She doesn't have the sense God gave a goose!"

Rose was splashing the dishwater with the gravy skillet to illustrate Claire's enthusiastic denouncement of her mental capacity when impulsively, she turned away from the sink and, wiping her hands on her apron, went into that part of the room she considered her parlor. An old brown horsehair sofa with crocheted doilies on the arms and back sat against the long wall to her left with a low table in front of it. Facing that were a straight-backed upholstered chair and a plain wooden rocker with two bright-colored throw pillows in it. A brass floor lamp stood at one end of the couch and a library table sat against the front wall between two tall windows that looked out over the street.

On the wall above that table Rose had hung some pictures—one of them in an oval tin frame. She took that one off its nail and dusted it tenderly with her apron. Then she held it close while she studied the portrait. She and Jack in sepia and all their youthful exuberance were smiling back at her and the love and joy in their faces made her heart swell to bursting right here and now, with gratitude for God's goodness in bringing them together. The picture was taken in a real studio in Jackson the day after they'd run away and got married, and Rose was wearing the pale blue silk dress Jack bought her that very morning at Miss Anna's Dress Shoppe in Maysfield. Maysfield was the town Jack worked in then, and he was renting a pretty little one-bedroom cottage for them to live in. So that was where they married and that was where they spent their first night together. But the next day, Jack wanted to take her someplace special on a short honeymoon, so they drove to Jackson, which was the state capital and the biggest and most exciting place Rose had ever seen outside of her geography book at school.

She studied the picture intently as she did with regularity, to conjure up all the happiness and absolute ecstasy she had been feeling on that glorious morning. Sometimes, in the lean years since they left Maysfield, that overpowering sense of being in Paradise with the man of her dreams was hard to come by, unless he was right there in the room with her. Then, even if he was mad and wouldn't talk to her, she felt as safe and secure and beloved as any woman who'd ever walked the face of the earth. Jack Nash did that for his woman. He gave her that certainty of his unwavering strength and courage and competence. And of his loyalty.

Then Rose noticed her reflection in the glass covering the portrait and she started giggling, "And lotsa people think I'm *prettier* than you are too, Sister Claire!" she boasted out loud, tilting her head coquettishly. "I will admit I *might not* be as smart as you, but *smart* ain't everything. I know how to love my man and keep him happy! And I am always aware of your notion that I am a *fallen woman* because I *enjoy* lovin' my man," she smirked. "And he's not just any man either. It had to be Jack Nash, the most no-torious rascal in the county!" That spirit of joy overtook her again, and Rose danced a little jig, "In *three* counties!" And then she was laughing. *"In the entire state of Mississippi!"*

The next moment her thoughts turned back to what was common gossip in her neighborhood in those days. That Jack was the real honest-to-goodness *flaming youth* that the circuit preachers ranted against, a *devil* that fathers and husbands sat up at night to ward off, with their shotguns at the ready, and the man every sinful woman and girl no matter her race, religion, nor age, daydreamed about and hoped she'd be the one he chose to ravish! Rose held the picture at arm's length and looked into Jack's eyes. "O my darlin' Jack" she whispered, sliding the tip of her tongue between her lips, "And to think— I'm the one that won you!"

She hugged the picture to her bosom and turned her eyes again to the gloom outside the window. But she wasn't seeing the low, dark clouds or the bits of icy sleet or even the roofs of the buildings across the street.

June 1927

Rose was 13 years old and back on the farm in Dobbin—she was breathing hard and sweating and fighting to get loose in the steamy, shadowy dark of her mama's bedroom where she had been dragged kicking and screaming after Papa found her in the lean-to hay shed with Jack Nash's bare muscular arms holding onto her.

Papa was going to kill him. He even got the gun down from its rack over the back door ... but Mama had a cooler head and she told Brother to get the horse whip from the barn and encouraged Papa to whip him instead.

It could only have been guilt that kept Jack from taking that whip away from the old man because he was certainly powerful enough to have done it. But he took his punishment without a whimper.

Rose hadn't witnessed the whipping, but she could hear the leather cut the air and crack across Jack's back and an occasional swear-word drawn begrudgingly past his clenched teeth. All the while Rose was fighting like a bobcat, and she never did know exactly who or how many of her brothers and sisters betrayed her trust and held her there that afternoon. They knew they had been in a battle though, before it was over and they straggled out of there bloody and gasping for breath to lick their wounds. Truth be told there was never another time in the remainder of her life in Dobbin that anybody tried to subdue Rose Sharon Saylor. She could chuckle at the memory, but nobody had been laughing then. When Papa had exhausted himself and his rage, they hitched Jimmy the mule to the wagon and lifted Jack into it and then Brother drove him to his Daddy's farm and dumped him at the end of the lane with nary a word to anyone.

It was nearly a year before he ventured near Rose again. In fact he kind of disappeared altogether for a time. At least nobody could say where he was—or anyway, nobody would tell Rose.

She touched the photograph to her lips and kissed it. "But I never wasted a minute worrying whether you'd come back, my sweet darlin', I just knew that sooner or later you had to come back to me. *Sooner or later!* " But that wasn't exactly the truth, because Rose had spent that melancholy season wallowing in a deep and dark despair.

Now she took some more time to study the photograph, remembering her surprise when her new husband took her to a real professional photographer's studio right there in Jackson and they had their wedding portrait made. And now, truth be told, that picture was Rose Sharon's most treasured possession. After Jack Nash, of course!

Rose sighed and hung the tin frame back on its nail. Then she returned to the sink and finished the dishes. After dumping the dishwater down the drain, she started her regular cleaning and straightening-up routine. She surely was in an unusual nostalgic mood this morning and was finding it difficult to keep her mind on anything except the past. It seemed especially joyful to dwell on those dusty, sultry summer days and nights, some of which were so sweltering the only way you could sleep was to wring out the sheets you laid on in cold well water. It was hard to think there could have been heat like that anywhere when she was practically freezing to death right now in another of those awful Chicago winters. Of course, lying close to Jack and twining her body around his was a lot more comforting in this climate.

Rose happened to notice the alarm clock while she was straightening up the bedroom and realized it was later than she thought. So she slacked off on the cleaning and started to gather a load of clothes for the weekly wash.

Mary Jean, the lady who rented them their part of the building had a wringer-washer down in the cellar and she let Rose use it on Monday mornings between 10 and noon. That was a real blessing from God or she'd probably have to do it on a washboard in the bathtub and God forbid she have to go back to washing persnickety Jack's white shirts on a washboard! She smiled recalling how fine he looked when he was wearing one of those crisply starched white shirts.

April 16, 1927

Then without willing it, Rose was back in Dobbin again on one of those late spring days when the sky is such a pure bright blue it swells your heart to look into it and all creation sparkles like sunshine on the ripples in the river. The leaves on the trees, the petals of the wildflowers, even the dust in the road—the very earth itself—twinkled and glittered just as though God had crumbled stars in his palm and blown the dust all over the world.

Rose lay back on the bed and closed her eyes, visualizing that day again, living it again.

It was the 16th of April, a Saturday, and the year was 1927—the very day Jack Nash took notice of her for the first time. Rose had turned 13 in March but Jack was already a man. He'd been a freshman in high school when she started the first grade, so he never even knew she existed. He had no notion that Rose had set her cap for him when she was barely 5 years old and still playing with her baby dolls.

Whenever Papa would let her—after Jack had smashed her mud pies and she had sworn to marry him one day—Rose would ride in the wagon over to his house when Papa went there to talk business with Toby Nash. Jack wasn't there more times than he was, but once in a while he'd amble over to the wagon and lean on it, listening to the older men's discussion while he chewed on a piece of straw or some clover. Sometimes his gaze would drift in her direction and sometimes he'd even smile at her, but he was only smiling at a skinny little sharecropper kid. He wasn't even sure whether it was male or female, and he couldn't know the passion that burned for him in that little heart beneath the bib of her shabby, ill-fitting overalls.

But Rose wasn't worried about that because during all those evenings Papa had spent reading to his family out of the Bible, she'd learned the one thread of truth that wound through all the scripture was that you dare not doubt God's word! *If he said something, you could swear by its truthfulness. If he made a promise to you, he was going to keep it, and there wasn't any way anybody could deny or question that or change his mind, either. It followed in Rose's mind that when she talked her prayers to God and asked for some blessing, it would be hers. Maybe not in that day's mail but in God's time. It would surely come about in God's sweet time. So Rose kept right on believing and growing up and waiting while Jack Nash went on with his life, graduating from high school and working his daddy's land. He even started at some college or other but for some reason nobody talked about, he didn't stay there long.*

And every now and then he rode his horse down the road past the Saylor house. That horse was a skittery black mare named Honey with a white splotch that sort of resembled a bee on her forehead and sometimes Jack had to talk real soft and gentle to her just to keep her from flying out from under him. That mare was so spooky, people got to calling her Wild Honey, and nobody would dare ride her but him. Sometimes Jack would lift his hat when he rode past. He always wore a fine gray Stetson that Papa said used to belong to the old Mister Nash, his granddaddy, and sometimes he would even stop and talk awhile to whichever Saylor happened to be outside at the time. A couple of times he even asked Papa how his daughter was doing, but that probably wasn't too promising a development because Papa still had three daughters living in his house at the time and Jack Nash never did ask for one by name.

Ida Belle was gone. She had joined the Baptist Church when she was 16 and a year later she up and married their newly widowed preacher. Claire Louise was long gone by then, being the first-born daughter and almost 14 years older than Rose. Sister Claire married that insurance salesman named Walter Bradley when she was 18 years old, and he moved her to Chicago two years after that. Walter got himself a job with an insurance company up there and in a few years he was rich and owned a fine house and even an automobile in which they would drive down to Dobbin on holidays and summer vacations—though they preferred coming back in the winter. Claire Louise would drive everybody crazy with her prideful stories about what they spent on food and clothes and overstuffed divans and at the same time rant and scold those sharecropping sisters of hers for coveting a pretty new dress or a pair of patent-leather shoes. And she was even worse about preaching God's Wrath *and calling down his fire and brimstone on everybody. It appeared that God wanted the very finest for Claire and Walter while he demanded sacrifice and downright impoverishment for the rest of the family. And, at least lately, it was always Rose Sharon who got the worst of it.*

And that was because Rose grew up and never bothered trying to hide her feelings for Jack Nash.

And on the evening of that perfect April afternoon in 1927, Jack Nash started falling in love with her—though at the time he most likely would have denied it.

Rose had turned 13 in March of that year and she was still spending at least a portion of every day daydreaming about Jack and what she would say to him if that day turned out to be the day when Destiny finally threw them together. Rose Sharon, being the baby girl with three older brothers and four older sisters, was considerably spoiled, especially by her Papa, who found in her sass and her beauty a little respite from the ugliness of his sharecropper life and the sorrow that his once pretty and spirited wife had grown old too soon and resentful from overwork and too many pregnancies. The fact that Rose was sandwiched between two sets of twin boys and had been "the baby" for four years before the birth of the last child, who'd turned out to be another boy, hadn't done anything to change her family's partiality. Her family's tolerance left her with free time to indulge her fantasies and flirtations because she wasn't expected to work as constantly nor as hard as her siblings—indeed, most of her duties were related to day-to-day housework and helping her little brothers with their schoolwork—chores she could put off until she chose to do them. She was a natural procrastinator anyway and rarely even scolded for it. To waste her time daydreaming was never looked upon in the same way such behavior by her siblings would have been. And so it continued even when she became a teenager.

Parts of her Jack Nash daydream were very repetitious, but now and then she'd come up with some thrilling new fairytale ending that would make the long-awaited encounter even more momentous. Today was that kind of day, and there were two reasons for it. The first was just that the day was so perfect. The second reason was that a lot of the gossip she'd heard lately was causing her serious concern that Jack Nash would marry somebody else or get himself tragically "maimed" before she got her chance at him.

The road she walked this day marked the boundaries of her papa's land, and it edged the fields in sharp cornered turns. You couldn't see very far in any direction, and that gave her a feeling of isolation and a certain security because nobody could see her from far away either. In summer, corn and cotton were growing in the fields on either side of that stretch of road. It had just been planted in mid-March and was not tall enough yet to hide her. But between the field and the dirt road where they'd had all year to grow, weeds and wildflowers were taller than she was and made an almost solid hedge that helped conceal her from any nosy busybody who might be looking out the window of one of the few farmhouses out there in the distance or thinning out the plants in one of the nearby cotton fields—an occurrence that concerned her, just in case her daydream really did come true this day.

Because if Papa knew what she was planning, she'd probably never get out of the house again, for sad to say, Papa didn't much like Jack Nash any more. Truth be told, he cursed every time he spoke his name and opined time and again, "That boy is a big disappointment to me!" And when he was talking to Brother and didn't see any womenfolk around, he said a lot worse things. That was how Rose heard the rumors in the first place while she was in the hayshed reading and trying to get some privacy away from her little brothers. Brother and Papa had come in from the fields to work on something in the barn. The hay was stored in a little lean-to shed at the back of the barn, and Rose liked to dig herself a kind of nest on the far side where she could settle down and day-dream to her heart's content—and read over and over the books that Clair Louise had left behind. Years and years ago, before Rose was even born, there was a well-to-do aunt of her Mama named Aunt Isobel of Natchez—long dead now, who favored Claire Louise and sent her all kind of story books.

Some of them were fairy tales that Claire didn't especially approve of so she hadn't taken them with her when she married. And because Rose's sisters weren't readers, Rose kind of considered they belonged to her now and she'd read them all, again and again, over the years.

On this particular day, she hadn't paid the menfolk any mind until she heard Jack's name mentioned and then her ears stood up like Papa's hounds did when the screen door opened. Brother's voice had a peculiar sly note, an edge that brought to Rose's mind the gossipy women who cackled and whispered their tall stories to each other after Sunday evening church meetings.

"Well, I reckon one thing's certain. Ol' Jack'll be lucky if he lives to see twenty-five. Somebody's bound to shoot him one of these days." Brother was the one doing the talking. Papa didn't say anything.

"Just night before last somebody caught him in a compromisin' position with Jasper Moore's old lady. I cain't recall her name just now, but she's Ruthie Moore's step-momma, and Ruthie and Jack been messin' 'round since grade school." Brother snickered, and Rose could imagine the sly look on his face when he glanced over to see if Papa was properly incensed.

And he was. He snorted in disgust. "No!" he said and clicked his tongue.

"Sure as Christmas!" Brother continued gleefully, and Rose scowled. "You was always jealous a' Jack," she thought, "ever since you was in grade school and Jack was so pop'lar and you never even had one sweetheart!"

And Brother kept laughing and talking. "The latest tale is that he's got four or five sets of mommas and daughters scattered around the county so he don't have so far to go to change…" and the nasty word he used shocked Rose so badly she gasped and so doing, sucked in a goodly amount of hay dust and then couldn't stop choking and coughing. That was when she started preparing to die because death would surely be her fate for having eavesdropped on Papa's personal and private conversation. Miraculously though, they didn't even notice. They were both too absorbed with their slandering!

And Brother just couldn't stop laughing, though Rose knew Papa wouldn't regard it as funny. "You ought not take so much pleasure in a man's sinfulness, Brother," he said sternly. "Nor in the ruination of our womenfolk."

But Brother roared with hilarity. "Our womenfolk?" he sputtered. "You reckon he's ever bedded your old floozy cousin, Hester Goode? I've heard you tell some stories on her yourself, Pa."

Papa's voice sounded grim "It was wrong of me to speak disparagingly of our blood kin, Brother, and you ought not remind me I done it." But then he lowered his voice and there was a chuckle in it. "Still I don't reckon that boy's had any trouble findin' women up to now and he'd have to be damn hard up to go after Hester!"

Rose was stunned. To hear Papa make lightly of any kind of sin was so shocking that she bolted upright in the hay and bumped her head against the wall. Surely they would find her out that time. But there was another miracle and she was spared death a second time that afternoon.

And Brother just went right on talking once his laughter had subsided.

"I heared he's messin' with bootleg too."

"Now that is serious, Boy—he's real apt to get hisself shot, foolin' around with moonshine."

Rose glowered and sensed defeat. Papa didn't hold with alcohol even when it was legal so that part about finished all hope of ever getting his permission to marry Jack Nash. "Papa ain't never gonna let me marry no moonshiner!" She was certain of that. But then she brightened. "I guess I just have to run off with him and do it." And thus her future was decided.

"You prob'ly don't remember" Papa was saying, "but Jack's granddaddy was a woman chaser all his life. If the truth were told, there prob'ly ain't but a few famblies in these parts that don't have a Nash bastard in some closet or other."

Brother, who had been silent for a while, whistled—"I know of a few of 'em myself, Pa."

But Papa seemed not to have heard him. "I guess the boy comes by it natur'l. It's a real sorry shame though." And then he sighed so loudly Rose heard it from her hiding place, and said for the millionth time, "That boy is sure a big disappointment to me."

As the summer progressed, those rumors had blown about like cottonwood silk and every time she heard one it was worse than the one before it. They were gonna shoot him ... or lynch him ... and the one that really scared her ... some husband over by Natchez was getting together a posse to come and castrate him. Rose was a farm girl and even though her Papa was protective, she knew what that word meant and it froze the blood in her veins. Time was running out. She had to get to him somehow. And that was what made the dusty road in the middle of the fields her next to the last hope. Her hopes were always "next to the last" because she didn't intend ever to give up hope altogether—no matter what! Jack rode his horse down this road often, and if he would just ride through there today, she had a plan that would drive him right into her waiting arms. Time was running out. If that man from Natchez got to him before she did, there wouldn't be any reason to keep daydreaming about Jack Nash! Heaven help him!

So she watched the sky get bluer and bluer as the day moved into late afternoon and then late afternoon started down toward sunset and twilight came on. The shadows got longer and longer, and the dusty gray road turned purple, and pretty soon all the color was gone from the sky and she could barely see the road at all. Bright stars twinkled in the black dome above her head but she didn't look up to see them. Her hope was gone! She'd tramped back and forth and up and down that miserable dirt lane until her feet hurt and her head ached and she was too depressed to remember or even care what her perfect plan had been. Filled with despair, she flung herself down to sit in the dust in the middle of the road, pulled her knees up to her chest, buried her head in her hands and started to sniffle. If she was the type, she thought, she could really feel sorry for herself. Hers was a wasted life. There'd never been anything else of importance in it except Jack Nash and she had never wanted anything more or longer then she wanted him, and now, when she was finally of an age to get some good out of him ... some crazy jealous husband was going to ruin him. And it was all his own jack-ass-stupid fault! Why couldn't he have waited for her to grow up? For Rose knew positively that she was the only woman on earth to love him the way he was meant to be loved. She knew without a doubt that her love was created by God only for Jack, and if she never got to share it with him, it would just shrivel up like a raisin and fall down dead into the sand. And so would she!

Being so deep in thought and with her head down on her knees like that she didn't notice the rabbit dart through the brush at the edge of the road and when it passed her close enough to stir the air against her bare legs she was so startled she cried out and thrust herself straight up in the air—and as a quirky fate would have it, directly under the nose of that wild black mare who reared and twisted and bucked until she'd tossed her hapless rider, saddle and all, into the ditch.

It all happened so quickly that Rose couldn't put it all together in her head, and so she just stood there staring into the dark, calling on Jesus under her breath, while the pounding of the horse's hooves (which she hadn't heard at all coming at her) and its terrified screaming whinny grew faint in the distance.

Then from the ditch to her left came the sound of hard breathing and a voice so righteous and condemning she thought it might be God himself, except that she couldn't imagine God using that kind of language.

"You crazy sonofabitch—are you tryin' to kill me?"

Then, even in the middle of her panic, Rose's heart jumped with joy as it tended to do at the sound of Jack Nash's voice. But almost instantly the joy evaporated. She was the "sonofabitch" he was talking about! If Jack Nash was still lying in the ditch it meant he was not altogether undamaged and seeing as how it was her fault he was there, her name would probably be a curse to him throughout eternity. Not only had she brought him to the humiliation of lying helpless and dependent on his assailant; worse even than that she had driven his beloved mare right over the edge into madness. Wild Honey probably wouldn't stop running till she got to the Atlantic Ocean and drowned just like those pigs Jesus sent the demons into.

"I got a rifle aimed square at your head" Jack said. "Move over here slow and easy so I can get a look at you." But Rose stayed where she was. It was too dark to see her and she reasoned if she didn't say anything he'd never know it was her.

"Who the hell are you? Who put you up to this?" But she didn't know how to communicate without talking so she couldn't answer him.

"Well, shit then, it don't matter who you are" Rose could hear him struggling and thrashing about raising a big cloud of dust that drifted across the road. But his efforts appeared useless, "Shit! Just get over here and help me out of this ditch. I think my damn leg is broke" And then he reminded her, "And keep in mind I got a rifle trained on you."

Rose thought that if she took off real fast down the road the dark would swallow her and like as not his bullets would miss her or anyway do less damage so she took a cautious step or two in that direction. But her love for him wouldn't let her go.

While she was deciding, he hollered at her again. "If I have to get back on the road on my own, I swear to God, I'm gonna hunt you down and hang you!"

And that decided her. Carefully, Rose made her way back to where his voice was coming from. She could see the dark hulk of him lying among the weeds, but she couldn't make out his face so she felt pretty confident she would remain nameless. And that notion exhilarated her. She would be Jack Nash's guardian angel and it would be her secret. He would never know!

"Shit," he said incredulously when she got close enough. "You ain't nothin' but a kid! Who put you up to this?" After a while, when she didn't answer, he snorted and waved his arm to motion her closer. "Okay, don't tell me. I don't give a damn who you are, just get this saddle off my legs so I can get on my feet."

Rose bent down and got her hands on the saddle but then she was close enough for him to get a hand on her and in a stunned voice he said, "You ain't no kid! You're that sassy little red-headed Saylor girl!"

Horrified, Rose forgot her plan to be silent—jerked straight up and backed off. "I plum well know who I am" she flared.

"I reckon you do, little girl!" he snorted and reached toward her." Just get this damn saddle off me and you can be on your way." A cracking in his voice told her that he was in physical pain.

Rose felt sincere compassion for the man, and terrible regret, but she stood her ground and tried to explain. "It was a accident," she said contritely. "A ra—somethin' ran 'cross the road and scared me." She thought it best not to admit it was only a rabbit. "And I was thinkin' so hard, I didn't hear you comin'."

"What's a little girl like you got to think so hard on?" he queried, and she knew he meant to be nice but having him call her "a little girl" lit her temper. Still, she had sense enough to keep her mouth shut this time and she went ahead and hunkered down to tug at the saddle. Jack was trying to help her but it didn't much matter—because where he was pinned the ditch just happened to slope away at a sharp angle so that his chest and head were downhill from his hips and legs with the saddle on them. All that pulling and scraping was hard on his leg, which was bent at an unnatural angle and caught underneath it—as was a lot of the rest of his lower parts, and he'd grunt and clench his teeth now and then trying not to let her know how much she was hurting him. Rose was not exactly frail, but she was small and not especially athletic and the knowledge that her efforts were hurting him, made her start to cry.

"O sweet Jesus," she said as she struggled with it. "I just cain't do this!" But then all of a sudden it was lifted and moved aside and Jack was praising her accomplishment, though his voice sounded cranky. She figured that was from the pain her efforts had wrought.

"It must have been a angel come down and helped me," she admitted modestly. And she really believed that was what had happened.

Jack struggled to raise his upper body and took some time then to study his leg. It was plain he'd need help removing his boot but after one feeble pull, Rose refused to be a party to it. The pain it caused him made him moan something awful and she just couldn't stand hearing that.

"You're gonna have to help me" he said, and by that time they'd both got used to the dark and could make out each other's expressions.

"No, I ain't" she said, and she was thinking what if his bones were sticking through his skin and what if his foot came off with his boot.

"I can't do this by myself," he said.

"A doctor has to do it!" she said frostily and was about to walk out of the ditch and get back on the road, when she felt herself spun off her feet and dropped across his lap and then to her horror Jack Nash started to spank her. Spanking her on her behind with the palm of his hand just as though she was a baby and he was her papa!

The humiliation of that was too awful to be borne and she struggled desperately to get out of his clutches. Pretty soon they were wrestling around there in the weeds like a couple of hound dogs.

"You're a mean man, Jack Nash!" she gasped, "And I'm glad you got throwed in the ditch!'

Though she could hardly believe her ears, he started laughing then. "Well, so am I, Sugar. If it hadn't happened I wouldn't be getting all this huggin' and lovin' on."

Stunned by the implications of what he said, Rose pushed herself off him and slithered out of his reach. He was weakened by the laughter that shook him or she'd never have gotten loose.

He had to struggle to catch his breath in the midst of all that hilarity and pain. "Now are you ready to do what I asked you?"

"No!" She said wiping away angry tears, but then she decided she ought to explain why. "It hurts you too bad."

"Well, shit!" he growled. "What do you suggest I do with myself, then? Scratch out a big hole with my fingernails and fall in so you can bury me and forget all about our little encounter in the moonlight?"

"Just don't make me pull off your boot."

Jack snorted. "Okay. Have it your way" and then he told her to get to her feet. Once she was standing, he grabbed onto her and tried to stand up using her like a climbing post. She was indignant and pushed him away and started toward the road again. She had a notion just to walk off and leave him. Let him lie there in the ditch until he rotted and decayed back into the dirt he'd come out of. There really wasn't much he could do about it if she decided to run off, she smirked.

But then Jack's voice reached out and took hold of her throat. "Get your useless damn butt back down here, you little pissant! You're the reason I'm layin' here in the weeds with a broke leg and my god-damn mare spooked off someplace in the next county. So you're the one who's gonna get me outta this mess!"

Well, she reasoned, in a dark panic, all he said was true—it was her fault. He could probably get her put in jail, or maybe even hung if she went off and left him to die. Cautiously, she returned to his side and immediately he grabbed onto her again. Only this time he made her bend down and got his arm around her neck which kind of made her nervous. But she straightened up as she was told and he sort of came up with her. As soon as he put some weight on his bad leg though, he went back down cursing and gasping. And Rose just kept praying. Jack Nash wasn't a real big man, but he was near 6 foot tall with muscle. It was all she could do just to keep from collapsing under him, and the only thing that kept her on her feet was fear and dread. Regardless, in the end it was pretty much the same as with the boot, he got to his good foot, but the other one just dragged along the ground and there was no way she could haul him up and walk at the same time. Besides, she wondered what on earth was she going to do with him if she did get him back on the road? She sure couldn't carry him all the way home.

"Maybe I ought to run to my house and get us some help?" she suggested hopefully."

Jack loosed his grip on her and sank back on his good knee and she didn't give him time to argue. As soon as she was what seemed to be a safe distance away and before she got out of earshot she turned and hollered at him. "You think you're so smart, Jack Nash. When my Papu hears about you laying your hand on my backside, you'll probably have to marry me!"

As his maniacal laughter faded away, Rose noticed he was no longer paying her any mind. Instead he was looking off down the road and his head was cocked to one side as if he was listening for something. "Shush!" he told her. It wasn't long before she heard it too. The soft thud of hooves in the dust, still a ways off, but coming on fast. Wild Honey was coming back! And Rose was nailed to the road! Her fear of that crazy mare was big enough to take away every bit of sense she had and she just couldn't make herself move out of its way. And anyway where would she go? Then Rose saw her. A big undulating black shadow coming out of the dark and bearing down on her like a steam engine. Rose could hear her labored breathing and still she stood there like a statue.

The thing that moved her at last was the sound of Jack's voice, quiet and calm but urgent, calling her to come to him. She turned and ran back to him and with the beast almost upon her she leaped off the road and into the ditch streaking around Jack to stand behind him—putting his body between hers and the mare's. From there she kept a wary eye on the beast, prepared to bolt if she made a move toward her. Jack kept his face turned to the horse but he motioned with his hand for Rose to step closer to him. Then he leaned on her and started to pull his body up just as if she was a fence post again. She tried to get loose but Jack stopped her. "Don't you move a god-damned inch further!" he ordered. "You got me into this mess and you are gonna get me out of it!" He was leaning hard on her but still down on his knee with his bad leg bent at a crazy angle beside him. He allowed himself one lengthy groan and then he got a better grip on her and she dared not protest. By then, he was talking in the same gentle, soft way to the mare and by then she was standing in front of them just up the ditch a little way.

"If I can get hold of the reins, I can pull myself up," Jack was telling Rose. "Just get me over to her." At the same time he kept talking low and easy to the horse. Rose did the best she could but she was no stronger than she had been when the ordeal began and she was a whole lot tireder.

"O sweet Jesus! She prayed again, but silently this time so as not to get Jack any more riled up. "I just cain't do this!"

though she was pretty sure she'd do it—or else. Then like a miracle, Honey moved to meet them, and Jack grabbed the reins and lifted most of his weight off Rose. Then he leaned against the mare and let go of Rose altogether, and that was when he gave her a sharp little jab with his hip which Rose thought unkind as well as uncalled for.

"Now, get my saddle!" he demanded and Rose rebelled. "I cain't" she wailed. "It's too heavy!"

But Jack's patience had reached the end of its rope. "I'm gonna say this one time, slow and easy, little girl, and then I'm gonna get mean! Pick the damn saddle up and toss it over your shoulder—get down on your hands and knees and push it with your nose, or pull it with your teeth—I don't give a damn how you do it—just get me my god-damn saddle!"

Rose sucked in a breath and then ceased breathing altogether for a time while she contemplated throwing a tantrum-fit! That always won her arguments at home—but not likely with Jack Nash. He'd just get meaner and curse at her. And call her a brat! And a baby—

That was when the breath she'd been holding drained out of her in one prolonged moan of capitulation and she made up her mind she would lift that saddle. Even if it killed her. She was gonna pick it up and swing the dang thing straight up over Jack's head and drop it square across the back of his crazy old mare.

And with super-human strength, born of fear and rage, that's what she did—with a little help from him.

The ordeal of getting Jack onto the horse however, might have gone on forever except that Papa and Brother showed up looking for Rose because of the late hour. There was a nasty smirk on Brother's face and ugly suspicion in Papa's pale blue eyes when he held his lantern up to get a good look at Jack's leg, but the terrible noises Jack made while they were removing his boot and the hideous red and purple and yellow-green swelling that stretched all the way from his toes to his knee convinced even Papa that Jack Nash, at least on this one occasion was truly an innocent victim. And because he felt it was the Christian thing to do, he wouldn't let anybody leave the scene of the crime until Rose Sharon apologized for her part in it. And truth be told, that took a long time. For Rose

Sharon had a stubborn streak wide as the Mississippi, and Jack Nash had hurt her pride. He was in grave need of medical attention by the time she relented and he was able to ride out of there. Even at that, he wouldn't let Brother accompany him. Rose figured he was so happy to be rid of the Saylors, he'd have dropped dead with a smile on his face anywhere along the road back home.

December 1933

"Poor Jack." Rose opened her eyes and smiled, remembering that night. Jack Nash had spent a big part of his life under a heavy cloud of suspicion.

But then she caught sight of the alarm clock on top of the bureau again and instantly she was on her feet. The morning was flying past and she'd miss her wash time if she didn't hurry. With a swoop of her arm she pushed the pile of dirty clothes she'd collected into a pillow case and flipped it over her shoulder; then she left her apartment and hastened toward the back stairs.

It was two buildings Mary Jean owned—looking at them from the street the grocery store occupied the one on the corner, and a small shoe repair shop took up the front half of the building to its right. The back half of the second building was used as storage space for the grocery, and the second floor where the apartments were located spanned both buildings. An enclosed staircase between the two stores led from the street to a landing off which both apartments opened and then continued on toward the back, where the stairs leading down to the grocery was located near a rear exit into the alley. The basement stairs were built against the back wall of the grocery at a right angle to the main staircase and the door to it opened between the other two exits. The Nash apartment was in the front above the shoe repair shop and Mary Jean's apartment was at the back. The second floor above the grocery had once been a doctor's office but had been empty for years and was rented out occasionally for wedding parties or neighborhood meetings.

Rose breathed in deeply of the musty smell peculiar to basements and cellars, mingled with the scents of steamy soapwater and damp clothes drying on lines that crisscrossed the long narrow space—she found it comforting. In the corner at the end of the stairs there was a partially enclosed coal bin, and a monster furnace with big pipes growing out of it in all directions like the tentacles of an octopus almost filled the front half. A laundry sink, the washing machine and adjoining rinse and starching tubs were crowded along the inside wall.

After Rose got the clothes agitating in the water and the rinse tubs filled, she sat down on an old wooden bench that was pushed against the side of the stairs. She thumbed through some magazines Mary Jean kept there to pass the time till the clothes were ready to rinse and hang. Rose loved to read the movie magazines, but she took her greatest pleasure from the romance periodicals that called themselves "True Love Stories" and "Secret Love" and "Secret Romance." Some of those set her heart racing and gave her goose bumps. She'd often thought about writing up her and Jack's story and sending it off to one of them. She believed their story was a lot more interesting than most and a lot more *passionate* than any of them.

Today, to her disappointment, Rose found she'd already read them all, except for one that she thumbed through without much interest. *Fashions!, of all things—*she turned up her nose with scorn. *In this day and age with everybody so hard up!* She herself hadn't had a new dress since … but it was best not to think about that. And then her thoughts turned to the blue silk Jack wanted her to wear tonight. That dress was a real *store-bought* one. The first she'd ever owned that hadn't belonged to somebody else before her. Up to then all her *new* dresses were homemade and never what you could call stylish. Not that she'd cared about that—until she married Jack and learned there was a whole other world out there. And Jack bought her a slew of new dresses when he was making money at the lumberyard. That blue silk was the first, though, and the most beautiful.

Jack let her pick it out herself at Miss Anna's in Maysfield, which was the finest ladies' wear store around.

Truth be told it was so fancy they spelled "shop" with two 'ps'
and stuck an 'e' on the end of it! Rose giggled to herself. Jack
had, right out of the blue that first morning after they'd run off
and got married, announced to her that he was going to buy
her the prettiest dress in town. And then he took her to Miss
Anna's Dress Shoppe and told her to pick out whatever she
wanted and never mind the cost. When she put that dress on
and came out to see how he liked it, he just stood there and
stared at her with his amazing blue eyes like she was a big
plate of meat and potatoes and he was hungry. Then he said to
the saleslady, "Don't put that in a box, she's going to wear it,
and bring us some silk stockings and a set of your best
undergarments." And then he asked the lady to show Rose some
"high heeled dancin' slippers!"

By then there was a whole crowd of ladies standing around
just gawking at him, and that was the first time Rose felt a little
twinge of jealousy. But that was okay—knowing it was she he
loved made her proud and playing jealous was just kind of a fun
game. Anyway, that purchase was unbelievably extravagant and
maybe it was even sinful to spend money like that, but Jack
wasn't much took-up with sin or with the Bible either, for that
matter. He pretty much did whatever he felt like doing. Not that
Rose worried a whole lot about his lack of religion. She was
certain salvation would come to Jack Nash one way or another.
God knew how much she loved him, after all.

When Rose had pinned the last sock to the line and
emptied the washer and rinse tubs, instead of returning to her
lonely apartment, she opened the door next to the one she had
just exited and stepped into the bright and bustling grocery and
meat market run by Leo and Viola Wesselman, the couple she
now considered her own family. Jack's too, since neither of
them had any blood relations who claimed them anymore. And
today, because there were in store customers and Viola was
busy filling their orders, Leo put Rose right to work packing
boxes with delivery orders. Thus what was left of the morning
passed quickly into afternoon when all three of them took their
lunch in turn, upstairs with Mary Jean as had been their
practice for years. That was so Leo and Viola didn't have to go
far from the store when it was open and Mary Jean didn't have

to eat alone. Nowadays, if Jack was working, Rose usually joined them. And today, being excited and all, she almost did that one thing Jack told her not to—though she had to bite her tongue a passel of times to keep from blabbing his secret.

And then sure enough, Jack got that job he was hoping for. And Rose thanked Jesus, although she never was sure exactly what kind of job it was. And she was kind of disappointed because by the time he got home that night, it was too late to go anywhere to eat and too bitter cold for a romantic stroll. But she had dressed up like he'd asked her to and so Jack turned the radio down low and they danced to celebrate anyhow. With only the lights from the street to illuminate the parlor, they could pretend they were in some swanky hotel ballroom. Just before they went into their bedroom, Jack whispered in her ear that they had just taken the elevator to the twentieth floor, and then he led her across the room to the window and with his arms around her they imagined they were looking out at beautiful Lake Michigan all a-shimmer in the cold blue moonlight.

January 1934

It was about a month after that when Jack was finally able to take her to supper at The Wine Cellar. After they were seated and he was studying the menu, he nodded with his head to indicate the others in the softly lit room and told her in a quiet voice that these were the sort of gentlemen he was working for. Rose breathed a sigh of relief. The men all wore expensive-looking suits with white shirts and ties, and their shoes gleamed like Abigail Nash's polished silver. It was plain that they made a lot of money, and Rose thought they must be prosperous businessmen, maybe even bankers! Whatever they were, they could afford to pay Jack fair wages, and she decided that all the money he was spending on their dinner tonight wasn't sinfully extravagant after all.

With a happy sigh, she turned her attention back to her husband and smiled proudly. All these well-dressed gentlemen and their fine ladies *who wouldn't even meet her eyes but looked right through her chair as if nobody was sitting in it* might have intimidated her, but it was plain that Jack was undaunted. He looked like he ate there every day and he knew exactly what those foreign looking words on the menu meant and just what to tell the waiter when he asked which wine they would like with their dinner. And she noticed none of those snooty ladies looked right through *his* chair. But that made her proud too. Because he wasn't looking back at a one of them. He was making it real plain that he considered her the most beautiful woman in that room. The look in his eyes said that! Heck, it just about shouted out loud how special she was to him and how much he was in love with her. What if her dress was almost six years old? It looked better on her tonight then it did when he bought it because she filled it out better now. And her legs in those fancy high-heeled pumps would look as good as anybody's when he spun her round on the dance floor later. Everything was perfect tonight and this one night made up for all the lean times that had gone before it. Rose knew it was the beginning of a brand new life for her and Jack Nash!

Truth be told, Jack was a lot easier to live with after that. He wasn't scared anymore once he had money in his pocket and he could pay all the bills. Jack was such a prideful man. The only bad part of their life after that was that he was almost always gone. Rose couldn't count on him to be home at any certain time of the day or night and it never was all that clear to her *why* he couldn't be at home. He told her he was driving a car for his boss. And once he told her he was a sort of bodyguard, and Rose guessed that with the state the world was in anybody who had very much money probably needed a bodyguard since so many people had nothing. So she tried not to press him. Besides, Jack's temper went off like a firecracker from too many questions. It was wiser on her part to accept his vague explanations than to suffer his wrath.

And there were other matters that cried out for her attention.

One most especially.

Rose had noticed a rather peculiar (for her) aversion to breakfast lately. Sometimes even the smell of the lard in the skillet awaiting the egg assaulted her stomach so violently that she spent minutes in an agony of dry heaves. Or worse, upchucking last night's supper. At first she guessed she was catching something. There was always some disease or other going 'round in the neighborhood. But gradually a new thought worked its way to the front of her mind.

The notion didn't come easy because she'd been married going on six years already and not having conceived in all that time she felt pretty sure there was something wrong with her and that there would never be any children for her and Jack. Coming as she had from a family where babies grew every summer like the crops, it seemed impossible to have relations with a man for five and a half years and *never* get pregnant. It had not mattered much to her and seemingly not at all to Jack, who had never once brought up the subject. Their life together was so perfect they didn't need a baby to complete it, and if the desire ever did cross her mind, it never stayed long. Rose was content giving all her love and attention to Jack, and she relished the fact he had nobody except her to love.

But the morning sickness had been going on for almost two weeks and now it was time for her monthly to start and nothing was happening. She was fearful and she was excited. Jack didn't have a hint to what was going on and she wasn't at all sure she wanted to tell him. At least not until she knew for certain it was true.

The strain of indecision made her kind of testy though, and he noticed that and the way she cried so easy about everything. But Jack had never spent much time with a pregnant woman so he couldn't put it all together. And he was gone so much of the time, anyway. Rose felt tears well up just thinking about how lonely she was. Well, she consoled herself, if there really was a baby started inside her, it would settle *that* problem. She wouldn't be alone anymore while he was away days and nights at a time.

February 1934

As the days passed, being pregnant became more probable in her mind and eventually by the third week in February and a second missed period, Rose decided it was a sure thing. During that time of uncertainty, she began readjusting her priorities and moving herself from the familiar and pleasant path she had been traveling with Jack onto a much more complicated road twisting with mysterious bends, around which she couldn't see until she turned onto them. She was looking down a road full of ruts and potholes that she feared she might fall into somewhere along the way. Still, the notion of having Jack's baby thrilled her when she let herself think about it. After all, a baby was the visible sign of their love for one another and the flesh and blood result of their coming together in their love. In the end of her contemplation on the subject Rose decided that a baby was the most blessed gift God could have given her to fulfill *her* love and the *best gift* she could ever offer Jack. After that, the thought of telling him started to make her tingle all over with excitement.

A whole new world was opening before them. Money was not a problem anymore. Jack's wages were more than fair. He could pay the bills and keep his pantry full and was even talking about a house and furniture. He had already started to spend money on clothes because he needed to dress well on his job and every time he came home he brought something special for her. They even went out now and then to see a movie or to eat at a restaurant, and whenever his boss let him bring the car home, they'd go for a drive out into the country past farmhouses and through little towns that reminded her of Dobbin. Even in her childhood, before the hard times came, Rose had never enjoyed such good and carefree times, and certainly never had such a free attitude about spending money.

And Jack was so happy! He loved doing whatever it was he did and wearing one of his perfectly ironed white shirts and a suit to work. He loved buying her things, especially extravagant little trinkets and jewelry she didn't really need; he loved having a car to drive her around in and showing her off when they went out. And most of all he loved being able to hand Mary Jean the rent money on the first of every month and still keep a big roll of bills in his pocket.

Oh yes indeed! God was good to them! Rose felt like throwing open the window and shouting "Hallelujah!" Even the dreary gray skies of winter couldn't bring her down!

There was going to be a baby! A little boy, maybe ... she hoped ... who would look just like his Daddy. Another Jack Nash for her to love and cherish! The joy in her heart just had to find an outlet and pretty soon she'd be dancing around the room praising God and thanking him for all her blessings. Now that the baby had become real to her she couldn't wait to tell Jack about him. To see the look of wonder on his face. And then the happiness and pride that would fill his beautiful eyes. She could hardly imagine how proud he would be. Jack Nash, a daddy! Finally!

But he didn't come home.

As she lay alone in their bed that night the tears began again and she let them flow for a time. It felt good to give in to self-pity and be sad for a change; giving Jack *"the what for,"* blaming him and yelling at him in her imagination. But that didn't last long—as she hollered at him, in her mind's eye he repented and embraced her and before she knew it he was making love to her. She opened her eyes in wonder. "Rose Sharon," she admonished herself, "you are really hopeless." And so she lay there, her cheeks still wet with tears, smiling to herself and marveling at the depth of her love for her husband and at the happiness that swelled her heart with just a thought of him.

How had she ever won him? What had she ever done to deserve such happiness? It was always a wonder to her that she had won the love of the one and only man she ever wanted. Her earliest memories were of him. And God had given him to her! To honor and obey ... to have and to hold ... to love forever! For Rose knew even death would not part them. And now they had truly become one and made a baby together and that bound them even stronger.

"O my sweet Jack!" she turned toward his side and hugged his pillow against her body. "Come home, Jack. *Please hurry home.*"

While she caressed his pillow her mind wandered backward again to the first time she saw him after that disaster on the field road, while his leg was still encased in plaster...

April 1927

It was the next Friday, almost a week later. She was walking home from school and as was her custom, lagging far behind her brothers. She tended to meander, head thrown back, chin stuck out, voice raised in a lusty tune with her molasses-can lunch-pail swinging on her arm. But today her concentration was focused on some hawks drifting in circles above the field to her left. The sky was cloudless and the air was still. And the strangest thing! She wasn't even thinking about HIM! For probably the first time in her life, too. When suddenly... there he was, right beside her. She thought her song must have covered the sound of the mare's hooves. But she hadn't heard her that other time either so maybe that fiendish beast meant to sneak up on her.

Surprise, delight, excitement, dread, panic, and finally embarrassment followed one another in rapid succession across her brain while he reined in his horse and trotted along with her. There was a strange grin on his face, and she wasn't sure she felt safe being alone with him.

With her eyes squinted against the western sun, she studied his face.

He bore her scrutiny with grace. "Good afternoon, Rosy" he said and he even tipped his hat to her.

Still studying, she nodded. "Same to you, Mister Nash."

Jack frowned at her and then he looked up at the sky and rolled his eyes. "Mister Nash?" he echoed in an incredulous voice. "Do you see my daddy out here somewhere?" Then he gave her a grave stare. "You can still call me 'Mister Nash' after our frolicsome little romp out there in the moonlight the other night?"

With a shrug, she corrected him. "There wasn't no moon," and then quickly asked, "What would you have me call you?"

He bent toward her and snapped the reins against her arm. "Well, Miss Prissy 'There wasn't no moon' Pants, I feel like we had a real intimate relationship started out there in the ditch and we ought to be at least on a first name basis, if not 'honey pie' and 'darlin'"

His voice sounded sincere but there were those wicked crinkly creases beside his mouth and an ornery glimmer in his blue eyes. So she narrowed her eyes at him and then turned her face forward. "Well, I sure ain't ready for no 'honey pies' or 'darlins'." And she continued to meander slowly homeward though her heart was pounding and her knees were shaking and the field to her left had started to pitch in the wind.

He didn't say anything else but he kept crowding her toward the ditch with that ill-tempered mare of whom Rose suffered an awesomely unnatural fear; but she was determined not to show it to Jack Nash, who might be even crazier than his horse. For as much as she was attracted to his manliness she was not blind to his odd and exotic mindset and enough of his exploits had been bandied about to ensure her awareness of his lack of self-discipline and good sense.

Finally he tired of the silence and snapped the rein at her arm again. "Why don't you just climb up here with me, Rose Sharon, and we'll have you safe and secure at home in just a couple a minutes?"

That was the first time she ever heard him say her proper name and the sound of it on his tongue almost made her swoon. She was also surprised that he knew it, and wondered if he'd always known or if he'd asked around. Between that and the invitation to climb aboard Wild Honey, she couldn't stop the shudder that shook her body and she turned her head to see if he had noticed.

He was staring down at her with his mesmerizing eyes. "Well?'

"No thank you" she said and shuddered again, that time because of her irrational refusal to what would very likely be the one and only invitation she would ever get from him.

Jack breathed another exasperated sigh. "Well, shit, Miss Rose Sharon Saylor," he said and pressed that old gray Stetson to his chest while he performed a most exaggerated bow. "I can't get down and walk with you, because some scaredy-cat Miss Prissy Pants caused my horse to throw me and bust my damn leg!"

Rose stopped walking then and turned to face him. He was still bending toward her with his hat pressed against his chest. The funny little crinkles and the glimmer were gone, though. Undoubtedly his mood had shifted. They stared at each other for a time, and she wished she could tell what was going on behind his eyes.

At last she took a deep breath and jumped off the cliff. "My heart does belong to you, Jack Nash, if you want it or don't—and I'm plum sorry and ashamed about your horse throwin' you. I wish I could go back and change that but I cain't, and I would be happy to ride up there with you but I'm scared plum to death," she shuddered again, "of that horse. I sure never wanted you to know that, but standin' here with you lookin' at me, I just cain't pertend anymore." She wanted to go ahead and tell him she loved him, but her courage failed and her voice just faded away.

Somewhere a dog was barking. Somewhere a mourning dove mourned. Somewhere to the north a train whistled at a crossing—but there on the road to Rose Saylor's house, a heavy silence lay—a heavy, brooding silence.

The man on the horse sat as if turned to stone. His hand still clutched the hat against his shirt and his body still bent slightly toward her. The only noticeable difference was that his mouth had fallen open.

The girl in the road hadn't changed either except that her focus moved down from his eyes to his dropped-open mouth. Maybe if she was really blessed, God would split the earth and she would fall in.

Eons passed before time finally started to move again, and Jack's mouth closed, his hand placed the hat back on his head and his body sat tall in the saddle. He patted Honey's neck absent-mindedly while his eyes searched the sky, the horizon, the cornfield, the road in front, and the road behind him. Then when he finally ran out of places to peer he looked at her again. Only this time the mirth in his eyes spilled over and his mouth began grinning and then laughing out loud. Petrified, Rose could only stare—stunned and horrified and humiliated, so naturally she started to cry. Flinging herself away from him she stomped off down the road. "You are a mean man, Jack Nash and you are as crazy as your horse!"

Her voice came to him filtered through his own laughter and though he tried to stop he just couldn't. Finally he and Honey started to trot down the road after her. When he rode beside her again he leaned far down and grabbed hold of her arm. She was fighting him until she realized her body was dangerously near the mad mare's head so she let him lift her off her feet and drag her onto the saddle in front of him. Rose drew back as far as she could just in case Honey chose to reach her head around and take a hunk out of her and that placed her tightly against Jack's chest but she was so frightened by the horse she didn't notice his nearness until his laughter had subsided and his voice began to seep into her consciousness. It came from right above her ear and she was suddenly aware of the pressure of him and his arm around her. After that whatever he was saying didn't seem to matter all that much. And the way he was holding her and the charming sweetness of his tone assured her she was in capable hands and exactly where she wanted to be all the rest of her life.

Understanding and accepting that, Rose let herself relax and just melted into him, and when she did she felt a shiver of excitement pass from her body into his that made her go all weak and trembly again. And Jack Nash held her like that while Wild Honey, trotting solidly under them, brought her home.

Jack left her at the side of the road near her house after planting a little kiss on her cheek at the last moment before he lifted her off Honey's back. Truth be told, it was so unexpected and so brief that later, except for a burning that wouldn't go away, she couldn't be sure it hadn't been all in her *imagination. The only conversation she remembered was him asking her how old she was and her answering that she'd be fifteen—but she didn't say when and he didn't ask.*

But that he said he would see her again the next evening was real enough and that set her to floating about a foot off the ground, a sight that, miraculously, nobody noticed and that was just as well too, because Papa would never accept Jack Nash as a fit suitor for his daughter. Rose knew that whatever relationship she might have with Jack, it would have to be their secret. But that fact didn't deter her in the least. Truth be told, the only problem in her life at that particular moment seemed to be that somewhere along the road home that afternoon, she had misplaced her lunch pail.

And so it happened, that the darkly handsome blackguard, Jack Nash, the unprincipled rogue of the entire countryside who had been the ruin of countless women and girls—he who had scurried from bed to bed with the insatiable appetite of a depraved wastrel and who was the prime example of moral corruption shouted about amid hellfire and brimstone from pulpits and in revival tents all over the state lost his incentive, whatever it was that had driven him, and sowed his last wild oat!

And the end had come out of nowhere and not altogether to his liking. He was still a month away from his 21st birthday, and had at least consciously no desire whatsoever to quit his wild and free existence to settle down, mate, and father children. Indeed, to his way of thinking, when he finally took the time to think about it, the only thing that could possibly have caused him to be so inclined, was one of those love-charms conjured up by that old herb-woman in Brewster's Wood. There had been some who tried that. He was sure the Saylors were a superstitious lot, and in his rare unclouded moments he did entertain the notion she might have put a spell on him. When he was feeling otherwise, he really didn't give a damn!

And all the while, he was hugging and kissing her and working up to things Rose knew shouldn't be allowed until after they stood before the preacher. It got so bad that evening in the hay shed she had to whack him a good one with her knee and the ensuing fuss he made was what drew Papa's attention and led to that beating with the horsewhip.

It was a long, sad time that followed that incident of course, because Jack just disappeared for a while. It was as if Brother had dropped him off the edge of the world that terrible evening instead of at the end of his Daddy's lane. Nobody mentioned his name and Rose feared she'd never ever lay eyes on him again. And having been with him like she had, that was a fate worse than death to her. She didn't know if he was afraid to show his face around because he was so terribly shamed by the whipping or if he just hated her so bad for letting her daddy catch them. Not knowing why or where he had gone was a cross she could hardly bear ... and her prayers got desperate! There was no soothing her during those terrible months. She became like a thing possessed, brooding and aloof, or growling and hitting and biting. Her brothers and sisters walked large circles around her and even Mama, Papa and Grammaw Saylor avoided too close an encounter.

Summer and Autumn 1927 to early spring 1928

Wallowing in bitter resentment, Rose refused to lift a finger around the farm, and come September, she started her final year of grade school, still determined to earn her diploma and prove Claire Louise wrong in her cold-hearted estimation of Rose's intelligence. That accomplishment being the only ambition in Rose's life other than becoming Jack Nash's legally wedded wife.

Her uselessness that year stuck out like a rowboat in a desert and she figured they might all gang up and kill her for being so lazy, but dying was about the only thing left to look forward to. Then, for some reason her family let her be, and the months piled up—Thanksgiving passed, Christmas came and went, and then a new year began and there was still no word of him. Jack Nash had been gone almost seven months and there still wasn't anybody who would admit to knowing anything at all about him. He could be dead by now and likely he was—

1927 was the summer Rose saw Grammaw Ida Belle just up and die one oppressively sultry August afternoon.

What Rose did mostly during the winter of 1927 and early spring of 1928 was walk the field road, forward and back, watching the days pass from sunrise to sunset. Sometimes she'd sing sad songs and when she ran through all she knew by heart, she made up her own words and sang them to the tunes of the songs she knew. Sometimes she'd take a paper and pencil and go hide in the hay and write long love letters to Jack, which would end up breaking her heart because she knew he would never read them. It was also during that dismal season that Rose shot up three inches taller and developed a truly-curvy figure, along with some other more serious and uniquely-woman modifications.

But it was most remarkable the way her family let her alone. She supposed it was because she had acted so ferociously at the start. They might have been scared she had got herself a devil, messing around with Jack, or become fixated on some other of their superstitious notions. It was a blessing to be let alone, though, so she didn't do anything to try to change their minds. She was to learn later that Papa had feared she was with child and was so relieved when she wasn't that he told the family to just let her be and not press her for anything till she got over being hurt. Papa figured he'd seen the last of Jack Nash anyway!

April 13, 1928

But fate knew different! And on April Friday the 13th, a month after her fourteenth birthday and just a few days before her graduation on Wednesday, he was back!

Suddenly without any kind of warning there he was on the road beside her again. Only this time he was driving a car! Her relief was so overwhelming she thought she might swoon and she did get a mite dizzy and sag against the door when he opened it. But right away, he stepped out and got her in his arms and was kissing her and squeezing her. Eventually he loosened his grasp on her, leaned back against the car, and stood for a while, just grinning at her and telling her to "stand back" so he could get a good look at her, and oh my—did he ever look her over—up and down, and down and up! Then he said, "Dammit, Rose Sharon, you are a sight for sore eyes!" And then he reached for her hands and put both of them to his lips and kissed them a hundred times. "Shit, there ain't nobody could have convinced me I'd ever miss anybody like I been missing you."

"Where did you go off too?" Rose's pouty mouth got thin and tight when she asked that. "Nobody would talk about you."

But Jack just shook his head, and kept grinning, "Maybe I'll tell you sometime." And then he motioned her to get in the car and when she did he slid in after her.

She settled herself and then started looking around at the car's interior. "This is real nice, Jack. Is it yours?"

"More or less" he grinned and the dimple lines in his cheeks got deeper. Then he stretched back in the seat and reached into the pocket of his trousers. "I've got a present for you." And before she could take a good breath, he had grabbed her left hand and was sliding a ring on her third finger.

"You and me are gettin' married today, Rosy." And then his cobalt blue eyes narrowed while he watched her face for a reaction to that statement.

He was pleased to see she wasn't repelled by it or even all that surprised, but she did seem to be stringing up a bunch of questions or conditions or something back there behind her eyes. "Well?" he asked, a little subdued by her lengthy silence.

At last she nodded and her face broke into a wide grin. "I am real relieved to hear that is your intention, Jack Nash."

Within minutes they were in front of her house and she was sliding out of the car behind him and following him up the steps to the porch, through the screen door, and into the kitchen where they found Olivia Saylor dissecting two frying chickens for the midday meal. Several boy-children of differing ages cluttered the room and saturated it with a noisy chattering not unlike monkeys in a jungle to which Ollie seemed oblivious.

But looking up to see Jack Nash in her kitchen did give her a start, though she managed to show nothing of her surprise and the only thought that came to her was "Thanks be to God, Papa is still in the barn!"

Rose, who in her excitement may not have shown the sense God gave a goose, forged a path through her brothers toward her Mama, with her hand stuck straight out so that Jack's ring glimmered and gleamed like the morning star for all the world to see. "Look, Mama," she said and her smile lit up the room.

Ollie's eyes went from the ring back to the chicken without a word. She knew her lack of reaction was a big disappointment to Rose, but she really didn't know what to say.

Minutes passed, and Rose and Jack waited in silence, watching dust motes drift through the rays of an almost blinding mid-morning sun that was pouring into the room through the wide-open, curtainless window behind Mama. But everybody else in that big square kitchen continued as they had been before the interruption. Gradually, Rose began to draw back her hand while her smile faded away. It occurred to her that maybe all those others in the room were not real people at all. Maybe they were just her imagination. Maybe she was still out there on that hot dusty road praying for Jack Nash to come back from wherever he'd run off to. Maybe Jack and his car and her ring were nothing but another of her crazy and desperate daydreams.

Rose sucked in a deep breath and exhaled slowly. She looked away from the mesmerizing sunlight, breaking her train of thought. Of course Jack was real and so was that ring on her finger ... she would not let her family ruin all the joy of this most perfect moment of her life.

With a resigned smile, she turned to Jack and one shoulder lifted in a hopeless shrug. He shrugged back and waited for her to decide what move to make "Well," she said finally, "it's plain to see nobody here cares one way or another about us, so we might just as well go ahead and do it."

She gave her Mama one last angry and disappointed glance and started walking toward the door.

Admiration for her feistiness made Jack grin, but instead of following her he moved close to where Ollie was standing, her face still without expression, staring down at the chicken parts on the table in front of her and the knife in her hand. The woman stiffened with shock though, when he slid his arm around her shoulder and hugged her to his chest.

"Now, Miz Olivia," and his voice was as soft as moonlight and as comforting as music, "I know you got some bad feelings toward me and I can't say they are altogether undeserved. But your Rosy has gone and made a new man of me. I guess you probably think that's a lot of bullshit..."

Olivia looked up then and saw he was shaking his head, "I didn't mean to say that—I mean—those words ..." He feared he might actually be blushing.

But then he felt her body sag against his and he breathed easier and smiled. "But since your old man horsewhipped me, I have done a whole lot of growing up. I moved out of my folks' house and I been working on my own. I got me a real pretty little house and a car and I aim to take very good care of your lovely daughter. I aim to marry her, Miz Olivia. And I haven't wanted to marry anybody in my life before." Then, with his natural arrogant charm restored in full measure, he turned her toward him and cupped her chin in his hand, raising her face so she had to meet his eyes. When she did and her weary brown eyes met his fire-lit blue ones, she had an instant awareness of his virility and for a split second of her own sexuality. She felt a sensation in the pit of her stomach she had not experienced since she was a girl and a whole passel of unseemly memories assailed her. With a desperate need to disassociate herself from such improper thoughts, she cast her eyes down, but then she was looking at his muscular young body and that gave her even less peace. So she closed her eyes and shook her head.

"Won't make a bit a difference to Rose Sharon's Papa. He's a hard man and he's got his notions and ain't nobody ever changed his mind yet. Leastways, nobody I ever heard about. Rose Sharon should of knowed better than to encourage you!" Her eyes flashed wide open for the first time then and looked into his and he saw the dispirited hopelessness of a lifetime of submission and resignation in them. What he wanted to do in that moment was grab her up tight and love her like a woman yearns to be loved. But that was an outrageous idea considering who she was, so he let go of her arms and she turned back to the chicken.

By then she was nervous, and she kept rubbing her bloody hands on her apron, wiping them again and again, while her heart pounded and tears of frustration threatened to gush down her cheeks. "What kind of a devil does this boy have to make me get them kind of feelin's?" she wondered. And for the first time she understood why all those women had always been after him. He really knew how to make a woman feel loved.

And then a smile began to tremble on her lips and she took a chance and looked at him again. "I reckon he can't stop Rose Sharon from marryin' you though, lessen he chains her to the wall. She's always had a mind of her own. You're gonna find out she's just about as stubborn as her Pa is," and then her eyes crinkled and some of the years went away. "But I wonder if you don't know that already?" And while their eyes studied and came to understand each other she couldn't help thinking how much Rose was going to enjoy being loved by a man like Jack Nash and recalling her own marital experience at the tender age of 14 as at best dull and at worst a repelling duty, she rejoiced at her youngest daughter's good fortune.

Jack called Rose's name then and she opened the screen door and looked in at him. "I don't want to do no more talkin', Jack. Let's just go on."

But he motioned her back inside and she came reluctantly to stand in front of him.

"Your Mama wants a farewell hug."

And though Olivia was hardly a hugging woman, she took a step closer and put her arms around her young daughter but just to please Jack, and Rose hugged her in return for the same reason.

Jack had an arm on each woman's shoulder squeezing them together and feeling a great deal of satisfaction at having brought a peaceable end to the encounter; he was grinning when he bent to give Rose a kiss on her cheek and then he squeezed them again.

"Well, you got my blessin', Rose." Mama had tears in her eyes, and the boys who had been scattered around the room seemed drawn suddenly as if by a magnet to crowd together around her. In those few moments an eerie blue silence descended and for a while all of them clung together as if enchanted—until something occurred to Olivia and she squeezed her daughter's hand, "But what about your diploma? You get it in just a few days and you made such good grades..." Jack feared a change of mind coming—maybe even from Rose herself who had not as yet given a moment's consideration to what she might be giving up by running away with him. Time stopped and his attention instantly focused on finding an argument to convince her she really didn't need a diploma while everybody's eyes turned expectantly to Rose Sharon.

Then, too late, they heard the sound of boots on the porch and the squeal of the hinges when the screen door swung open.

Art Saylor stood there in the doorway appraising the situation and instead of letting the screen door slam shut, he pushed it wide open and stepped to one side.

"This here door is open boy, and I'm gonna stand right here and hold it that way so's you can walk outta here. And then you'd best run quick as you can to that automobile out yonder in the lane and drive like a bat outta hell back to wherever it was you came from."

When nobody moved he spoke again. "I'm speakin' to you, Jack Nash. I'm warnin' you to get your heathen ass off my property! You ain't wanted here!"

Olly instinctively moved backward, freeing herself from Jack's arm, and the three boys moved along with her, still magnetized by her knees.

Rose's first reaction was fear, but that passed quickly and she rushed to gain control of the situation.

"Jack is goin', Papa, and I am goin' with him. We just come to say we was leavin'. We are gettin' married!" She took Jack's hand and pulled him along with her as she crossed to the door. When she passed her father she held out her left hand and shoved the ring under his nose. "There's no use you sayin' we can or we cain't. We don't care squash blossoms if you mind or don't mind. We love each other and it's all the same as done!" She moved on out the door and Jack, grinning and cocking his head in Art's direction, followed directly behind her. "Goodbye, Papa," she said without looking back. "I wish you coulda been happy for me."

Art Saylor was angrier than he had ever been in his life. Angrier even than when he'd laid the leather to Jack's back to punish him for taking liberties with Rose Sharon. He fumed and blustered and turned to look at Olly who cringed behind him; she was hardly more than a dark shape with the bright sunshine behind her and the younguns stacked around her like cordwood. "Why didn't you stop her?" he hollered and his voice had a crackle of despair in it. But when he got no answer his face screwed up with rage and he kicked open the screen door and roared out at them. "I'm gonna kill you, you son of a bitch, if my baby girl ain't back up these steps in half a minute." And over his shoulder he motioned to Olly. "Get me my gun, Woman!"

He said it three times but Olly just stood there staring at him—at his long, thin, sun-burned body with its sharp bones poking against his baggy overalls. At his yellowish-gray hair lying in damp and straggly wisps along his neck. And when he turned to see what was taking her so long, she looked at those cold, pale, watery eyes above a thin-lipped mouth that only barked harsh orders to her or preached hell and damnation at her and she shuddered.

Then she heard the automobile engine start up and heard it speed away, and her exhausted body sank down onto a kitchen chair. A memory of that moment when Jack Nash had touched her chin and looked into her heart flickered across her mind and she couldn't help smiling. Rose Sharon was going to know what it felt like to be a woman all right, being loved by a man like that one—being married to Jack Nash and having his babies.

She sighed and realized she was smiling. "Get your own gun, old man," she said softly. "And while you're about it, why don't you just go ahead and shoot yourself!"

Rose was smiling too now, just remembering it. Two years ago, in the early spring, her brothers the twins Andrew and Joseph, big strapping boys who looked older than their 17 years, came to Chicago with some buddies looking for work. They spent several hours with her and Jack and related what had occurred in the farmhouse after she and Jack had driven away, and everybody had a good laugh over Papa's comeuppance. But Rose felt sorrow too, for Mama, who had to put up with her husband's meanness all of her life and never even had anybody to complain to. As for her brothers, they weren't long in Chicago—they quickly got homesick for the South and hopped a freight headed in that direction. The last Rose heard, they were working in Tennessee.

March 1928

As for her own marriage, being the wife of Jack Nash was just about as pleasant a thing as going to heaven without having to die first. Anyway, that was how Rose felt about it.

He moved her to Maysfield, which was just far enough away from her family to suit both of them and where he was working in Raymond Delaney's Sawmill and Lumberyard. And it was plain to Rose the first time she met Mister Delaney that he thought Jack was the best thing that ever happened to that burg. "Jack keeps everybody up on their toes trying to keep step with him," he told her with a sincere nod of his head. "That boy's the hardest workin' youngster ever set foot on this property." And then he went on to tell her how he treated every customer as if he were the only one they ever sold anything to. "It's gettin' so they won't do business with anybody but that tall, good-lookin' dark-haired kid ... That's what they tell us when they walk on the lot. 'I want that tall good-lookin' dark-haired kid to wait on us'." And then he grinned and winked at her. "That boy's got charm!" he said and then he leaned his head down to hers and spoke in a loud whisper, "That boy could charm the devil right out of his pitchfork, M'am. And that's the truth. And you can take whatever Ole Ray tells you as gospel!"

He just couldn't stop bragging on Jack, and pretty soon Rose was all puffed up with pride. It was an entirely different world over here in Buck County where people had an altogether different opinion of Jack Nash. Here he was treated with respect and looked on as honorable, which he surely deserved to be. The only thing Mister Delaney said to her that even got close to how people slandered him back home was that an awful lot of ladies had started coming in with their husbands to pick out their lumber. And he laughed when he said it, like he knew they just came in to get a look at Jack. Truth be told, in Raymond Delaney's opinion, it was a great bit of luck to have hired him, and amusing to boot!

At home that night when she told Jack how Mister Delaney had bragged on him, he grinned real big and pulled her down onto his lap. "Well, Sugar, that man just wastes more time givin' compliments! He couldn't say enough about my sweet little wife either! 'She's got the prettiest color hair I ever saw,' he says, and all day he's asking this fella and that, 'Did you see the color of her eyes? They're like shiny new pennies,' he says, 'hidin' behind the longest curly black eyelashes I ever saw!" And then Jack kissed her. "I may end up havin' to fight him for you, Rose Sharon."

But Rose knew he wasn't serious about that. The one thing she knew for certain was Jack Nash was way too sure of himself and his way with women to ever get jealous. When some man looked at her with admiration or even with lust in his eyes, Jack just stuck out his chest and grinned. Jack Nash proudly considered their leering a compliment to his taste in women.

And she had come to know that Jack liked the way she looked, too. That probably had more to do with his marrying her than anything, although she was aware that the fire of her character and her down-to-earth sense of humor and bull-headed perseverance helped seduce him. But to a man with Jack Nash's appreciation and love for women, looks made a mighty big difference when choosing the one he would spend his life with. He told her himself that of all the women and girls he'd loved, and he assured her there weren't anywhere near as many as he was renowned for, Rose was the only one who crept into his dreams afterwards. And the only one he couldn't just put aside and forget. Ten months away from her had only made that fact more evident and in the end he had to return, in spite of the humiliation of their last encounter. He admitted he was even fearful she might not want him anymore and he'd been jubilant enough to shout "Hallelujah" when she said yes, except he didn't want to mislead her into thinking he'd "got religion." And they laughed a long time about that.

Jack appreciated the fact that she went away with him, even though it got her disowned by her Daddy and made her an outcast to all her family. There was no doubt in his mind that Rose Sharon Saylor was in love with him so he drove her away to Maysfield that afternoon and got a justice of the peace right there in town to make everything legal. Then he took her to the little one-bedroom house he was renting and that was where they spent their first night together. Rose liked to relive that night over and over in her memory and she could recall every single minute of it to this day. Nothing before or since had been as scary or as awesome or had affected her as profoundly. It was as if Jack Nash had only one purpose in life and that was to love her. That was how he made it seem anyway, and that appeared to remain his purpose even after all these years. Rose knew she was the luckiest woman in the world!

March 11, 1928

The next morning he took her to a café for breakfast and then to that fine ladies-wear store in town—Miss Anna's, where he told her to pick out the prettiest dress they had and never mind the cost. And that was what she did. But she didn't dare look at the price tag because she knew she'd probably faint if she saw what it said. It was plain enough that the store was expensive. Rose picked out several dresses, and the saleslady led her away to a room in the back with a curtain instead of a door and helped her try them on.

She didn't bother to go out and show them to Jack, though, except for the blue silk (that was what the lady told her it was), which she fell in love with the instant it touched her skin. The material was kind of thin and it had its own special undergarment built right in and that was made of a slinky material you couldn't see through. The entire thing was as soft and light as moonlight and that was what the color brought to her mind. A pale light blue that was the color of moonlight.

Jack's sky-colored eyes got real big when he watched her walk up from the back of the shop and his smile came on like the sunrise. "Dammit, girl" he said in a low voice when she got close enough for him to take hold of, and he slipped his arm around her and raised her up on her tiptoes in a big hug, "I swear you look good enough to eat!" And then he looked over at the saleslady. "We'll take this one and don't worry about a box. She'll wear it home."

By then a bunch of customers were standing around gawking at them, and Rose had started to blush. But Jack just gave them all a friendly grin and walked her over to the counter, where he asked the saleslady to pick out a set of her best undergarments and make sure they were in Rose's exact size. Then he leaned across the counter and whispered something to the woman, who smiled and led Rose back to the room with the curtain door where she helped her out of the dress so she could slip into the underwear. And just before he paid for everything he told her to add a pair of silk stockings— even down to the garters, and "some high-heeled dancin' slippers" to the list.

That was the best time Rose ever had in a dress shop. Truth be told, it was the first time she'd ever set foot in one but it wasn't the last. Jack bought her a new dress just about every payday after that but never another one so special. And once they were out of that store, he put her into his car and as they were driving away, he insisted she put on the stockings and dancin' slippers right there in the car while he drove her all the way to Jackson. It was just a little honeymoon present, he told her, and while they were sightseeing they ran across a portrait studio and impulsively, Jack took her hand and they went inside. With his winning ways, he talked the photographer into taking their picture right then and there and that was how that portrait in the oval tin frame, her most treasured possession, came about.

That was the spring of 1928, and the world had never looked brighter.

1929

But as Rose soon learned, nothing ever stays the same and neither had those good times. In the fall of 1929 came "Black Friday" and although it didn't bother them much at first, eventually the lumberyard stopped selling lumber. After a while, nobody could afford to build anymore. Ray kept Jack on as long as he could; Jack even worked a while at half wages, but finally the day came when Raymond Delaney had to shut it down and sadly bid the young folks goodbye and good luck.

Jack tucked his tail between his legs and kissing his pride goodbye along with his house and furniture, drove Rose and a few personal belonging back to his Daddy's farm in Dobbin.

And sadly, Art Sailor hadn't been the only disgruntled father in the wake of Jack and Rose's elopement.

Tobias Nash had reeled in disbelief at the news. Surely his son, coming from an educated, well-to-do family with a long and noble history, could do better than a sharecropper's daughter, never mind how pretty she might be. Surely there was some town girl—maybe the banker's daughter, Beatrice, wasn't it? Or Jasper Philpot's girl. Jasper owned the whole west side of town. Or even the Reverend England's daughter. At least there was some prestige attached to the clergy. Anybody but an unschooled, coarse-mannered, sunburned, share-cropper's daughter. How would she ever fit in with Abigail and the girls? Especially, the daughter of that self-righteous son-of-a-bitch who humiliated the whole Nash family with the lashing he gave Jack. If Jack hadn't been so set on keeping that incident quiet, Art Saylor and his brood would have been dumped across the county line in the clothes on their backs and penniless that very night—and then this disaster could never have happened. There had been talk of disinheriting and disowning and other more or less drastic retaliative measures, but in the end it had come down to "Just keep her in Maysfield and out of your Mother's house."

Jack figured that would be easy enough. If they didn't want Rosy, they didn't need him either. And he was willing to spend the rest of his life sans Daddy and Daddy's money.

But then, who could foresee such a terrible Depression. There was suddenly no place to go except home. And although he wasn't welcomed back like the prodigal son, at least the door wasn't slammed in his face. Or in Rose's either. So for a time they settled into his old room and Rose busied herself alongside his Mama and his sisters in the house and learned to keep her opinions and her notions to herself. It didn't take her long to get used to a household run by housekeepers and cooks, though—nor to miss the luxury of leisure when they were let go, which happened very soon.

On one occasion she got up the nerve to walk down the back road to visit her own Mama. She had stood for a long time by the creek in the seclusion of a stand of willow trees a little ways behind the barn while she prayed for courage. After several false starts up the lane toward the house, she was about to give up altogether and go home to the Nash's when somebody called her name from the direction of the barn.

"Rose Sharon! Is that really you?"

Rose stared into the dusty-dark and finally made out a form standing on the half-wall that divided the horse stalls. The girl had her hands on a beam in the ceiling to keep her balance and had been looking into a swallow's nest that was mudded against the rafter. It was her sister Flora. Flora was seven years older than Rose, but there was something wrong with her mind and she was slow. She still acted like she was 5 or 6 years old and sometimes she would throw fits and act like she was crazy. Most of the time, though, she treated Rose like her big sister.

She was smiling now. "Come up here Rose Sharon and see the bird nest."

Rose crossed the barn quickly to pause in the passageway in front of the stalls and contemplate whether she wanted to take a chance on soiling her dress by climbing the wall. "Come on, Rose Sharon." And Flora's voice was already sounding stressed. Rose figured any minute she'd start screaming at her and then all hell would break loose up at the house.

"I'm comin'!" she assured her and grabbed onto the top of the wall, swinging herself up to straddle it. Quickly she shimmied to where she could grab hold of a post and pull

herself up on her feet. Once she was standing on the wall she reached for the beam and worked her way to Flora's side.

"Look in the nest," Flora instructed with a grin, her good nature restored.

And Rose looked into an empty nest.

"The baby birds are all gone" Flora said with a shake of her head and a wistful smile. Rose patted her arm and nodded.

Then Flora sat down and slid off the rail, and Rose followed her.

"I really been missin' you, Rose Sharon. Where you been keepin' yourself?"

Rose hugged her and kissed her cheek. "I'm a married woman now, Flora," she said proudly. "I'm livin' with my husband."

But Flora shook her head and laughed at that notion and then, without warning, she was aggressively pulling her toward the house. Rose resisted. "Let's stay here and just talk awhile, Flora." She tried to keep her voice gentle and reassuring while she struggled against her sister's single-minded determination, knowing it would be impossible to make the girl understand her reluctance to see the rest of the family.

"How is Mama?"

"Mama's up yonder in the house. She wants to see you."

"Is Papa here?"

"Oh Rose Sharon! Papa's up yonder in the house." And then she gave up pulling on her and got behind her instead and tried pushing her up the lane. She had dug in her heels and was butting Rose with her head and it was all Rose could do to stay on her feet. Flora was bigger than her and outweighed her by more than 30 pounds and she had the tenacity of a bull-headed child.

"Silly Rose. You silly Rose!" She was shouting it over and over, making a game of it. And her giggling was catching. Despite her concern about being discovered, Rose started giggling too while she struggled and wrestled against her sister.

Then, all of a sudden Flora stopped everything and stared seriously into Rose's eyes. "Mama misses Rose. Mama cries for Rose Sharon."

"Did Mama say that? Flora, did she say she misses Rose Sharon?"

The girl's lips formed a contentious pout and she shrugged, "I don't remember." Then the seriousness passed and she started to giggle again. "I know Mama wants you to come see her. Let's go home, now! Pleeeeese, Rose Sharon?"

But Rose was full of dread and in spite of her eagerness to see her family again, the dread was winning out. "I think I better not right now, Flora. I think I better go away again." And she tried to disengage Flora's hands from hers. She was not having much luck, though, until Papa's angry bellow snatched Flora away from her as neatly as if he had reached out and plucked her up.

"Stand away from that harlot, Flora, and get yourself up to the house!"

Rose watched as Flora raced up the lane, passing her father who was bearing down upon her and a frenzied panic exploded within her. She saw herself flying apart into a million little bits and pieces, and what was left of her mind was telling her she'd better gather everything up and put herself back together before she could turn away and run from him—back to the safety of Jack Nash's arms.

"Sweet Jesus! Sweet Jesus! Sweet Jesus!' She prayed as Art Saylor narrowed the distance between them.

When he faced her at last, she had a moment to look into his eyes and she saw anger there so menacing she couldn't even comprehend it.

"You're my Papa!" she cried incredulously. "How can you hate me so bad?"

"You're no daughter of mine, you Jezebel! You are a curse on the family name!" And he reached out and grabbed hold of her arm with one hand while the other slashed through the air and smashed against the side of her head. Rose felt her brain slam against the other side of her skull, and she thought she was going to pass out, but he struck her again before she had time to do that and then with murderous rapidity, twice more.

Rose had begun to slide downward and except for his hold on her would have fallen into the dust at his feet. The sunny afternoon darkened and Rose wished for a quick and merciful death.

Flora had created a storm of curiosity with her agitated state when she climbed onto the porch, and when Olly realized it was Rose's name she was screaming over and over amid the tears, a terrifying black cloud of fear descended upon her and she darted off the porch past her daughter and down the lane that disappeared behind the barn. She didn't believe her eyes when she saw her husband hunched over and clutching the child's limp body with one hand while he punched her again and again with the other.

Olly screamed out his name but he seemed not to hear her. "No! No! Don't hit her anymore! Stop! Stop! Stop!" She was already breathless from the running and screaming but her husband took no notice of her. When she reached the place where her daughter sagged against his legs she swung out her arm and hit him with all her strength—a tigress protecting her cub, and he withered before her like a piece of severed grass in the August sun, dropping Rose on the ground at his feet.

Olly fell to her knees to embrace and examine the girl. She was bleeding from her nose and her mouth and Olly feared she was already dead. Tenderly and with a desperate and terrified prayer on her lips, she cradled Rose and rocked her while she pleaded with God not to let her die. When she was sure that Rose was still breathing she looked up at Art Saylor and warned him with her eyes to keep away. Time was moving in slow motion for her. Maybe it would never move normal again. If Art had hurt Rose in any permanent way, time might just cease altogether.

An agonized moan slipped past Rose Sharon's broken lips and her eyes flew open. They were so full of fear that Olly's anger exploded and she cursed her husband but her focus returned instantly to her daughter who was calling Jack's name. "Jack, Jack," the girl whispered in a voice weak with pain. "He's gonna kill me!" And then Olly started to fear the girl had been struck blind because she seemed not to see her even though she was looking directly into her face. "Rose Baby. My little Rose Sharon. Can't you see me?"

Then Rose looked right into her eyes and the tears started pouring. "Mama, Papa tried to kill me!" Olly drew her close to her breast and rocked her some more. "Everything's gonna be okay, Rose. You're safe now." And then unconsciously, she began humming the lullaby she had sung to quiet all her babies across the years.

After a while she looked up and saw her husband was still standing in the same spot staring blankly at nothing and her face twisted with scorn. "You'd best find somewhere to hide, Old Man. When Jack Nash sees what you done to his wife, like as not he'll come to kill you!"

The rest of the family had made their way down the lane and Mama sent Grace to fetch a basin of water and a towel and they tried to wash the blood off Rose's face without causing her any more pain. Then they put some pillows and a blanket in the wagon and with Mama stroking her hair and Brother driving the mule, they made their way down the back road to the Nash farm.

Brother suffered real dread at the notion of bringing Jack Nash's woman back to him all bloodied and broken, and it took all his Mama's bullying just to keep him in the wagon. She wasn't too joyous about meeting up with Jack under those conditions either, but there didn't seem to be any other way to get Rose back home.

When Rose got calm and quiet, she started to ask questions of her Mama in a shaky voice. "I know Papa hated Jack after he caught us in the hayshed, but why cain't he forgive him now that we're married?"

Mama shook her head. "Ain't no tellin' why a man thinks the way he does. Their reasonin' tends to be a mystery most times."

But after Rose had asked the same question three or four different ways and Mama had evaded a direct answer the same number of times, Brother spoke up from his seat at the front of the wagon. "Fer cryin' out loud, Ma, just tell her the truth. All the rest of us know why he's so mad at her."

Rose saw Olly lay a displeased look on her eldest son and then sit in silence for a while, staring down into Rose's eyes.

The Nash house was in sight down the long lane when she finally spoke again. "Your Pa had four little girl babies that grew up lovin' and honorin' him like a man's daughters ought. They gave him all their respect and treated him like a man feels *he ought to be treated. Like the Bible says, a man has the right to be honored and obeyed. And nary a one of them ever put another man ahead of him!"* She paused for a moment and looked down at the bruised and swollen face of her daughter and then she sighed and started talking again.

"But his baby girl, the one he loved better than all the rest put together," she paused to take a deep breath, *"better even than me—"* and then she paused again, *" before she was even done playin' with her dolls, she had turned all her love and respect toward another man, though he was still just a boy back then. But in such a brazen way, your Pa couldn't even purtend it was just some little-child crush. Rose Sharon, you spent so much of your attention and love on that boy, you just broke your Papa's heart because he couldn't find any place for him in yours. And then when Jack started down the road to perdition at such a young age floutin' all of God's commandments that your Papa reverenced, you being so attached to that boy just stuck in your Daddy's craw with him being so helpless to change your mind. So there was nothin' he could do but stand by and watch you both go down into hell. It nearly killed him, Rose Sharon."*

Rose heard Brother snort and mutter something and saw her Mama glare at his back.

"What did you say, Brother?" Rose sobbed.

He didn't answer her, but Mama sighed and said, *"Brother thinks your Daddy had an unnatural affection toward you."*

"I ain't the only one. Gracie and Ida Belle and Claire Louise think it just as much as I do!"

Mama's sigh sounded so weary. *"They just resent how he always favored you, Rose Sharon. It is true he loved you most. But there weren't no sin in that. Jacob loved Joseph most of all his sons."*

"And look at all the trouble that cost his family." Brother's voice was bitterly sarcastic.

When Olly spoke again, her voice revealed a profound sadness. *"Your heart always belonged to somebody else, Rose, and your Pa was just disappointed—disappointed and heartbroke jealous like any man might be for the one he holds closest to his heart."*

Brother snorted again and went on with his grumbling, but Rose stopped listening. The notion that it was too much love that made her Daddy beat her almost into the next world didn't make a bit of sense to her and struck her as outlandish! She figured it was just another case of Mama trying to come up with excuses for her husband's meanness.

Lucky for Brother and Mama, Jack was gone when the wagon pulled up to the Nash front porch and Olly didn't have to make too detailed an explanation to Abigail, who felt that anything was liable to occur when a couple of ignorant sharecroppers got together. "Best to let sleeping dogs lie," she cautioned her daughters afterward, when they wanted to pry into the particulars. She saw that Rose got to her room and dispatched Sally to fetch her a pitcher of cool water and some fresh linens so she could clean away the smears of blood and dust and then left her alone the remainder of the evening.

It was dark by the time Jack got back, and since Rose feigned sleep, he didn't light a lamp or disturb her in any way.

By morning, although she looked awful, she felt much improved and was able to talk him out of, or at least postponing the killing of Art Saylor.

But Jack never again would allow her to go anywhere near her family.

After that, there was another period of good times, though it was discomforting to put up with the Nash prejudice against her family and their patronizing attitudes. But Rose was adaptable and nothing kept her down for long. Maybe she couldn't have meals alone with her husband or spend long, quiet evenings alone with him in front of the big fireplace in the living room, or ever be alone anywhere in that big old house except in their bedroom upstairs, where truth be told, they weren't all that much alone anyhow, with Molly's room on one side and Sally's across the hall.

But they could go for walks together, and there were several secluded and secret places they could stop along the paths they took. Places remote and beautiful where their natural inclinations could surface and be satisfied with complete privacy, and were! And Rose never stopped thanking God for letting Jack Nash fall in love with her. Sometimes her happiness scared her, how even a thought of him would thrill and excite her, and the sound of his name lit a fire inside her. When she watched him bounding across the yard in the evening to meet her on the porch, the animal grace of his smooth gliding long-legged lope made her skin tingle and sparks twinkle up and down her spine. It was entirely likely that no mere human should be so happy. She couldn't imagine that even heaven would be more perfect. And maybe just thinking that was a sin. Still, she couldn't change how she felt. And as long as Jack Nash was with her, nothing in the world could bring her down. Not as long as he was nearby, and not even if he was far away, as long as she knew how much he loved her.

Jack was running the farm for his Daddy again. And the Depression wasn't getting any better. In fact, it just kept getting worse. Lots of farms were being foreclosed on. Lots of houses in town, too. And stores were closing, and banks. Nobody seemed safe from the ugly black fingers of that evil demon that kept reaching farther and farther into the countryside touching more and more people Rose knew—lots of whom were leaving their land and even their wives and kids and moving off to places like Chicago and California.

Claire Louise and her husband, Walter, had gone to Chicago some years before, not too long after they married and Walter had worked his way up in the insurance business. They were well off before the Depression hit, but Rose didn't have any way of knowing how they were faring lately. She knew that several people from the Dobbin area had gone to Chicago in the last year hoping that Walter could find work for them. Rose and Jack seemed pretty safe, seeing as how Toby Nash's farms had been in the family for generations even before the Civil War and were not likely to be lost. There sure wasn't much of an income anymore, though. Nobody could afford to buy anything the farmers harvested. But at least you could always grow your own food. "Something to eat and a roof over your head" was enough to give thanks and praise to God for during those lean times.

But then, the worst that could happen, happened.

1930 Winter and the Spring of 1931

Rose knew something was going wrong at the Nash farm. She could feel extraordinary tension whenever Mr. Nash was around. Whatever was causing the stress was never talked about or even hinted at, but where there used to be laughter and gay evenings around the supper table or in the parlor after supper there was now a dark and ominous quiet. Voices hushed when either she or Jack entered a room. Looks were exchanged that were fearful or angry ... or what? Rose was deeply puzzled, but Jack had no answers for her and she dare not question his family. So she watched and waited for some clue to explain the mystery but none came. Many days passed in that deep purple twilight. Rose felt the darkness of night coming, but it dallied and that strange twilight lingered. And the days turned into weeks, until months had passed. And still the darkness waited to fall and she became more and more fearful of its coming.

Then one especially oppressive, sultry evening in early spring, a storm came up. It was so violent with the wind ripping limbs from trees, and lightning and thunder crashing and rumbling and cracking that the house started shaking with a strange and alarming vibration that filled Rose with foreboding and dread. She lit a lamp in their bedroom because the flashes of lightning jarred her so badly coming out of the pitch blackness of that night. And the tempest went on and on. "Jack, I'm gonna lose my mind if this doesn't stop." And Jack was uneasy himself, though not unduly. But neither of them could sleep, so he held her in his arms there in their four-poster bed and sang to her. All the bawdy ballads he could remember. Eventually she was laughing with him at the ribald stories the songs told. Toward dawn the storm passed and the house settled down to an occasional creak. Jack blew out the lamp and they both slept.

And it was to an unexpectedly harsh world that they awakened.

Downstairs in the parlor, sometime during that terrible night, Tobias Nash had taken a gun and put it to the head of his wife, *Abigail Butler Nash*, and squeezed the trigger. Then after he saw for certain that she was no longer alive he pressed the same gun to his own temple and ended his life as well. There was a long letter of explanation on a lamp table between the chairs where they slumped.

Sally and Molly, their two daughters, had found them like that after they came down for breakfast to discover the kitchen cold and dark and empty. Their search took them to the master bedroom, where they commented jokingly to one another that because the bed was already made it was plain they were no longer in it and from there they broadened the search to the barn and smokehouse and stables. The last place they looked was the parlor because that was the last place anyone would think to go so early in the day.

The sight that confronted the two young women in that room was one that Sally the eldest would carry with her into an institution for the insane some years down the road, and Molly the social butterfly would carry through three doomed marriages and into a slow death in an alcoholic stupor, abandoned and alone in the elegant New Orleans townhouse she had received in her second divorce settlement.

Of the three Nash heirs, only Jack would overcome the memory and he alone seemed to be the cause of it. The letter told the story.

When Jack, after having been beaten and humiliated by Art Saylor, ran away from Rose and his Daddy's farm, he threw his saddle on Honey's broad back and rode west. He got as far as Texas, where he happened upon a dance hall and got blind drunk. Before he'd sobered up again, somebody started a fight over somebody's girlfriend and somebody got killed. Jack, being a stranger and incoherent, was the most convenient suspect and he was subsequently arrested and charged and pretty well convicted even without a trial. Feelings against him were high and he was in a dangerous situation. He needed the best lawyer money could buy and maybe a juror or two and perhaps even a judge. It would take a massive amount of cash to save him.

Toby Nash was very well off, but that much cash wasn't just lying around the old plantation or even in a bank account, so to get the money quickly he mortgaged his farms. That was no big deal at the time. He would pay it off when the crops came in. The money got into the lawyer's hands and Jack got acquitted and moved on. He wandered around Texas for a while, worked here and there until he found himself in another triangle and decided to mend his ways. He moved to Maysfield, a mid-sized town in Northeastern Mississippi, got himself a job, turned his life around and came back to Dobbin, where against his family's wishes he picked up little Rose Sharon Saylor, took her away with him, and married her.

In spite of the family's fears, all was well enough—until the stock market crashed, the business market turned bad, and the crops couldn't be sold. So there was no money to pay back the note and no way to acquire the money to pay back the note. Toby had exhausted every hope. The bank was going to foreclose. No amount of talking or compromising, no old friends or family to come to their aid. No hope at all. Everything was lost, and Toby and Abigail could not and would not cope any more. There would be no bread lines for them, no poor house ... and most of all, no having to look up to a worthless sharecropper as being better off than they were. Theirs had always been a cultured, genteel, and noble lifestyle; their families had always been highly respected by everyone. They could not accept dealing with poverty and want. The only thing left for them to do was take out the big gun and shoot each other. So sorry, Sally! So sorry, Molly! So sorry, Jack! You no longer have a big fine house to live in. You no longer have all that land and the tenant-farmer-families to work it. You no longer have crops to harvest and sell. You had better pack your suitcases and hit the road. It's every man for himself now. Please forgive this awful mess we are leaving you. Goodbye and Good Luck!

And so it was that Master Tobias Nash and his faithful wife, Abigail, who had so recently been mighty pillars of society in their little corner of the world and prime examples of the virtues of honest labor and Christian faith, who had always treated their tenants with justice and mercy, became little more than a bad memory and an everlasting dark spot on the parlor carpet.

After he saw to the burying and was able to settle his sisters comfortably in the city of Biloxi with the help of sympathetic family friends, Jack Nash decided to leave Dobbin. The story in the letter became common gossip and nobody wanted him around. Some people felt his questionable character was responsible for his parents' suicide. Some had old festering resentments because of his notorious reputation with women, and some who were strict teetotalers had heard about his alleged moonshine connection. And then there were some who weren't so sure he shouldn't have been hung for that killing in Texas. Whatever their reasons, at the wake and funeral Jack saw plain enough he wasn't wanted in the neighborhood. He was utterly friendless and even his sisters, especially his sisters, both of whom had once doted on him, wasted no time in booting him out of their lives. Without his Daddy, whose prestige and reputation as a gentleman had up to then been his defense and protection, he was at the mercy of anyone who held a grudge against him.

So the day after the funeral, Jack made his plans to move on. There wasn't anything to hang around for anyway. Everything belonged to some bank somewhere and would undoubtedly be sold for a pittance to somebody sooner or later. The tenants would go on working the land. They'd just be giving Tobias Nash's share to the bankers. There wasn't any work, and he'd just as soon have a whole lot more miles between Rose and her family, who seemed now to be uncomfortably near. And with all those who saw him as a murderer, it didn't seem unthinkable that somebody who hated him anyway, somebody like Art Saylor, might just blow him away some dark and gloomy night and get the neighborhood's thanks and glory to boot.

Being poor was not something he relished either. Rose would handle it, he knew. Rose would handle anything that came along, but he wasn't really that adaptable himself and moreover he didn't care to be. Some things just weren't acceptable and being poor was one of those things. So he decided to do what dozens of his neighbors had done. Go north to Chicago. "Anybody can get rich in Chicago" was a promise he'd heard bandied about by young men of his acquaintance *while he was still in high school. Well, maybe rich was too much to expect right now, but at least there was work there and he wasn't ashamed or afraid of hard labor. So he and Rosy packed two suitcases and left Dobbin forever. He'd found a man from a nearby town who was driving up there in his car. So Jack sold his jazzy Chevrolet soft-top for what cash he could get and they hitched a ride.*

It took two days driving straight through, and the man turned out to be a crook. He tried to drive off with their suitcases when they made a rest stop in Memphis, but Jack caught him and after a serious discussion behind the gas station there was no more trouble.

April 1931

In Chicago, the man drove them directly to Sister Claire Louise's great big elegant, yellow and white mansion, which turned out to be in a very comfortable neighborhood. Both Jack and Rose were surprised at its grandness.

Not wanting their crooked friend to impose on the Bradley hospitality, they hurried him away as soon as he dropped them off in front of the house and made their way up the wide walkway to an impressive Victorian-style front porch. Once they reached the security of the front door, Jack's natural confidence and pride returned in full measure and he grinned gleefully at Rose Sharon. "Well, Sugar, we have done it! We are on our way to the good life!" And then he pressed the doorbell. "Look around you! What do you see little Rose Sharon?" He pressed the doorbell again and by then Rose was practically bouncing up and down and she just kept smiling and shaking her head as if she couldn't believe any of it. "Shit! Sugar, the world is beautiful, ain't it?" and he pressed the bell a third time. "Give us a year, maybe less, and we'll have a house like this. And we'll have our own automobile again." He tilted his head toward a fine, shiny black car in the driveway. "Don't it feel good, Rosy? Dammit! I sure feel good!" And he leaned his head toward her, flashed her a big grin, and whispered *"Maybe you ought to start thankin' that man upstairs you're always talking to."*

Then he hugged her and she had just raised her head for his kiss when somebody pulled open the heavy front door. It didn't open wide, though, just enough to see Sister Claire's skinny face peering at him with those unpleasant watery blue eyes of hers; that was when Jack noticed how much she favored her old man and a foreboding shudder shook him. But being naturally optimistic, he thought maybe she didn't know who he was so he pushed Rose up in front of him. Then Claire Louise made a strange moaning noise and appeared to be undecided on whether to open the door further or close it altogether.

Rose smiled sweetly at her big sister and Jack grinned happily, and they both leaned forward anticipating their invitation inside. But Claire all of a sudden was outside with them and she was pulling the heavy door shut behind her. It made a soft solid thud and something about the sound froze the blood in Rose's veins and sent a stabbing pain through her heart. She didn't look at Jack but she knew he was feeling the same chill move over him.

Claire's face looked a lot like Papa's, and her voice was full of a similar poison. A lethal poison that was killing all the hope and the joy and the love that had just started to grow again in the two of them. The poison poured out all over everything and would have utterly destroyed them had not Walter Bradley, curious about his wife's disappearance, opened the door and interrupted the flow of venom.

Claire Louise went right on talking while he stood behind her and when he realized the gist of her words, his face darkened and in a low and angry authoritative voice, he told her to shut up.

But Claire Louise was undaunted and with her neck stretched back to get a look at him, she growled. *"These are my people, Walter. This has nothing to do with you!"*

"This is my house, Claire, and I will say who can come into it!"

"These two will never come into my house, Walter!"

"My house, Claire."

"My house, your house, St. Peter's house!" She was hissing and flailing her arms by then. *"Whose-ever house! Jack Nash will never enter into it."* She looked so malevolent and sounded so deranged that Jack backed away and pulled Rose with him.

But Walter stepped out the door and took Jack's arm *"My wife is having some kind of serious mental collapse, Jack, there's no other explanation for her action. And you mustn't take anything she has said seriously."*

But Jack did take it seriously. *"Thanks, anyway, but if she feels so strong against us, we don't want to come in. We'll find someplace else to stay till we get on our feet."*

"Oh come on, Jack! I won't hear of it! We've got plenty of extra bedrooms. Of course you'll stay with us. And just as long as you need to."

Then suddenly there was complete silence; it was as if the world had stopped turning. Rose stood stunned, staring at her sister and marveling that she could be so mean and ugly. Surely it was all a mistake. Surely it was some terrible misunderstanding and she hadn't meant to say what it sounded like she said. To come up to your relative's front door full of good feelings and love and to be met on the front porch without even a *"Hello, how are you?"* and ordered to take yourself and your suitcases back where you came from, was just too outrageous. Even Claire Louise wouldn't be that nasty on purpose. And Rose decided to give her another chance. She really believed she'd jump at the chance to apologize and make up for the bad feelings and explain that she really didn't say what it sounded like she said.

So Rose smiled at her again. A trusting and hopeful smile. *"We didn't get a chance to say anything, Claire Louise, but Jack and I came up here to Chicago to get work because we've had some real bad times back home. Jack's folks lost everything and there's no jobs anywhere. But we won't be no burden on you and Walter. We just need a place to stay until Jack finds work and a house for us. Surely that won't take us long in a fine big city like Chicago is. If you could just put us up till we get our own place. Jack's got some cash."* She grabbed his hand and held onto it. *"We will be glad to give it* all to you. And I can help around the house ... cleanin' and washin' dishes, and cookin' too if you'd like..." Her voice started trailing off into nothingness when she realized that Claire's face was still frozen in the same hateful expression and that her eyes, though she met them straight on, held no mercy at all.

Rose turned hopelessly to Jack who looked beaten and then back at her sister, who crucified her to the wall with a look. "I don't care where you go, Rose Sharon—just get off my porch, take that man and your suitcase, and go away from here. This is a big city—" She had more to say, but Walter took her arm and moved her aside. "Claire!" he was so astonished by her invective that his reaction time was sluggish. But she wasn't ready to back down—she pressed forward instead and thrust her face close to Rose's.

"Our Papa warned you not to marry Jack Nash, and you betrayed him and ran off with that heathen! My loyalty is to my Papa and I don't care if you find a place to stay or not. I just want to make it clear to you that Walter and I will not use our money to keep Jack Nash in whiskey and tobacco. He can sleep in the gutter for all we care, and since you chose to share his bed you can sleep right there beside him!"

With that, Jack picked up the suitcases and turned on his heel toward the steps. Rose followed without a word.

Walter took a moment to squeeze Claire Louise's arm until she whined with pain and then he called after Jack. "Wait! Wait a minute! Jack! Don't go anywhere yet! Get in the car ... my car's in the driveway. Get in it! I'm going to call some people I know and get you a place to stay."

Jack turned toward the car and then looked at Rose. "What should we do?"

"Get in the car," she whispered.

April 1931 to December 1933

Walter Bradley was a big man, and tall, with wide shoulders and a broad chest. He stood 6 or 7 inches taller than Jack Nash and was raw-boned without a speck of fat on him—and the man's heart was as big as he was. He was so distressed about Claire Louise's mean reception of them that he thought they could never make up for it. But he did. He found them an apartment that very afternoon, moved them into it and paid 3 months' rent so they could keep what cash they had, and by that evening he even had Jack lined up for a temporary job loading and unloading trucks at a warehouse not too far from the apartment. They had two rooms and a bath above a shoe repair shop with two tall windows in each room overlooking the street. Their landlady, Mary Jean Turner, owned both buildings. Her husband had operated the shoe repair shop, and the grocery store to its right on the corner was rented out to the Wesselmans, a middle-aged couple of German descent. Mary Jean had lived in the front apartment herself for years until the recent death of her husband, when she moved to a smaller apartment at the back of the same building. Her door was at the other end of the landing, and she mostly used a narrow back staircase that went right down to the grocery store or outside to the alley. Walter had known her for years, and also the Wesslemans—he had sold all of them insurance when he first came to town. That was how he knew Mary Jean had a vacant apartment after her husband died.

The warehouse wasn't that great a job, but it brought in some money and it kept Jack busy. Gradually, as they came to know the neighborhood better, a lot of little odd jobs became available, and their life settled into a pleasant routine again. And very soon Rose started helping out in the Wesselmans' Grocery.

Leo Wessleman was in his middle 50s and not much taller than Rose, with a powerful oversized torso and short muscular legs. He was exuberant and gregarious and seemed to have the strength of a bull; he was always proving his vigor by hoisting heavy cases of canned goods onto his shoulders and heaving weighty grocery boxes into the delivery truck—"showing off," Viola called it, with a smile and behind her hand. She, on the other hand was quietly efficient and retiring, fragile as a wren and about as colorful. But she was the sweetest lady Rose had ever met; Viola had immediately set herself the task of playing mother to the girl and once she did that, Rose never had another real worry about anything. Before long, Leo had taken the part of father to both her and Jack and from then on they were *"the kids,"* and whatever they needed was theirs. Neither Rose nor Jack had ever had such unconditional love given to them before, and they were so charmed by the Wesselmans they couldn't do enough for them in return. All in all, theirs was a most satisfying relationship.

Before long, with Jack working every day, Rose was spending almost all her spare time in the store. She developed a special kinship with Leo because he was so outgoing and kind and she had never been able to relate to her own father that way. Leo encouraged her to open her heart to him, so she did. He understood her even better than Jack did, because his was the same spirit of attachment to the earth and all natural things. They shared their most secret selves. He understood her need for solitude sometimes, the joy she experienced when she walked barefoot in the grass or freshly turned soil, which was not easy to come by where they were. The alley behind the store had a patch or two of dirt with a few sprigs of grass shooting out of it, but it was mostly graveled over. And except for an occasional fleeting whiff of the wet earth just as a shower begins, Rose never got to enjoy that most pleasant fragrance. There just wasn't enough real dirt anywhere near them.

But together they watched the seasons change that first year. It was already autumn before Rose knew it, and there were a few scrawny trees squeezed between the alley and the backs of the buildings. Rose had to admit she'd never seen such pretty colors as those leaves turned. But there weren't any geese flying across the night sky, or if they were, you'd never have seen them with all the bright lights. And you'd never have heard them with all the city's noise. And the migrating birds that flew low across the fields back home, twisting and turning all of a piece like a giant bolt of dress goods, were flying elsewhere as well.

That first winter was nothing like anything she'd ever experienced before. It was ungodly cold … a piercing cold that penetrated her heaviest coat to chill her to the bone and freeze the marrow in it. And for a while she didn't believe she could stand it. For a while all she wanted to do was fly south herself. But Jack laughed at that notion and shamed her out of it. Then, one strangely hushed and windless evening brought the first snow and Rose found it mesmerizing and so beautiful that she spent the first hour racing from window to window just watching it fall; fat floppy flakes that looked like scraps of lace drifted haphazardly in the still air like drunken butterflies. She felt caught in a dream and she couldn't turn away until it had covered the street and the sidewalks and frosted the tops of street lamps and automobiles and drifted over garbage cans and crates to hide all the ugliness in the alley. Jack had rushed her down the back stairs and opened the door to the alley so they could reach out and catch some flakes in their bare hands and on their cheeks and hair. Everything was changed as if by magic into mysterious shapes of spun sugar that glittered and sparkled in the lights of the city.

The snow fell all night and most of the next day, and that dirty gray city was absolutely transformed into a fairyland, all rose and blue and deep purple depending on the time of day and the slant of the sun, when there was one. Rose and Jack played in it, she rubbed her cheeks with it, she tasted it. Jack showed her how to make snowballs and they made them in the alley and threw them at each other. And at the deliverymen and Leo and Viola and Mary Jean, and they got stung right back. They even made a snowman and Rose opined how much fun her brothers would get out of playing in the snow with her.

Yes indeed! That first snow was a glorious revelation to Rose and an adventure of epic proportions for the young lovers from Mississippi. But the beauty passed soon enough when the soot and salt and crush of feet and vehicles turned God's lovely gift into a nasty brown slush that got pushed here and there and melted and froze and melted and froze as it snowed again and again and more and more piled on top of it. Snowplows pushed it up out of the street onto the sidewalk, and shopkeepers shoveled it back off the sidewalks and into the street, and winter went on and on and on until the notion of ever having found it beautiful became a ludicrous joke.

Leo had shared all these new experiences with Rose and Jack, and he enjoyed the seasons more than he ever had before, because they shared them. The other thing he and Viola shared with Rose was a simple unquestioning faith in God. Jack left God and religion to the womenfolk. He didn't doubt there was one, but he didn't see any connection between that God and himself. He had managed to repel Rose's attempts to church him from the very first month of their marriage and in such a forceful manner that she hadn't approached him about it again. Not that she was a church-goer herself, it was mostly Bible reading and now and again a revival or a visit to a particular preaching.

Now, though, with the Wesselmans' support she was going to church fairly often and the weird thing was … the thing that would have caused her Papa to skin her alive … she was going to a place called St. Mary's—one of that Roman Pope's churches. A *Catholic* Church. Even Jack's eyebrows kind of raised up at hearing that. Not that he knew anything about it. Or cared either, but there'd been so many years of hearing people tell about the wickedness and Godlessness of that "Papist Religion" that he just naturally shrank from it. He did ask her a few questions and he did remind her of the way her people felt about it, but she reminded him that she didn't have any people anymore. That they'd all cast her out, so she felt like she was free to make up her own mind about that church and anything else that took her fancy and he just shrugged and agreed that every word she said was exactly true.

So Rose went to church with Leo and Viola. She helped out at their store, and Jack worked at the warehouse and shoveled snow and did odds-and-ends repair and maintenance jobs here and there. Rose cooked his meals and washed his clothes and mended and ironed his shirts and kept his house in order. And all the time they were able to be together was spent loving each other. Holding onto, kissing, and caressing each other. And when they couldn't be physically in contact, they loved one another with their eyes.

The only way Rose could have been happier would have been to live in the country again. To dance with feet bare upon the tender earth, to feel again the thick mowed grass in the

Nash front yard tickle her unshod toes. For Rose was a child of nature and she had a fierce need to absorb whatever strength, whatever mysterious life force it was that came only from direct contact with the earth, with the soil—something that concrete, asphalt and tar-covered gravel prevented her from absorbing.

Thus time passed. Money didn't come any easier. Jack went through some periods of depression when his natural optimism, good humor, and trust in the goodness of life and his pride in the power of his manhood rose and fell with the amount of money he earned in any given week. Most of the bad times would end with Rose sweetly counting off the marvels he had accomplished so far, and between the recitations her sweet mouth would kiss away the weariness, the sadness and the depression while her body nestled close to his and everything in her made love to him. Jack never knew about the despair that would rise in her heart when he descended into one of those dark pits. She hid from him the desperation that threatened to overwhelm her whenever he … her rock … started to disintegrate. Still, neither of them ever gave up on their dream of better times and it was that dream, and Rose's faith in Jack, that kept them and saw them through the hard and lean years.

All through the rest of December and into the New Year of 1934, Rose couldn't stop regretting her rashness on that morning when she brought up her sister Claire Louise and the Christmas presents. That was one of those *spoiled-little-girl tantrums* she succumbed to with disheartening regularity, and it was downright mean on her part to rake up again all those bad feelings for Jack.

During her reminiscing today, Rose recalled a cold and rainy November afternoon the first year in Mary Jean's apartment, when the memory of Claire Louise's vicious rejection of them was still fresh and bloody in her and Jack's minds. Jack was still at work and Rose was preparing supper when there came a soft but determined rapping at her door. When she opened it she was pleasantly surprised to find Walter Bradley standing there, but the pleasure-part evaporated instantly when she noticed her sister trying to hide behind him.

November 1931

After sighting Claire Louise, her first inclination was to deny the woman entrance. So some minutes had passed before those proper Southern manners she had picked up during her sojourn with Abigail Nash kicked in and she stepped aside and motioned them both into her home. Walter embraced her warmly and immediately began an explanation of Claire's visit—Claire stayed just inside the door, plainly ill at ease and nervous to the point of shaking while keeping her eyes on the windows across the room and away from Rose altogether.

"I know you probably would rather we didn't come around, Rose, but I can't have you living right here in the same city with us and not be concerned about your welfare. You are the only family we have close by so unless you really despise the sight of us, I hope you'll see fit to spend some time with us."

He saw that Rose was smiling but her face looked drawn, and the smile wasn't reaching her eyes. He closed his eyes for a moment and took a deep breath. "There is no excuse for the way you and Jack were treated that day on our front porch. No excuse and no explanation that anybody who isn't living with bitterness and prejudice in their hearts could accept or understand." He reached out and took Rose's hand and held it to his chest. "So we will certainly understand if you can't or choose not to forgive us right now. But perhaps you might forgive us when more time has passed? Perhaps later you will be able to find forgiveness in your hearts—Jack, too?" He looked back at Claire who was still staring toward the windows. "At any rate, Rose Sharon, that is our purpose in visiting you today. We come to apologize with shame and humility and to ask your forgiveness."

Then he squeezed her hand before letting go of it and called Claire's name. His gentle voice had taken on a firm edge.

When she turned her eyes to meet his, he nodded. "It's your turn, Claire."

Claire Louise looked as though she wanted to bolt out the door and down to the street. For one instant Rose thought she might even prefer taking a quicker way—out the window rather than humiliate herself with apologies. But eventually, she started talking and although she still couldn't meet Rose's eyes and was instead staring at the top of her apron she did speak the words Walter asked her to. Near the end of her monologue, her breath caught and her voice cracked and unbelievably to Rose, tears started to run in little rivulets down her pale, bony cheeks.

After a while, her voice came back and it was shrill with desperation. "I'm so ashamed, Rose Sharon!" she shrieked and looking down started to fiddle with the clasp on her purse, finally opening it and rummaging around until she came up with a handkerchief. "And everything Walter said is true. There is no excuse for the things I said or for the way I acted." She looked up at Rose and met her eyes for the first time. "If you can never forgive me it will be exactly what I deserve. And I won't blame you. Walter says I am nothing but a "whitened sepulcher" and a "hypocrite" because I call myself a Christian and I pretend to 'pray with the tongues of angels but I have not love' and all of that is true, except I really couldn't see it until last evening when the Lord spoke those very same words to me when I knelt to pray."

Rose was flabbergasted! She almost dreaded Claire Louise's skinny cold arms around her and she feared that was her intent, so at first, she was more aware of her own thoughts than of her sister's confession. While Claire held herself in check Rose's brain went over and over the tearful sentences until they sank in and then her mouth opened and made a pretty little circle of surprise. But instead of grasping onto Claire, she threw herself against Walter and hugged him. Pretty soon her own tears were making a wet spot on his coat and with some embarrassment she backed away and shook her head at both of them in turn. She couldn't recall ever having anybody apologize to her before and the experience was staggering. She remained speechless for some time, but Walter was smiling by then, and he looked at Claire and nodded his approval. Then Claire took another deep breath and dabbed at her nose with the handkerchief.

"I came here to say I'm sorry and ashamed and to beg if I must, that you forgive me and that you will not hate me anymore."

Rose just stood there with her mouth open.

Claire Louise's face screwed up again and the tears, which had abated some, gushed down like rain water from a drain pipe. *"If you can't forgive me, Rose Sharon, I'll just have to accept that as God's punishment."* She stopped talking long enough to blow her nose. *"And I will just stay away and pray that someday things will be different. Walter has been at me ever since ... ever since the first day you were here, to try to make it up to you. And to Ja ... your husband, too"* She was having some difficulty saying his name. *"And I knew as soon as Walter drove you away that day that I had sinned grievously. But it is so hard for me to admit my sins. Even when I know them in my heart. It's so hard for me to admit when I am wrong."*

Rose still didn't know what to say. Maybe Claire really was sorry or maybe Walter Bradley had made her so miserable she had to "say" she was. Whichever was true, Jack wasn't likely to be so quick to forgive. Should she? It wasn't Rose's nature to hold grudges or to stay angry. But out of loyalty to Jack, who had been badly hurt and humiliated by Claire Louise's meanness, maybe she ought to let her stew in her own juice a while longer.

"Oh sweet Jesus," she thought, *"please give me wisdom!"* and then she looked squarely into Claire Louise's pale wet eyes. *"I ain't sure what to say Sister Claire. My Jack was well-nigh crushed by your mean mouth, when all we came to ask you for was some neighborly hospitality. I feel like he's the one you hurt the worst and he's the one you ought to be beggin' forgiveness from. For my part, you're my sister and I cain't hate you. I know that sooner or later I'll forget what you did and I'll forgive you. But I don't think I can do it today. Not today, yet."*

Claire Louise nodded. *"I can understand that, Rose. What I did was terrible ... awful! I don't know if even God will ever forgive me."* And then she was weeping again. She looked at her husband for encouragement but he was frowning at her *and now he shrugged. So she looked at Rose again. "I am not the same woman I was all those months ago when I sinned against God and you, Rose." Her shrill voice softened then. "God has turned it to my good," she continued. "He has shown me what a miserable hypocritical life I was leading and how far I have to go just to be the least of his disciples. I feel that now I am truly on that straight and narrow path of which the Bible speaks. I feel like I've spent 30 years fooling myself, thinking I knew God when I had not the vaguest idea who he was or what he wanted of me."*

While Claire was confessing, Rose looked past her to see Jack Nash enter and close the door behind him. His dazzling blue eyes took in the scene before him and Rose could see he was torn between greeting Walter and booting Claire to the end of that "straight and narrow path" she was walking on.

Claire Louise's voice trailed off to nothing when she realized neither Rose nor Walter were listening and were looking at something in back of her. So she turned in that direction and recoiled instinctively at the sight of the man she had abused. Jack's wide, electric-blue eyes passed over her, unnerving her even more, but he chose not to acknowledge her presence. Instead he reached out his hand to Walter and in one long stride was in front of him shaking his hand and grinning a warm welcome.

"If you ain't a sight for sore eyes, Walter, I don't know who is!" Then he turned his head to look at Rose while he was still pumping Walter's hand. "You got some coffee made?" And then he looked at Walter again. "Rosy made some apple cobbler a day or two ago that tastes like the angels baked it. Sit down over there at the table and she'll get you a plate." He let go of Walter's hand and motioned to Rose to get the coffee on while at the same time moving across the room to stand behind her, squeeze her against him and kiss her cheek, letting his hands slide across her breast as he left her.

Rose had automatically obeyed, and the room and its occupants waited in silent anticipation while all eyes watched her fill the pot with water, set the percolator basket inside, and measure the ground coffee into it—she was so flustered she couldn't remember how many spoons to add, but she went ahead and pressed the lid on top, set it on the burner, and struck a match to light it. When the blue flame appeared, Jack rubbed his hands together and with a movement of his head motioned Walter to take a seat at the kitchen table. He saw Walter look anxiously at Claire, who seemed so ill at ease he almost felt sorry for her. But he had made up his mind she wasn't even there and he behaved accordingly. Walter observed that Jack seemed not to have noticed her at all. She was invisible to his eyes.

Walter didn't know what to do. Perhaps he had presumed too much bringing her into Jack Nash's house without some sort of preliminary discussion. He'd been a long time away from the bitter and unforgiving feuds of some of the people back home. Maybe he should have handled this differently.

He studied Rose's face seeking her thoughts but she revealed nothing. Then again he turned his eyes to Jack. He was so young and so sure of himself. His dark head was tilted back, showing a strong chin and a wide angular jaw, high well-defined cheekbones and an almost hawkish nose. Those striking blue eyes were certainly extraordinary, looking out from behind heavily lashed lids. His hair, dark and straight and cut a little longer than was the current style, gave him a rugged unkempt look, but Walter imagined that was part of his charm for the ladies. His smile was disarming and wide, showing all his teeth. Walter thought Jack Nash looked a lot like an untamed and high-spirited stallion, straining against the reins of civilized humanity, who was apt to rear up on his hind legs and stomp a fellow at the first opportunity.

Sensing his contemplation, Jack slid his eyes to meet Walter's and with a quizzical expression asked, "Did you say something, Walter?"

But Walter shook his head, still puzzling about what his duty was to Claire in that uncomfortable situation. Finally, he took a deep breath and came right out with the question. "Jack, I can see now I made a serious blunder barging into your home like ..."

Jack was shaking his head and he raised his hand to signal silence. "Hey, Walter," he said, and his smile was sincere. "You're welcome in this house anytime. As a matter of fact, I feel real honored that you think enough of me to care to come at all." He looked over at Rose who was just setting some cups and saucers and pie plates on the table and started laughing. "I know some of the things I'm supposed to have done make me unsuitable company for righteous society, and most of them walk across the street to avoid my shadow." Then the grin waned and he gave Walter a serious nod. "but I'm not so ill-bred that I'm ungrateful for the kindnesses you showed me and Rose Sharon in our hour of need."

Walter's eyes moved uneasily from one to the other of them and his smile looked embarrassed. "Please Jack, don't mention it! Really! What I did was no more than anybody would have done for family. There's no need to be grateful..."

Jack stuck out his chin and snorted. "But I believe there is need. To my way of thinking ingratitude is an ugly trait. But the point I'm getting at, Walter, is that while I'm indebted to you and couldn't like you more if you were my own blood brother..." he paused and shook his head while his eyes iced over. "I can't even look at that wife of yours without wantin' to puke."

Rose was as stunned as anybody else in the room, and she almost slid to the floor in a faint—the table being right there to hang onto was her salvation. She heard herself say his name but she had no idea what she intended to follow up with had he answered her.

As it was, she and Walter and Claire Louise just stopped breathing and stared at him, and he looked from one to the other of them with blue ice chunks where his eyes ought to have been. And it was plain he didn't care squash blossoms what any of them thought about him or his sentiments.

"You understand, Walter, I've had nothing but grief from Rose Sharon's family. That crazy old man of hers like to beat the shit outta me with a horsewhip one time. And then I had to practically kidnap the girl to make her my bride while that old man stuck his head out the screen door squealing like a stuck pig and pointed a shotgun at my back—. And then one day Rosy wanted to see her Mama again so she walked over there to that house by herself one afternoon and the damn sonofabitch grabbed this little girl and beat her with his fists *until she was bloody and unconscious and would've killed her if Olly hadn't got him off her. And I never lifted a finger after any of this shit to get back at him. And the only reason I didn't was because I love Rosy so much and that was what she wanted. I 'turned the other cheek' like she wanted me to do...."*

Then he turned his head to look at her and his blue eyes heated up a little while the tip of his tongue licked at the corner of his lips. Momentarily, he was facing Walter again. "But when that wife of yours opened her front door and without so much as a 'Hello, how are you?' cursed me and her own little sister to hell's damnation and sent us and our suitcases to sleep in the gutter 'for all she cared!' that was, so to speak, the old straw that broke the camel's back." He tilted the chair he was sitting in until it was standing on only one leg and then he spun around in it to face Claire Louise, who was still standing where she had stood when he first stepped into the room.

The shock of having his attention on her so suddenly gave Claire no time to turn away or even to avert her eyes, which got caught on his, and once riveted by that intense blue stare, could do nothing but stare back at him. Which she knew instantly was a huge mistake. The man was a devil exactly as she had always suspected and now quite naively she had put herself in a place where he held all the power. But even as she thought that, she had to acknowledge, at least to herself, that his beauty was striking and his audacity disarming. That was the moment she decided it was no wonder someone as young and innocent as Rose Sharon had been snared in his trap.

Claire Louise believed herself wise in the matters of the flesh and the devil, even though she had no experience with either, except in Biblical terms, which didn't have all that much to do with the real world. She believed every bit of gossip she'd ever heard concerning Jack Nash, and knew he was a lost soul, but she had regretted her un-Christian treatment of him and Rose Sharon simply because it was un-Christian and she felt shame and humiliation knowing Walter had seen her betray all her own preaching on the subject of loving as God loves. That was why she had agreed to apologize. But now she was regretting the apology.

Rose could see what Jack was doing, but she doubted Claire Louise had ever had a man look at her like that, so she wouldn't have the slightest notion what was going on. Rose glanced at Walter who was looking at his wife and probably wondering why she was staring at Jack like she was. Rose was so sensitive to Jack's sensuality she could feel the heat even when it wasn't directed at her. But neither of the others in the room had a clue to his spitefulness. He was out to humiliate Sister Claire, by muddling her thoughts and bringing her to a realization that she was just as capable of the sin of lust as he was. Rose was certain he didn't know Claire Louise Bradley, though. She was just like Papa as far as sin went. She knew what it was and she knew how to fight it, and even a man with Jack's charm wouldn't tempt her. That was what Rose thought.

But Jack saw confusion and wonder at the strange feelings she was experiencing and he got up from the chair and in a couple of his long, rolling strides stood right there in front of her and his whole demeanor was that of a tomcat on the prowl. Nobody except Claire Louise could see his face anymore and she didn't recognize it for what it was ... but she reacted unconsciously. And Rose, watching her from across the room, thought she just might throw herself into his arms and demand satisfaction.

By then Jack had started to chuckle and he stepped around her, allowing his body to brush hers, as he swaggered to the bedroom door where he turned to grin at her. "You see, Sister Claire? You're not on that straight and narrow road after all. You're still down here in the shit with all the rest of us sinners!"

Then, he lifted his arms and locked his hands above his head and after an obviously feigned yawn he turned his back on them and announced over his shoulder that he was going to bed. "As soon as you get rid of Sister Claire you can come to me, Rosy. I do believe I've worked myself up to something." And then he was laughing. Just before he got out of her sight, he turned back one more time and spoke to Claire Louise. "Oh! just so you understand me, Sister Claire, so there's no doubt as to my meaning, I'm gonna say this slow and easy one time and then I'm gonna start getting mean. I don't ever want to see your sorry-looking ass in my house again!" He clicked his tongue two times and then he was gone.

He returned a moment later, however to see Claire still staring after him with her face flaming red. He wasn't sure if it was shame, embarrassment or fury that colored it. But he smiled at Walter that time, and his manner was sincere and charming. "Walter, you're still welcome here if you care to come." And then he disappeared a final time, and Rose was left to pick up the pieces of the evening—which seemed like an impossible task.

Claire Louise was weeping again, and Walter had risen from his chair at the table. The coffee was bubbling against the lid of the pot, playing its cozy little kitchen ditty, and Rose stared at it, utterly discombobulated. She felt Walter's arm brush hers as he moved toward his wife, and she reached out and took hold of his sleeve.

"Walter, don't you want a cup of coffee? It's all perked now." She nodded her chin at the cobbler in its pan in the middle of the table, and added weakly, "And a piece of pie?"

In spite of his distress, Walter grinned. "Rose, I really don't think this is the time for a cup of coffee. I think Claire and I better tuck our tails between our legs and run for home." He patted her hand still clinging to his shirt. "Don't feel bad, Rose. Jack's been abused—and badly, by the whole Saylor clan. He needs time to heal and forget."

Rose laid her other hand on top of his and her eyes searched his. "But you've been so good to us, Walter. I just cain't bear to see you get hurt."

He hugged her against his chest while Claire stayed in the center of the room staring at them through dripping red eyes. "I'm not hurt, Rose Sharon. On the contrary, I'm very sympathetic to Jack. I've had my own problems with Art Saylor."

He released her then and walked Claire to the door. She was whimpering at him and saying something in whining, broken sentences. Walter was nodding and patting her back as he maneuvered her out of the room. "I'll be in touch, Rose. Don't give Jack a hard time about this. He was driven to it."

Rose nodded her head and closed the door behind them.

Then remembering the perking coffee, she went to turn off the burner—luckily she caught it before it had all boiled away.

February 1934

Jack never did forgive Claire Louise, though she did venture back now and then, always stopping at the grocery store downstairs first to make sure Jack was gone and wouldn't be back for as long as she visited.

Rose didn't like keeping those visits a secret from her husband, but she liked even less the idea of him finding out about them.

And Rose believed that Claire Louise really did want to be a good Christian and that she wanted to make up with Jack. So she never told her to stop coming. It would have been pleasant to have a good relationship with the Bradleys. Then they could have visited in that grand house and Sister Claire was always wanting to buy things for Rose, which of course she couldn't because of Jack's bad feelings. And after that last December's argument about accepting her Christmas presents, Rose knew there would be no more offers.

So the years had passed and although Rose never did give up hope entirely for a real reconciliation, she got to where she didn't really believe it would ever happen.

But now! Now all things were being made brand new! And wasn't it grand how the Lord just planned everything out so perfect. At any other time in their marriage a baby could have been a worrisome burden. For so much of the time there hadn't been a spare penny for anything extra. Hardly enough for even the necessary things, but now since Jack had this really fine job ... they already had more money than they needed and he'd only been there a month. As hard as Jack worked and as likable as he was, the Lord only knew how far he could go! Soon they could get a house in the country or at least in a neighborhood with grass and trees and backyards. And little Jack (she just knew their baby was a boy made in the

93

image of his handsome Daddy) could have lots of nice little boys and girls to play with and go to school with, and later on there'd be a real special girl he'd love for all his life and eventually marry.

"O sweet Jesus!" Rose prayed over and over, "Thank you for being so good to me!" She could hardly stay in bed, there was so much going on in her mind. She felt there must be something she ought to be doing but it was not yet dawn and she hadn't slept at all. She probably needed more rest now. "Oh Jack, please come home." She said it out loud that time and hugged his pillow tighter and then she said it again and again, while tears of frustration leaked down her cheeks. After a while she started rolling back and forth clutching the pillow against her body and absolutely losing control.

"Jack Nash—I cain't stand it anymore. If you don't come home I'm going to Claire Louise's house!" She sat bolt upright in bed, realizing she had all but screamed the words out. Shocked at her lack of control she pressed the end of the pillow over her mouth while hot tears washed down to be absorbed in the feathers. She lost track of time passing while she sat there like that, her naked legs crossed under her, watching the sky through the windows grow pale as daylight began even though it was another cloudy one. It was then that she heard the creak of the front door swinging open and she listened to it close again and then she heard Jack's footsteps bringing him through the parlor to where she waited clutching his tear-soaked pillow.

He was surprised to find her awake and sitting up like that and even more surprised when he became aware of the whimpering sound she was making and then he saw her tear-swollen eyes.

Jack undressed quickly and was soon in bed with her, tossing aside the damp pillow and pulling her close into him.

"What's the matter, Sugar?" he asked. "Why the tears?" He wiped them off her cheeks with his thumb and looked deeply into her eyes in the dim gray light while he tried to imagine the meaning of them.

Rose couldn't stop sobbing. In fact it only got worse and worse the more he tried to console her. So he gave up trying to get an answer and just started kissing her eyes, her forehead,

94

her nose, and finally her mouth working her into a prone position where he could lie beside her and study the situation from a more comfortable angle. Naturally all that comforting and studying led to more and more intimate positions until it got out of hand altogether and Jack never did find out what was the cause of her tears. He did notice the soggy pillow however, and in a fit of self-indulgence just before he turned over to fall asleep he jerked hers out from under her head and replaced it with his chilly damp one.

The day had advanced into early afternoon before they awoke again. The sky looked even darker through the windows then it had at dawn and sure enough the air was full of snowflakes. Not those big fat lazy ones but tiny, sharp, swiftly falling bits that were almost ice. They were so thick Rose couldn't see across the street when she looked out and looking down she saw only a dizzying circular movement as the snow blew in every direction on a howling wind. It was not the kind of day she'd hoped it would be. She wished for sunshine and bright blue skies or even one of those softly dreamy snowfalls wouldn't have been bad, but this! This was ugly and dangerous and full of bad omens. Not at all the kind of day to tell Jack about his baby.

She turned her back to the window and rested against the sill. She could feel the cold wind right through the pane and it chilled her very soul. A feeling of dread washed over her. The same kind of terror she'd felt all those years ago when she watched Flora running away to the house and her papa pounding down the dusty lane toward her with the devil's own malevolence in his eyes.

Rose's body shuddered involuntarily and she flew across the room and back to Jack's side in the bed. He opened his eyes when her body touched his and he gave her one of his most dazzling smiles. "Feelin' better, Sugar?" He mumbled and his arms reached for her and pulled her closer. "I don't like it when you're sad, Rosy. It makes me hurt to see you sad." He kissed her and then laid his face against hers on her pillow. "You want to talk about it?"

Rose thought about that for a time, but when she finally talked it wasn't what she needed to say to him anyway. "I miss you so much whenever you go away, Jack. I cain't hardly stand it when you're gone."

He nodded. "I hate that too, Rosy." Then he raised up on an elbow and looked down at her. "I reckon that's about the worst thing about this job." He was tracing around her mouth with one of his fingers and she was beginning to want him to love her again. His eyes followed his fingers and when he traced around her eyes, their eyes met and she grabbed his hand pressing it to her mouth. "I love you, Jack Nash! I love you so bad I feel like I could die of it. I don't want you to be away from me anymore. I'd rather be poor again then have you away from me!"

Jack's sky-blue eyes widened with wonder. "Why, Rose Sharon! It pleases me to hear you say that."

She glared up at him. "You already knew that, you wicked man. The thing that pleases you is me bein' such a fool for you. You are just as mean today as you were the first time I told you how much I loved you."

His eyes began to crinkle, although his mouth turned very serious. "Come on now, Sweet Rosy! You break my heart when you talk like that. You think I don't know what a lucky man I am to be laying here next to the prettiest woman any man ever laid eyes on, not to mention the softest and sweetest and tastiest..." His voice drifted away as he lowered his head and closed his mouth once more over hers.

Darkness crept into the room very early that afternoon and as happy as Rose was to have Jack lying beside her, the strange dread of the earlier hour kept crowding in on her. She had a perfectly natural desire to tell him about the baby and she worked up to it three or four times during the course of the day, but somehow she never managed to get it done. She couldn't begin to understand what stopped her. Or why. She was so sure he'd be pleased and excited and happy. Wouldn't he? Maybe it was just her own worries. Maybe she was a little jealous thinking she'd have to share him finally with somebody else. Even if it was her own flesh and blood. Well, she reasoned to herself, it *would* be hard to share him, but she'd adjust to it. You just did what you had to do.

Eventually it was evening and Jack was suddenly hungry. They hadn't eaten all day. He jumped out of bed and was dressed in a flash. "Come on! Come on, Sugar! Let's go to Gertie's and get us a sausage sandwich!" He went to the wardrobe "What you want to wear?"

Rose sat up in bed and was immediately overwhelmed with nausea and no matter how she tried she couldn't stop the gagging and retching that ensued.

Alarmed, Jack rushed to her side. "We don't have to eat sausage!" His eyes told the confusion he was feeling. "A bowl-a chili, maybe. O ... Well, shit!" he cried with exasperation, "Gert don't serve nothin' that ain't swimmin' in grease!"

Rose would have liked to laugh but she couldn't stop retching. Jack helped her out of bed and into the bathroom where she tried to relieve herself of whatever caused the heaves, but there really wasn't anything in her stomach. The only thing she'd eaten since Jack left two and a half days ago was one old dry biscuit!

Jack was getting scared. "Rose Sharon, what's the matter with you? Do you need a doctor?" He started for the door. "I'm gonna get Viola. She'll know what to do."

But Rose called him back. She had to tell him now. That is if her stomach could settle long enough for her to talk. She sat near the edge of the bed, letting her feet dangle over the side and holding a pillow tight against her stomach. The retching gradually subsided as she willed herself calm, and as soon as she was able, she reached for his hand and pulled him down beside her. Jack's arms slid round her and her fear ebbed slowly away. They sat like that in silence for a while and she didn't want to ever move out of the circle of his arms.

Eventually, though, he turned her to face him. "Rose, I'm gonna see you get to a doctor tomorrow. You scare the shit out of me when you get sick. It ain't like I can't afford to pay a doctor, now."

Rose sighed deeply and plunged into her story. "It's nothing to worry about, Jack."

"Well, I think different. I think I want to worry about it."

She tried again. "I've been tryin' to tell you all day, Hon," and then she paused and got lost for a while in his fantastic eyes. When she could see her silence was starting to annoy him, she blurted out, "We got us a baby started inside-a me."

Jack's expression didn't change but there was a tremor that passed through him and ended right in Rose's heart. She felt that awful dread settle down on her again and somehow it was cutting her off from him.

His voice was quiet and calm. "How do you know that, Rose? For sure, I mean?"

"Lots of things, Jack. A woman just knows."

She felt nervous and testy and it came through in her voice. "You can just take my word for it, Jack. I got your baby in me."

Jack's arms were still around her and his hands were clasped together holding her tightly and she felt his arms stiffen and then move still closer about her. His voice was soft and his lips brushed her hair. "I never wanted any babies, Rose. All I ever wanted was you."

She twisted in his arms and pulled his head down to hers. Her mouth opened upon his and she kissed him with fearsome desperation. "Please don't say nothing you cain't take back, Jack. Please don't. It will take a little gettin' used to, is all. It ain't nothin' we cain't work out. It's my baby, Jack. And it's your baby. It's gonna be more for us to love—that's all."

He didn't pull away from her physically but she sensed his leaving her in a way that was even more terrifying.

"I don't want a baby, Rose. I never did want a baby. I never *will* want a baby. All I want is you!"

She rested against him in silence, putting words together in her head, and then she took a deep breath before she finally spoke again. "All I ever wanted was you, Jack."

She felt his body relax against her and then he started laughing. "Well, shit then, Sugar! There's no problem. All we got do is get rid of it!"

It took a moment for what he was saying to sink in, and when it did Rose's heart fell into the pit of her stomach and a weird weakness overtook her so that she just crumpled onto the bed, bringing Jack's body down with her. He seemed to realize her disintegration as he let go of her and raised up to look into her face. But she closed her eyes so she wouldn't have to look at him.

"A baby is a gift from God" she whispered. "You cain't just '*get rid*' of it."

Jack wrapped his hand in her hair and jerked her head hard, so she had to open her eyes and look at him, and that time his voice was as hard as stone and as cold as death.

"A baby is a piece-a shit that happens when a man f----s a woman, Rosy" His anger was so fierce it seemed obscene and Rose started to feel sick again. The retching that followed seemed to disgust him and he let go of her hair and rolled across her to the other side of the bed and got off. She didn't move from where he left her but she listened to him throwing things around in the kitchen and pacing the floor. She was so afraid! She had never been more afraid. Not even on that day Papa beat on her so badly she figured she was done for. At least back then she knew that even if she died, Jack loved her and would never forget her. Now she knew she was losing Jack and that was so much worse than dying.

Rose tried to get out of bed, but her nausea was so bad by then she couldn't move at all. Not even to turn over, so she lay on her side while her body tore itself up with all its gagging and retching that wouldn't stop. Tears came now too, so violently that her sobs rivaled the retching in jerking her body around. Between sobs and gagging, she whispered Jack's name like a prayer, loving him back into her arms—but he didn't come.

Finally she heard the door slam and knew he was gone. "Oh please, not forever, Lord!"

When hours had passed and her body had at last quieted and become still, she left her bed and went into the kitchen. She couldn't see what he'd thrown around. Everything seemed in its place, and only his coat and hat were gone. But that was all he needed. He spent days at a time on the job and never took anything but his hat and coat. She felt panic coming on. Hysteria. What would she do if he never came back!

She ran to the window and tried to see if the car he drove was in the street. There were lots of cars there, but from her place looking down on them, all heaped with piles of snow, she couldn't tell which, if any, was the one his boss let him drive.

"Well," she said aloud just barely keeping herself from screaming, "I just cain't stand this." She couldn't bear being alone in those two rooms. Before she went entirely to pieces, she'd better get dressed and go somewhere. Leo's ... maybe he could help her. She had to go somewhere. In a fit of fear she ran to the bedroom and frantically searched for her clothes. Where had she put them? She'd taken them off somewhere in that room. Why couldn't she find them? Eventually she had located her things and was almost dressed, having only her shoes left to slip into, when suddenly he was there in the room with her. In her panic she hadn't heard the door open or close. Now, at the sight of him her relief was so immense she got dizzy and felt herself sliding down toward the floor but then Jack's arms were there and she sank into them.

She couldn't stop the tears that started anew and so he held her to him and let her down gently onto the bed. "Jack, don't leave me! Please don't ever leave me again. I cain't live if you leave me. I don't even *want* to live if you leave me," she pleaded with him and clung to him and he let her.

Jack didn't talk at all, but Rose didn't care. Or even notice really, because his arms held her and his mouth kissed her and his hands caressed her and he loved her ... again and again that night after they both got undressed and back into bed, until at last she slept tucked under his arm and in perfect peace.

When she awoke she couldn't believe her good fortune. After such a horrendous beginning he was with her again. Everything was going to be all right after all. She knew he'd get used to the idea of a baby once the shock wore off. It was just that so many years had passed without one. He just hadn't expected it, hadn't been prepared for it, any more than she was. But now everything was going to be okay. Thank you, Jesus! She twisted under his arm and her body thrilled at the touch of his and then he was awake. She let him roll her over and kiss her again. When he raised his head at last his dazzling blue eyes dug into hers and his precious mouth smiled down at her.

But there was something different about it ... about his eyes and his smile. She couldn't name it but it made her wary.

"Rose Sharon, I gotta talk serious to you."

Rose felt her hair stand on end. Yesterday's awful dread was crowding her again.

"I did a lot of thinking last night after I left you. You know Rose, I love you more than my own life. There ain't nothing or nobody I want other than you. And if it comes to giving you up—it will be the hardest thing I'll ever have to do"

His words were terrifying her.

"But if you ain't willing to get rid of that thing growing inside you ... growing between us ... I'm leavin' you. And I'm leavin' you this morning." His voice cracked, and she wondered if this was harder for him than he made it sound.

"Oh cry, Jack Nash!" She screamed inside. *"Cry with shame for killin' me!"* And she reached for him and clasped both hands around his arm.

"I cain't let you leave me, Jack. I couldn't live without you. You might just as well go on and shoot me, because I'll die without you!"

He studied her beautiful face. He didn't want to give up that face. "I meant it when I said I never wanted any babies. I don't aim to make any compromises with that." He swallowed hard and blew out a breath, knowing what he had to say was not going to make her happy. "I went and saw Della last night." He watched her face screw up with disgust.

"That prostitute?"

"Yeah, Della from across the alley. Shit, Rose, I didn't go for that! But I know whores know where to go to get rid of babies so I asked her to come over here this morning and take you to whoever does that for the girls she knows. When she gets here you better go with her. If you don't Rose, you and me are done. I'll walk out that door and I'll never come back." He loosed her hand from his arm and touched her belly, "It's that baby, Rose. That baby you don't even know, or me. It's all up to you. You ain't gonna have both of us. I promise you that."

Rose stood up. "How could you just *leave* me? No matter what you did, I couldn't leave you."

"I don't want you to have that baby, Rose. I don't want some squalling brat suckin' on your tits or hangin' on your skirt or takin' up your time! *You are mine!* Every part of you belongs to me. All your love belongs to me. I ain't gonna share you with nobody!"

"But it wouldn't be like that. It would be your child. That's *part* of you, Jack—it's part of me! We'd be a family!"

"*Family*? Dammit, Rose Sharon! What would either of us want with a *family*? What has either of us ever got from our families except grief and hell. Families are just excuses to abuse one another. No thanks, Rosy. I don't want a family. I'm up to here with family. I want you. All by yourself. Nothing extra. Nothing *"growing inside."* Just you, Rosy. Make up your mind!"

Rose was frantic again. "You cain't leave me. You want me as bad as I want you—I know you do! You cain't just turn that off and go away. You'd go *crazy* same as me!"

Jack reached out and took her wrists in his hands. "You're right, Rosy. My body hurts already just thinkin' about losin' you. My heart will probably bust a thousand times and I might even cry every night and I will, sure as hell, whenever I hear one of those songs you go around singing all the time. And most likely when there comes one of those shiny autumn days or some big fat snowflakes drifting down out of this dirty-gray sky or when those long purple shadows start stretching across the road in the evening—" he narrowed his eyes and took a deep breath.

"There's a hell of a lot we got to remember each other by—but I guarantee you, Sugar, I'll dry my eyes and I'll move on, cause I ain't gonna put up with you having babies. There ain't no ifs, ands or buts about that. I want you to understand that what I say is for sure, so there's no confusion about what my meanin' is. I'm gonna say it slow and easy one time, Rose, so listen to me good!"

That was when he stopped talking for a long moment and just stared hard into her eyes. "Rose, I'm leavin' you this morning if you don't go with Della to that doctor. And I swear to God, I'll never be coming back"

Plainly, as far as he was concerned, there was no more to be said. Jack let go of her wrists and went about collecting his clothes. He emptied his bureau drawer with both hands, and raked his pants and shirts and jackets out of the wardrobe onto his arm and dumped them carelessly onto the bed. Then in a panic, Rose found her robe to cover her nakedness—it was new and even as terrified as she was, she took some time to feel its richness and admire its beauty—it was such a *soft* green chenille that Jack had surprised her with on Valentine's Day. Then, with her breath coming in sharp gasps, she followed him around the room, so close she kept bumping into him, while he picked up this and that odd sock and underwear and tossed them into the same old yellow suitcase they'd carried to Chicago together a little more than 3 years ago.

Had Rose not been in shock she would never have been able to bear such a scene as was being played out in front of her eyes, but through the Mercy of God a sort of bright fog came over her, maybe something like the fog Flora lived in, and it somehow took her mind away from her body so that even as she watched Jack throwing his clothes into the suitcase she could look at herself standing close-by watching him. And since her mind wasn't anywhere near her body, she wasn't able to think about the dying that was taking place or even to react to it.

Jack was packing and dressing at the same time. Rose watched his comfortably familiar naked body slowly disappear under layers of clothing and even in the dullness of her lost mind, she realized the same thing was happening to her marriage. And her life. Without mercy or remorse Jack was taking everything away ... didn't he know he was killing her?

Rose watched herself follow him around the room, even once or twice picking up something to place tenderly inside his suitcase. And when she did that, the real Rose saw Jack's head jerk up and his eyes study the face of the empty Rose who stood beside him. But he didn't say anything or touch her, and she just kept following him around. From the bathroom he took all his personal stuff, his shaving cup and brush, his razor and toothbrush and the pretty-smelling aftershave that she loved.

Finally when he was satisfied that he had everything that belonged to him, he pushed the empty Rose aside and went into the kitchen. She followed blindly behind him. Jack turned at the door to take one last look around, then he sat his suitcase on the floor, slipped into his sheepskin-lined jacket and the fur hat he'd been wearing on his new job instead of the cap with the ear flaps, and pulled Rose into his arms one final time. As he did that, the real Rose left her mystical realm and flew back inside her body. She melted into him, willing him back to her but he was not responsive. "I'm gonna wait down in Leo's store. Della will be up here shortly."

He let go of her long enough to reach for his wallet. She still clung to him. He removed some bills and held them in one hand while he replaced the wallet in his pocket.

Then she saw for the first time something that looked like fear in his expression though it was gone in an instant and he grabbed her hand, "This is enough to pay the doc." He laid it on her palm and folded her fingers over it. "When Della comes, you go with her. She'll take you there and see you get home again. She says there's nothin' to it, Rose. You won't even know what's happening. You're not far enough along to have any trouble, she says." His mouth was tight, his lips were dry. "When it's all over, I'll be waiting here for you, and everything will be just the same as it always was. You hear me, Sugar? I'll be *right here waiting* when you get back." He held her tight against him, her head tucked under his chin and he didn't move or talk again for a long time. Just held onto her and let the familiar loving feelings warm them both.

She hadn't argued with him, and he hoped that meant she was ready to do what he wanted. But he dreaded the actual question so he avoided asking it.

"I'm gonna wait at Leo's like I said. If I don't see Della in half an hour, I'll come back up here and wait for you." Then his voice caught on something in his throat and got real husky sounding. "But if Della comes to tell me you ain't goin' to the doctor..." He moved a little away from her, still keeping her in his arms, looking down at her, those bright blue eyes lingering extra-long in their appraisal—studying her face in case it was for the last time.

Then his mouth was on hers and his kiss and her response were both passionate and desperate and neither of them wanted to let it end. But everything ends, and Rose at last had to loosen her hold on her husband as he loosened his on her. With a final hopeful flash of grin, Jack Nash walked out of the room and shut the door forever on their life together.

Because Rose couldn't kill his baby.

She listened as his footsteps moved away from her and down the back stairs—she heard the door to Leo's store open and close while a fearsome panic—a desperate panic was growing inside her. She knew she was close to madness and at any second might plunge over the edge.

All at once the room was too small for her. She needed to break out of it. To run down the stairs and out into the street. But she knew already that even the street wouldn't be wide enough or long enough to free her. Where could she go? She needed to soar up and away *above* the street, above the city into the sky! But even the sky was too small to hold her grief! Where was there space enough to lose all this agony? All this pain? By then she was shaking violently. Not even the universe! Nowhere except in Jack's arms could she be free of it. Only Jack Nash could contain and hold her. Only his arms. Only his eyes. Only his love.

Then, out of nowhere came peace. It settled upon her quite unexpectedly with the realization that all she had to do to get him back was go with Della. With that knowledge, joy came flooding back into her empty heart. "Oh, sweet Jesus!" she sang and felt like dancing down the steps to tell Jack her decision—never even considering her nakedness under the robe. How long had it been since she felt joyful? How long had she lived in terror and despair? How long had fear been her companion? How long since she and Jack had laughed and teased and pleasured one another? Surely God had blessed her by giving her Jack's love. By giving Jack to her. He was surely God's special gift to her and here she was ready to throw it all away. Toss it away as if it wasn't the most important thing in her life. To do that was most likely a sin. To belittle God's gifts. A very major sin probably. Maybe even what Leo called a *mortal* sin. A sin unto death! *A sin unto death!*

Then the voice came just as if somebody was right there in the room talking to her and though she knew it was only her imagination, she listened to it.

"You're reaching for straws, Rose Nash. You know that baby under your heart is truly God's gift, and your love for that baby is your husband's only chance for redemption. You must not kill his child!"

In spite of her certainty that the voice was imaginary, it sounded so real that she couldn't help glancing about to see if perhaps somebody, Viola maybe, had slipped in unbeknownst to her.

"Is anyone there? Is somebody here?" She really didn't expect an answer and got none, but in the silence that followed, a realization came. Two realizations, actually. The first was that her panic and her madness had disappeared and a peace ... *"the peace that passes all understanding?"* had taken their place. And the second realization? That there was no way on God's green earth she could go with Della to that doctor.

The loneliness that followed Jack Nash going away was too deep to bear and too dark to talk about. If God hadn't given her the wisdom to spend her life minute by minute, not looking ahead or remembering behind, she never would have lived through it. Never lived past that first black week, but God was there for her and she prayed he was there for Jack too. For she knew that no matter how cold he had seemed when he walked away from her, he really did love her more than his own life, and his hurt had to be at least as bad as hers. Likely even worse because he didn't have a little baby growing under his heart, sharing hope for a better day.

That awful morning while she stood there waiting for the prostitute from across the alley to knock on her door, clutching Jack's folded-over money in her hand, tears pouring down her cheeks, down her chin, and onto her bathrobe, she couldn't help thinking about her beloved Jack who was probably pacing nervously below her—probably not far from where she stood. She could see him anxiously checking his pocketwatch, maybe smiling to himself as the minutes lengthened, growing more hopeful that Della wouldn't show her face in the store at all.

Rose wished she didn't have to bring such awful hurt on him, but there wasn't anything she could do to change any of it. *She couldn't kill his baby!*

When Della knocked on the door, though, she hesitated before going to it, and when she finally stood looking into the woman's dark, sooty eyes, she hesitated again. This was the moment! What she did now would seal her fate forever. *"Oh, sweet Jesus!"* It was hard to set that particular destiny in motion. The last thing on earth she wanted to do, the most distasteful to her, the most repugnant.

Della only shrugged when Rose told her she wouldn't be going with her to the doctor. "Ain't no skin off my nose," she smirked, "but your old man is gonna shit bullets!"'

Rose felt resentment that Jack had revealed so much of his feelings to that whore. "It's not any of your business," she told her, and the words were spoken in a tone of superiority. The woman who stood before her snorted as she turned and retreated toward the stairs, letting her words echo behind her— "Well, snooty lady, it may not be any of my business but I sure as hell heard more about it than I ever wanted to hear!" Halfway down the hallway to the back stairs that would take her down to the grocery store, Della turned a scornful face back to her.

"And any damn fool who'd give up a stud like Jack Nash for a snot-nosed squallin' brat shouldn't be runnin' around loose. She oughta be locked away on a loony farm instead of bringin' more dummies into the world!"

Rose felt like she ought to say something to that, but no reply came to her mind. And then it was too late as the door into Leo's Grocery was slammed against her.

A vision then filled her mind of Jack's beautiful blue eyes looking up to see Della stomp toward him with her doomsday message eagerly spilling past those petulant red-painted lips. Rose would never know for sure what that message meant to Jack. Did he cry or did he curse? Whatever his first reaction was, his second was Biblical. He shook the dust of their marriage off his feet, turned away and left that place, and at least as far as Rose knew never again set foot there.

It's possible that nobody ever loved a man the way Rose loved Jack Nash and it's probable that nobody ever hurt as bad as she hurt once he was gone and she knew it was her fault that he went.

She remembered the beginning, when she was a very little girl making those mud cakes for her baby dolls and the landlord's beautiful son accidentally stepped backward and smashed them to set her wailing in protest until she looked up into those eyes that were as pure and blue as if a piece of the spring sky had fallen into them. She was no longer a yowling little 5-year-old playing house but from that instant on and for all the rest of her life she was a woman in love. The mud cakes and the baby dolls lay forever after forgotten in the dust while she plotted and dreamed about the day (and never doubted its coming) when Jack Nash would look into her eyes again and know with the same certainty she had, that they were two halves of one whole and that neither would ever be anything without the other. And it had all come true—but Rose had never imagined the ending—that came out of a clear blue sky like one of those sudden summer hailstorms back in Mississippi; storms that never failed to tear up Mama's vegetable garden and demolish her flowerbeds.

When the first week without Jack was over, Rose knew she couldn't live through a second week. It wasn't that she merely *missed* him, it was that she wasn't *all there* without him. He really was the other half of her! She decided then to just go ahead and die, and she stopped eating, she tried to stop drinking too, but kept taking sips of water without thinking.

Then Leo and Viola and Mary Jean made some kind of pact to keep her alive, and they wouldn't let her alone long enough to die. Mary Jean threatened to put her into a hospital and force-feed her … that idea was so disgusting she had to give up and eat. Besides, Leo pointed out that if she were to die, the baby would die also and since keeping the baby alive was what caused Jack to leave in the first place, it really didn't make sense to kill the baby now and not get Jack back anyway.

In the state she was in, all that made perfect sense, so she set aside all thoughts of dying—for the time being at least.

But living didn't get any easier. Somehow Claire Louise and Walter got wind of her troubles and they came and demanded she move out of the apartment and into their house. She entertained that notion for a time. It might be easier not to miss him if she wasn't always seeing where he'd walked or sat or lain, but then a new thought came to her. What if he came back? What if without her, he was only half there himself, and what if he realized he had to be with her in order to just be alive? If he came home and she was gone and living with Claire Louise, he'd *never* forgive her. So she turned that offer down and found hope suddenly replacing despair. More than hope … an inner knowing that he *would* come back to her someday. And all she had to do was just stay where she was and wait for him.

Soon after that, she realized the money Jack left her was eventually going to run out and since she had to support herself now and pay a doctor to deliver her baby and maybe even pay for a hospital, she knew she had to get a job. She'd helped Leo and Viola at the store a lot during the three years she and Jack lived in the apartment, so now she asked Leo for a steady job. He seemed uncertain that he could pay her enough but he didn't hesitate to put her to work. Her morning sickness passed soon enough and she began to feel as good or better than she'd ever felt in her life. True, she had to be careful not to dwell on thoughts of Jack. It only took a word or a moment's reflection to bring back all the pain and sorrow and loneliness. But she managed pretty well for the most part, and having work to do was a great blessing. It would have been, even if she hadn't got paid at all.

With Jack gone, Sister Claire and Walter came over more often, and they brought pretty things for her and for the baby and even for the apartment. Lots of Leo's customers fussed and worried over her and brought her baby things. Leo and Viola were special blessings, though. They were the ones who held her in their arms and prayed with her and comforted her with their love. And with their love for Jack, because they cared deeply for him too and understood her loss.

They took her to church and they took her to their doctor so she'd get the proper care and so Jack's baby would be healthy and safe. Less than a month after she started her job, Leo raised her wages … more than double what she started with. She felt guilty about that because she didn't seem to be worth that much, but she couldn't talk them out of the big increase. So she just tried to work harder.

And so the months passed. She tried to find out something about Jack ... where he'd gone ... but nobody could tell her anything. She had never known the name of the company he worked for or even his boss's name. All she could recall was the name of a town, a suburb of Chicago, which Leo recognized and Walter did too. So several Sundays when the store was closed, she asked Walter to drive her there and just look around in case she might run into him. It was unlikely she knew, but she didn't think it was impossible. Rose's natural optimism was fighting its way back, and she expected more and more to see his beloved and familiar face grinning at her across a shelf of canned tomatoes or peas, or when she looked up from the cash register, or even when she opened the door to her bedroom.

At last it was September and her time was drawing near. Her pretty little shape had swollen into something that looked like an overripe pear and when she saw her naked body in the vanity mirror she was almost glad Jack wasn't around to see it. She could understand his revulsion about pregnancy now, because she felt a fair amount of revulsion herself. Especially as the final days drew to a close and her nausea came back with a vengeance and then diarrhea set in and a while after that some nasty hemorrhoids caused her miserable sleepless nights. Then her skin dried out and she itched everywhere. Every morning brought a new complaint and it was getting so bad that she started hoping she'd die in her sleep. Claire Louise came and stayed with her the last few days, and Rose didn't know if she was better off with or without her. Claire Louise did have a sort of calm strength about her these last few months, and since Rose was rapidly losing everything, she supposed her sister could be a help to her.

The day the baby finally chose to be born was one of the most perfect days Rose had ever seen. The morning sky was as clear and blue as Jack Nash's eyes and a warm autumn breeze billowed the new curtains Claire had hung just the day before. Rose knew a day like this back home would have been full of the songs of mockingbirds in the laurel oak trees and butterflies of every imaginable color would be floating from mounds of chrysanthemums at the side of the porch to the asters at the front and to the crape myrtle bush outside the girls' bedroom window.

There would be a special golden haze over the fields and crows and mourning doves would be sounding their calls in the distance. And the hooves of Jack Nash's horse, Wild Honey, would be pounding a soft thud along the field road, bringing him nearer and nearer to where she waited for him in the stand of willow trees that lined the creek a quarter-mile behind the barn, their special trysting place during those few months before Pa whipped him and he disappeared that other time.

All those sweet rememberings hushed when the harsh reality of the pain of labor set in though. And they came on with a crash—there would be no gentle learning pains for Rose Sharon. She knew this was some special vengeance conjured up for Jack by some witch-woman. He surely was making her pay for letting his baby live.

There was to be no hospital for Rose either. The bed where she lay to conceive this child became the bed where it was birthed, and it hardly seemed a fair exchange.

While Walter and Mary Jean paced and prayed in the kitchen, Viola and Claire Louise rubbed Rose's back and stroked her forehead until the doctor finally came and conducted Jack's baby girl down that long and winding road and out into a harsh and unmerciful world.

If Cynthia Jackleen Nash was not the most beautiful baby ever to be born of woman, there certainly wasn't anyone in the house that pre-dawn to suggest otherwise. They all *oohed* and *aahed* and praised her as they checked the petite 5½-pound, 18-inch-long infant. She had a perfectly round little head full of large eyes and just a bit of a nose above a tiny rosebud mouth. What little hair she had was dark, and when Rose took her one and only look at it in those wee hours after midnight, she thought the child was the image of its father and that almost made up for all the pain it took to get it born. But it was plain she was a girl and that broke her heart. After that realization, Rose didn't even care to look any closer. The ordeal was much worse than she had imagined and the only thing she wanted to look at ever again was Jack Nash's pretty face. In the final 2½ hours while Claire Louise, her strength all gone and bearing a headache that almost blinded her, knelt beside the bed praying desperately and without ceasing, Rose had screamed Jack's name over and over, cursing him in one breath and begging forgiveness that she had not done what he wanted in the next.

At the height of her pain she had decided to give this infant to Claire Louise and search Jack out to tell him she would never ever go through this again. Rose had seen her Mama give birth to at least three of her baby brothers and never had she given the least indication it was such a thoroughly nasty experience.

After they had cleaned her and the bed, they tried to lay that awful little creature next to her breast but Rose rebelled as violently as she was able in her condition and Viola, fearing for the safety of the child, held her next to her own heart instead.

And so while Rose slept away the memory, the people who loved her most rejoiced together in the kitchen and somewhere miles away, Jack Nash, blissfully unaware of all of it, turned in his bed and slid a hard-muscled arm across the bosom of his new woman.

But Cynthia Jackleen quickly won her mother's heart. When Rose awoke early the following afternoon, she noticed first of all the brightness of the day through her bedroom windows. The sunshine lit up the room with that pale golden glow peculiar to September and lifted her spirits instantly—and then she noticed the way the sheet stretched flat across the bed. That huge lump that had plagued her for so many months was gone! She felt so joyful at the sight that she sat up and threw her legs over the edge of the bed. She had started to stand when, without warning, pain shot through her lower belly and she became violently ill. Sinking back upon the pillow she closed her eyes and screwed up her face in agony.

"Jack! Damn you, Jack! Where are you when I need you?" Hot tears stung her eyes and then she heard it. A mewling whimper from the basket next to her bed. As she listened and as the realization poured over her that Jack's baby was in that basket, her mouth readjusted itself into a smile, and her tears became tears of thankfulness to God.

She tucked her legs up to her stomach and rolled sideways off the bed. This time the dizziness didn't come nor did the pain, so she sat on the floor with her back against the bed until she felt it safe to move closer to the basket. Then she scooted to it and looked inside.

The baby was so tiny and so neatly wrapped that she had a time finding her face—until she reached in and pushed back the blanket.

All she could do was stare. "Sweet Jesus! Jesus! Jesus!" she sang over and over again and was so rapt in the wonder of it that she didn't see Claire Louise come into the room until she was kneeling beside her. Sister Claire laid her arm around Rose's shoulder and squeezed her. "You certainly did it right, Rose Sharon. She's perfect and just beautiful. I wish God would have seen fit to give me one just like her."

Rose forgot every bad feeling she'd ever had for her sister and nuzzled her head onto Claire's thin shoulder. She was smiling so big her face could hardly contain it and she grabbed Claire's hand and squeezed. "It is worth it! It is worth all that terrible pain, ain't it, Claire? Oh! Oh! If only Jack was here. If only he could see her. He couldn't leave me if he could just see her. If only he had waited." She reached into the basket. Then Claire stopped her. "You get back into bed, Rose Sharon. I'll lift her out and bring her to you. You're not strong enough yet to carry her."

As Rose moved back to the comfort of her bed, Claire Louise gingerly lifted the little bundle from the basket and placed it into Rose's eager arms. Then she sat on the bed next to her baby sister and the two of them giggled and baby-talked while Rose unwrapped the blanket and examined the perfect little hands and feet, counting the fingers and toes.

After many moments, Rose bundled Cynthia up again and with fresh tears streaming down her cheeks leaned against her big sister. "Claire Louise, a baby really *is* a gift from God." She brushed away her tears. "Jack will see that someday." She nodded her head and squeezed her daughter tighter. "Your Daddy *will* come back to us one day, Cynthia Jackleen. Yes, he will! God will see to it!"

When Rose was strong again and before Claire Louise went back to Walter and her own home, she did her very best to talk Rose into coming with her. But Rose knew with more and more certainty that Jack would be moving back and she didn't dare be anywhere but waiting at home for him when he came.

Rose had saved enough money from the good wages Leo paid her that she didn't need to work for a while. But after the first month she found herself spending too many lonely hours doing nothing, so with Viola's blessing she brought the baby's basket downstairs to the store where she could keep busy and at the same time care for the infant. That proved to be a blessing for everybody. Viola and Leo adored the child, they were soon calling themselves Granny and Gramps, and Rose had some freedom from the loneliness and the complete responsibility of being a single parent.

From time to time, one male customer or another—unwed, separated, or widowed—would take an interest in Jack Nash's good-looking, deserted wife. Although Rose might not have been adverse to male companionship now and then, she was definitely not ready to become attached to anyone. And since it always seemed to lead to that, she finally had to turn away every special attention from the start. There were only two men with whom she dared spend any time after her initial bad experiences: Leo, whose love for her was pure and fatherly, and Walter, whose love, while it may have been less pure, was nonetheless safe and very solicitous. In fact, while his feelings for her were growing less and less brotherly, he himself was not aware of it until one Sunday when he was driving Rose on her rare but regular searching trip through those suburbs whose names she recalled Jack had mentioned, while Viola, Leo, and Mary Jean looked after Cynthia at the apartment.

It was pretty much accepted by Rose and Walter that they weren't going to run into Jack Nash anywhere, but the drives gave Rose a sense of hope and a feeling that she was doing something more than just waiting helplessly.

June 1935

They had started later than usual on that particular Sunday in June. A shower had passed earlier and the streets, still wet,

114

glistened while the late afternoon sun teased Walter and Rose, appearing and disappearing behind fast-moving cumulous clouds. The trees and lawns were aglow with the bright pastel green of spring and everything looked fresh and clean. Rose, nurtured by the warmth of the elusive golden sun felt her hopes growing just like all of nature around her.

Unable to contain herself, she commenced singing and her sweet folksy-soprano voice captivated Walter who started to harmonize with her. Rose had begun with some old-time spirituals she had learned as a child at revival meetings, but after a while Walter introduced some of the popular songs from the radio and pretty soon they were completely absorbed in the sound of their own voices. Rose was swaying rhythmically to the music and he was keeping time on the steering wheel with his hands. As their harmonizing got better Rose became more and more animated and less and less concerned with propriety until finally she was next to him, her knees almost in his lap, her left arm and breast crushed against his arm and her right hand on top of his keeping time with him on the steering wheel while her eyes watched his mouth form the words of their song. At the finish of an especially enthusiastic version of "Anything Goes," Rose broke into a fit of giggles and threw both arms around his neck and then, feeling emotionally reckless, she planted a big noisy kiss on his cheek.

Without knowing how he did it, Walter found himself with his arm around her pulling her tight against him and turning his head so her mouth was no longer against his cheek, but under his own impassioned lips. He felt her resist for a moment and then sag against him and as he persisted in his seduction, she melted altogether and her mouth responded with heat.

The harsh sound of an automobile horn broke into their moment when the car wandered dangerously into the left lane. It brought Rose to her senses, but Walter wasn't as easily deterred. He brought the car out of the traffic and to a halt against the curb without letting go of her even though she twisted against his arm. "Walter, please let me go. I didn't mean to lead you on."

He turned in the seat and pulled her back to him and his mouth was on hers again: there was no way she could excuse the kiss he was giving her as brotherly. It was a long time since Rose had been kissed that way and in spite of her own good sense and better judgment she was beginning to like it and since she couldn't seem to get away from him anyway...

After a long time he raised his head but was still holding her with one arm when he turned back to the steering wheel and pulled back into the traffic. She, on the other hand, didn't move at all, in fact she pressed herself closer against him and closed her eyes. If she tried really, *really* hard she could believe it was Jack's shoulder she was leaning against—Jack's arm holding onto her—even Jack's mouth on hers. She trembled with longing. Yes. Walter could be Jack for her, until Jack finally returned and sat in that place himself. Not a twinge of guilt assailed her at that adulterous notion. It didn't seem wrong at all. She wasn't after all, being in the least unfaithful. She wasn't lusting for Walter Bradley, her sister's husband. She only hungered for her own husband who was always and forever the only man she wanted to lie with. It wouldn't be wrong at all. It was Jack's body she wanted ... Jack's body she needed. Then, in her mind she was explaining to her husband...

"O Jack! You've been gone so long and I just cain't wait any longer. I just cain't stand bein' alone anymore."

Walter wasn't making any such excuses to himself. He knew it was Rose he had kissed and he knew it was Rose he wanted. Without turning to look at her, he started talking. "I know Jack was—*is*—very special to you, Rose. I can't begin to take his place and I don't want to try, but I can love you, Rose. I do love you. You have always been special to me. Extremely special! I've never known anybody like you." Then he looked at her, but quickly averted his eyes. "If I could come to you sometime and I could—*stay* with you for a couple of hours sometime..." There followed an uncomfortably lengthy silence. Eventually, he broke it.

"Claire Louise...." He said her name and then, nervous and agitated, he chewed on his lip a while. "Claire and I don't sleep together anymore, Rose." He made an odd sound of frustration. "This is all so personal and almost too shameful to talk about … but…"

Then he was silent awhile again and Rose waited patiently.

"Claire can't have children, you know." He glanced sideways at her. "So … so she says to have martial relations with no hope of conceiving a child is wrong. She's worked it up in her mind until she thinks it's sinful somehow and so she sleeps in one room and I sleep in another."

He was squeezing her so close it began to be uncomfortable but Rose waited for him to finish his explanation.

"Rose, you know I'm still a young man. I'm not 40 yet, Rose. I still feel the need sometimes—" and then he snorted, "to be honest, Rose! I feel the need all the time. And it's pretty strong. I've been tempted. There are lots of young women at the office and even some in our neighborhood. And I'm not a real religious man," he swallowed "Claire has her religion to fortify her. She goes to church three or four times a week, and I don't think she needs *physica*l love." He looked at her again. "You do though, don't you, Rose?" He waited for an answer but she didn't choose to give one.

Walter turned his face forward—it was no longer easy looking her in the eye. "I know you and Jack had a very passionate *love* relationship," and his voice lowered. "Doesn't your body sometimes ache for the touch of a man? It was plain Jack could barely keep his hands off you even in public, so he must have been very demonstrative in the privacy of your bedroom." He felt as if he was hanging onto a rope over a river and he was losing his grip—probably he'd slid too far already. "I'm saying this badly, but it's because I feel so strongly about it, and I feel ashamed and embarrassed now that I've put it into words. At any rate, I don't expect you to feel like that about me. I'll be *honored?* I don't know if that's the right word." When he finally turned his head to look at her, his expression was tense. "If you'll just allow me … just *let me love you* once in a while. Now and then. You can even pretend I'm Jack if it helps any."

They were stopped at a red light with three or four cars in front of them, and Rose listened without comment, though she was smiling. She already knew her answer. She was going to let him love her. She'd be a blessing to him and he'd be a blessing to her. Surely *that* couldn't be a sin.

Then suddenly her attention was drawn to a man getting out of a car at the curb two car lengths ahead of them. She watched him leave the car and hurry across the sidewalk into a store. She moved away from Walter to look at the sign above it. "Fletcher Pharmacy" she read and as she did she cried out. "Stop! Stop, Walter! Stop the car! It's Jack! Jack just walked into that store!" She was trying to open the passenger door and Walter grabbed for her.

"Be careful, Rose. You'll be killed!"

"Stop then! Stop this dang car!"

"I will, Rose! I will as soon as I find a space. I can't stop in the middle of the street."

"O sweet Jesus! Don't let him leave that store. O sweet Jesus!" She was praying frantically. Then she glared impatiently at Walter. "*Why don't you stop?*"

"I will as soon as the light changes. Right up there's a place," he pointed out, hoping to calm her. "Just keep your eye on the door he went in and we won't lose him."

It seemed to Rose it was taking hours to get properly parked.

"Oh! Please hurry, Walter! Please, Walter!"

As soon as she could she was out of the car and bouncing up and down on her toes, unable to bear the waiting. "Hurry, Walter, it's Jack! It's Jack after all these months!"

As soon as Walter's feet hit the sidewalk she was away. "Come on, Walter. The pharmacy!"

Walter hurried to keep up. "Are you sure it's Jack? After all this time you could be mistaken."

Rose threw a look over her shoulder that was at once offended and scornful. "Mistake my Jack?" and she thought about how many times she had looked upon that special stride of his with pride that he was her man and she snorted. "*Mistake*

Jack Nash? Are you out of your mind? I would know my Jack from the *sound* of his shoes on the sidewalk!"

They were at the drug store and Walter reached past her to open the door. Rose rushed inside with high expectations and he followed.

As her eyes searched the building, which wasn't large, a sense of doom settled around her. She didn't see him.

Frantic, she raced up one aisle and down the other. There were several booths near the back and all of them were occupied but not by Jack. Her eyes met Walter's when she turned and they were so desperate, he felt frightened for her.

"He's not here, Walter."

"I know. Maybe this is the wrong store. Let's look in the ones on either side of this. Maybe you made a mistake."

He tried to take her arm but she flung off his hand. "I didn't make a mistake. He came into this store."

"But he's not here. Just look around, Rose. It must have been a different store."

"No. It's not a different store. It's just me. I'm goin' crazy is all. I just *thought* I saw him because I wanted to so bad."

Walter looked up as a man in a white pharmacist's jacket stepped from behind the counter and greeted him. "Can I help you?"

Walter smiled and shook his head. "I guess not." And then he asked Rose, "What was he wearing? How was he dressed? Maybe this gentleman saw him," and then he asked the man if there was a back door.

But Rose had already turned away from him and was heading toward the exit. "Never mind, Walter. I was just wrong, that's all."

Walter shrugged over his shoulder at the pharmacist. "Thanks anyway," he said and followed after her.

Rose's disappointment was so great it made her bitter and angry and she wasn't the least receptive to his offers of help.

"Let's try these other stores. It can't hurt and you'll never forgive yourself if you just get back in the car and don't try to find him."

She flung away from him again and then noticed the car she'd seen the man get out of. It was still parked there at the curb. At least she hadn't imagined the car.

A desperate thought occurred to her. What if she got in that car and just waited for him. If it wasn't Jack she could say she'd mistook that car for hers. And if it was him … "O, Sweet Jesus, show me what to do!"

She walked toward the car as Walter, in spite of her attitude, went into the variety store to the right of the pharmacy. She watched him disappear inside and then recklessly jerked open the door to the car. She hesitated as she looked inside. A familiar fragrance wafted up at her and her heart began to race. It was Jack's aftershave! Nothing could have stopped her from climbing into that automobile after that.

Walter had exited the variety store and was looking up and down the street but being unable to locate her he decided she'd gone back to his car so he pushed open the door to the little cafe on the left of the pharmacy and went inside.

In the meantime, Rose was tearing that car apart, front and back, glove box, pouches on the doors.

There were papers in the glove box but nothing with a name on it. Nothing anywhere that would reveal the driver, except that fragrance.

Rose began to lose her courage. Probably hundreds, maybe even thousands of men in that town wore that same aftershave. What kind of proof was that? She was about to step back out when the thought occurred to her that the man she saw leave that car was the image of Jack Nash. That sighting was what led her to the car in the first place. So putting the fragrance and the man together, the chances got better suddenly and she decided to settle down and wait.

She watched Walter go past her and on down the sidewalk to where his car was parked. She saw him move back onto the sidewalk when he realized she wasn't waiting there.

He was agitated and worried and she started to feel bad for him, so while he paced up and down, her conscience made her open the door and get out. He saw her coming and he took note of the car she had stepped out of and he panicked.

"Good Lord, Rose Sharon! What do you think you're doing? You could get arrested for doing that."

Rose raised angry eyes and scowled at him. "Shut up, Walter! I think Jack was driving that car just like I thought in the first place and I'm gonna stay here till he comes back to it!"

"But he's not in any of those buildings, Rose. It *was* somebody else you saw."

Rose's teeth clenched and her hands coiled into tight fists. "I am not mistaken! It is Jack Nash!"

Walter threw up his hands and then backed away from her toward his car again. "I can't help you anymore, Rose. I'll sit in my car and wait until you're ready to go."

She made no move in either direction, just stood close to the wall in the shadow of the building and watched Jack's car.

Minutes passed and then it was an hour.

Walter walked over to her. "Rose, we can't stay here forever."

She shook her head. "Not yet."

So he sighed and went back to sit on the front bumper.

Another fifteen minutes and still no one came to the car. Rose looked nervously at Walter, who sat there glaring back at her.

After another five minutes she went reluctantly to him. "I've decided to go, Walter, but I'm gonna leave a note in that car. I'm gonna tell him I was here and saw him and waited and that I love him and want him back."

Walter nodded with some gratitude. He kept a notebook and pencil in the glove box, and he tore out a page and handed it to her along with the pencil.

She laid it on the hood of his car and started writing her message. "Dearest Jack Nash." It was short and to the point and when she finished she read it and added one more short paragraph after her name. "P.S. I lay every night alone and pray I'll look up and see you open our bedroom door. Please come home, Jack. I'm the same as dead with you gone."

She handed the pencil to Walter, who waited silently but with frustration plain in his eyes. Then she carried her note, folded neatly three times, to Jack's car. She had a moment of worry … what if it really wasn't Jack? That would mean she was baring her most intimate feelings to a complete stranger, but she pushed that worry aside. If it wasn't Jack, whoever it was would have no way of knowing who she was anyway and if it was, *as she thoroughly believed*, her beloved husband, than she *had* to tell him how she felt since this was the closest she had been to him in a year and a half.

Walter drove back toward her apartment in silence. Not only was he exasperated with her stubborn insistence she's seen Jack Nash and the hour and a half of useless waiting, but he was embarrassed with the memory of his humiliating attempt at seduction which was interrupted by her supposed sighting.

They were just a block from the grocery store when he finally got up his nerve to broach the delicate subject. "I think we should just forget what happened earlier."

Rose, whose thoughts were full of Jack and her note for him had a moment of confusion as she tried to imagine what he was referring to. So she only nodded

Walter glanced at her from the edge of his eye. "I am really ashamed, Rose. I had no business asking you a thing like that." He slapped his hand against the steering wheel. "I would like to make excuses for myself, but there aren't any. I just got carried away with my feelings for you." He sighed, "I just couldn't handle having you *touch* me. I felt like an adolescent boy with his first crush." Rose heard a self-conscious chuckle wrinkle his voice. "I am so sorry, Rose, and I feel like such a fool. I hope you know I could never have followed through on that—*proposal*."

Having the incident brought back to her mind gave her an embarrassed moment of her own and she felt her cheeks flush. She really had let herself get all worked up being in his arms and kissing him like that. She opened her mouth and took a couple of deep breaths before she could get her words strung together. "I reckon we both ought to give thanks to God that he stopped us in time."

Walter sighed with relief when she didn't say anything else. "You're absolutely right, Rose Sharon. We both need to give thanks to God!" She nodded, then quickly turned her face away from him. But he hadn't ended the conversation.

"We ought to just forget it ever happened, don't you think? Just pretend it never happened?" Actually, he sounded close to tears, and Rose didn't dare look at him for fear of that event occurring. But pretty soon he sighed again and his voice got back to normal while he explained, "I love you and Cynthia and I care deeply for Jack, too. I wouldn't want us to be afraid … or ashamed … or embarrassed to be with each other because of a few lunatic moments." Walter took a deep breath, exhaled, and then was quiet for a while until the grocery store loomed before them. Then while he was pulling up to the curb, he added quickly, "Rose, I want to be able to drive you places like we did today and not worry about what might be between us. God knows I could never screw Jack Nash's wife." After that he couldn't talk at all for a while but he was muttering curses at himself and holding onto the steering wheel so tight that his knuckles turned white. "I'm sorry, Rose. I'm just flustered. I hope you know I never use that kind of language, especially not with you!" He looked full on her for a few seconds and she took that time to look back at him and relieve him of his embarrassment.

"And I couldn't do that with Sister Claire's husband," her smile was comforting and sincere, because she was feeling fonder of him than she ever had before and Walter had already picked up on that.

"You're a very special lady, Rose Sharon," he nodded at her and then thought to himself that she *really was* a very special lady, and then he went ahead and told her what he was thinking. "You're *extra* special to me, too. I want you to know that I love you and that I might even love you in some illicit ways, but I'll never again allow myself to show it. With the grace of God, I'll never give in to that temptation again. I'm sorry. I'm truly sorry I put us through this."

Rose put her hand on his arm, and he looked at her with a sheepish grin. "I'd rather you stayed on your side of the car, if you don't mind. I'm not a real strong man, Rose."

She drew back and clasped her hands together in her lap. "All right, Walter. We'll be real careful from now on and I'll try not to be so casual around you. But truth be told, I feel so safe with you. And I feel so close to you that you might have to remind me every now and then."

Walter's grin widened. "You sure know how to make a man feel exceptional, Rose. I don't know how that foolish husband of yours can stay away."

Rose's smile faded and pain shot through her heart. "He sure don't seem to have any trouble with that, though. He stays away right well."

At about the same time Walter dropped Rose at her apartment, a door opened behind a curtain at the back of Fletcher's Pharmacy and Jack Nash, looking handsome and stylish in a slate-gray pinstripe suit stepped onto the same piece of worn linoleum that Rose Sharon had trod with such hopeful excitement a couple of hours earlier. He wore his dark gray fedora tilted rakishly forward across his forehead and his shoes were polished to a glassy shine. With a cocky grin, he tipped his hat to two young girls seated in one of the booths at the back and at the pharmacist in his white jacket and at the pretty blond clerk behind the counter as he made his way through the store and out onto the sidewalk. Then he entered from the curbside the same automobile Rose had sat in less than 30 minutes before.

Settled finally under the wheel he rolled down the window beside him and turned the key in the ignition. The car responded immediately and the engine hummed. Removing his hat he tossed it into the back seat and ran his fingers through his hair while he studied his reflection in the rearview mirror. He grinned and winked at his image, pleased with himself. It was then that he noticed the piece of folded paper, one end of which was closed into the glove box. His curiosity piqued, he opened the box and removed it. As he started to unfold it, an odd sinking feeling hit his stomach for no reason at all, and an inexplicable sadness came out of nowhere to lay heavy on his heart. With that awful sense of apprehension, he turned off the engine and took a long slow breath as he unfolded the page and glanced over the familiar handwriting that covered the paper. His worst fears were confirmed when he read the signature in her neat and painstakingly drawn little-schoolgirl's script.

"Oh, shit!" and Jack crushed the paper against the steering wheel while he stared out through the windshield, not seeing a street full of traffic or the lights just beginning to flash on as twilight faded. He was seeing Rose's face and not her happy face. He was seeing her the way she had looked at him when he turned away to walk out her door for the last time. "Shit! Shit! Shit!" He straightened the creases he had made and holding the paper between his hands against the steering wheel, he began to read.

"Dearest Jack Nash…" By the time he reached the signature and the P.S., he was wanting her again.

"Damn you, Rosy! How the hell did you find me?"

Suddenly fearful that she might be watching him from somewhere nearby, he began frantically looking around, his eyes straining at the other cars, the shop windows, the people on the sidewalk. But she wasn't there. How had she ever got to that particular suburb in the first place? Or was it some kind of black magic that put that letter in his hand?

He breathed another deep breath. There was no denying the fact that she could stir up the hot blood in him. Right at that moment, from just looking at her handwriting on that piece of creased notebook paper, his body had already started aching for her and his hands were shaking remembering the soft curves of her body, the fragrance of her silky skin. Jack's eyes closed and his mouth opened instinctively to close over hers.

But she wasn't there. He held the paper and absently bent the part that bore her name, pressed it to his lips and kissed it. "Rose, Rose," he sighed, "you do have the power to move me." His lips parted and he sucked her signature into his mouth, closing his teeth on it. For a long time he let his tongue move back and forth over that little piece of paper. That little piece of paper that she had touched and held and that now became her in his imagination. The day was passing into night. The stores along Main Street were all lit up now and the lane of traffic moving away from him was a string of ruby beads as tail lights slid past. And he just sat there holding that damn letter and kissing her signature while warm memories made his body ache, and desire and need merged in his loins. The urge to answer her prayer and push open her bedroom door was about to overwhelm him when a sudden thought saved him.

She hadn't mentioned the damn kid and so he'd almost forgot about it. Almost forgot the reason he'd closed the door on her in the first place.

With that thought, he took the piece of paper that was Rose's last desperate hope, out of his mouth and slowly and deliberately crumpled it in his fist. Then with one quick motion of his arm, he had tossed it out the window and into the street where the tires of a passing car immediately smashed it into the pavement.

"You just didn't love me enough, Rosy." He muttered with angry frustration. "This is all your own damn fault!" And then Jack Nash restarted the engine and eased the shiny black automobile away from the curb and into the line of traffic.

For the first few days after she left the note in what she was certain was Jack's car, Rose looked up expectantly every time the door to Leo's Grocery opened and all night long she watched the bedroom door, sure he was going to throw it open and walk back into her arms. Happiness welled up in her and she spent hours talking to Cynthia about her Daddy, making sure she'd know him when he made his return to their family. She took the wedding picture in the oval frame off the wall and brought it to her bedside table where she showed it to Cynthia Jackleen a hundred times a day.

"This is your handsome daddy, Jack Nash," she'd tell the child. "You got a lot to be proud of and look forward to. And you're gonna have lots of time to get to know him now."

For a long time there was not a doubt in her mind that he'd come home. And soon! Her faith was as strong as it had been when she was a child herself and daydreaming him into her life every waking moment.

But when days turned into weeks and weeks became months, her faith wavered and eventually she knew it just wasn't going to happen. The car must have belonged to somebody else after all. So after a while she got another nail and hung their wedding photo on the wall beside her bed—low enough so Cynthia could take it down herself for their evening prayers.

But the disappointments were getting harder and harder to bear each time and she found herself weeping out of control sometimes.

Leo and Viola did all they could to comfort her. Once they even suggested she go away for a while. Maybe she would like to visit her family in Mississippi. But Rose knew she didn't have a family in Mississippi anymore. Truth be told, there wasn't any place to go. And then she started having those strange feelings that she'd had the night Jack left. Feelings that the house was not big enough to contain her, so that she wanted to run screaming like a crazy woman into the street she knew wasn't big enough either and then wanting to soar up into the sky because there was nothing anywhere on earth left for her to cling to, only Jack Nash and he was nowhere to be found.

"I think Jack's not in Chicago, anymore, Leo," she mused one day. "I think he's gone away. New York, maybe. Or California."

Leo's brow furrowed, "You think he might have gone back to Mississippi?"

But Rose smiled at that notion. "No," she said with certainty. "He had nothin' down there anymore and anyway, he hated it there." She was stacking cans of soup and she paused sadly. "Maybe he's dead. Maybe he got killed in a car wreck or somethin'."

Leo slipped his arm around her. "Now, there's no reason to believe that, Honey. He's around somewhere. Sometime you're bound to see him again."

She smiled and shook her head. "I don't know anymore. I always felt so sure he'd be back. I just always knew it. But I'm not sure anymore. Truth be told, Leo, I'm scared he's got somebody else."

Her eyes looked desperate and she grabbed Leo's shirt sleeve with her hand. "Jack couldn't do without a woman this long, Leo!"

Leo patted her hand tenderly. "Rose, honey, it doesn't do a bit o' good to think things like that."

But she was frantic. "Leo, if he's taken up with some woman he might never need me again. He might *never* come back to me." Her eyes held so much fear and anguish that

Leo's own gentle eyes welled up with tears and he bent down to pick up the nearly empty soup box so she wouldn't notice. After he rubbed away the tears, he straightened up again. "If he takes up with some other woman Rosy, it will only show him how special you are. He'll never find anybody near as good as you."

Rose's smile was grateful, but she took no comfort from his words.

And Rose's foreboding that she'd seen the last of Jack was not her only anxiety. There was the terrifying possibility she'd seen the last of Walter as well because she had neither seen nor heard from him since she left that letter in the car she thought was Jack's. Viola had even wondered out loud about his prolonged absence, though neither she nor Leo ever asked Rose about it. And Rose was too scared she'd muddled her friendship with him to even bring the subject up to anyone. But the truth was that as soon as she stopped expecting Jack to come back into her life, she started missing Walter. She even went so far in her desperation as to wonder what it would be like to become his *"back-street woman."* That was something that had come up more than once in those *true-love-story* magazines of Mary Jean's. Rose couldn't be sure exactly what was expected of a back-street woman, but she was fed up enough with being lonesome to try it. If Walter ever came back, that is—which was beginning to seem as fantastic a notion as Jack's return. But Claire Louise didn't come to see her either so maybe they'd just decided to wash their hands of her. It wasn't as if Claire Louise hadn't done that a couple of times already.

At any rate, Rose had more or less given up on him when three whole months passed without even a word. And it almost broke her heart that neither he nor Claire even acknowledged Cynthia's first birthday!

But then one morning toward the end of September, there he was! And to her uncomprehending surprise, he had a boy-child on the car seat beside him. Rose just happened to be gazing out the front window of the grocery store resting her elbows on the counter during a few quiet moments between customers, when he drove up and before she had time to consider that she might be better appreciated if she showed less enthusiasm at his return, she had rushed out to meet him, jerked open the passenger door and found the child. Her mouth fell open in amazement.

"Where did this beautiful child come from, Walter? Where'd you find him?"

Walter's face was so lit up with joy he looked like a different man and he answered her instantly.

"Claire and I are adopting him, Rose. Can you beat that?"

"*Adopting* him? Are you tellin' me the truth, Walter? I cain't believe it. Why that's wonderful! That's the best thing could ever happen to you and Claire Louise." She lifted the boy into her arms and looked into his face. When she did her scalp began to tingle in a most unnerving way and the more she studied the boy's face the more she tingled. Finally she turned to look accusingly at Walter who had slid from under the wheel and was now right there on the seat in front of her.

"Where'd he come from, Walter?" she was asking in a cold and hostile voice that didn't sound anything like her.

Walter seemed not to notice. He just nodded and his grin got bigger and he started to answer her but she interrupted him in that same unnatural bone-chilling voice. "Cain't you tell who he looks like, Walter? Cain't you see who he's the spittin' image of?"

Walter's grin faded and he shrugged but he took some time to study the boy's face.

And Rose kept glaring at him.

Walter shrugged again. "What are you getting at, Rose? What are you saying?"

He studied the boy's face along with Rose, shaking his head. She watched him with disbelief. Finally she blurted out her suspicions through clenched teeth.

"Is there *any* way this child could belong to Jack Nash?" Her voice made Walter shudder because of the malice in it. It wasn't Rose talking.

Walter was shaking his head while his forehead furrowed into a disconcerted frown. "Jack Nash?" he said, and then he shrugged again. "I guess he might kind of favor Jack!"

But then he turned to look at her again and the grin reappeared. "But Rose, that's not possible! If he favors Jack, or if you see that in him, it's simply a freaky coincidence; there's no way on earth he could be Jack's boy. His mama and daddy are both known to Claire Louise. We got him through her preacher. Brother Browning from her church? She's known him since we came to Chicago, Rose. This couple, the boy's parents, are both very young and," he shrugged and shook his head, "*they* gave him to the preacher. They were having some problems they couldn't handle … they're both alcoholics I understand, and then the husband was taken off to jail for hitting the wife. Just a whole lot of problems and they were about to lose the boy to the state, so the preacher took him and he knows Claire and I can't have children so … Rose, there were lawyers and everything—it was all done according to the law!"

Rose's expression hadn't changed, so Walter made a move to gently take the child from her. "Well, anyway, that's where he came from and that's how we got him. It's a real miracle I guess, just like Claire says. Makes you take all that sort of stuff more seriously when you run into a real honest-to-goodness miracle of your own." He was fearful he'd have to forcefully remove the child out of her arms, and he knew that wouldn't be pleasant. So he stepped out of the car but kept his hands on the boy and waited for Rose to release him

In the meantime, he explained some more, "Browning knows we're pretty well off, so he came to us and we agreed to consider it. So he brought this little guy right over and we were just like you, Rose. We lost our hearts! Right then and there. He is a beauty, isn't he?"

Walter had eased the child away from Rose and now he moved toward the front of the car and stood him on the fender. "I never thought I could get this excited about anything again." He shook his head in wonder and then he reached for Rose's hand and tugged her closer so he could hug her and the boy together. "But I am damned excited now! I feel like my life has just begun. Like I was just born. Is that how you felt when you first got a look at Cynthia?" Rose nodded at him but her eyes were cold so Walter chose to ignore it. He threw his head back and howled. "I've got me a boy, Rose. My own son to raise up according to *my traditions* and *my ideals* and there is going to be somebody now to carry on the Bradley name. I never gave that a thought before." Walter's eyes were digging deep into hers and he sighed and clicked his tongue "Ah my little Rose-Sharon. A whole new life has opened up for me." He paused again, and then he was laughing. "And I'm *happy,* Rose. I think it's the first time in my life I've ever been truly happy."

Rose saw his eyes mist over and she deeply regretted her lack of enthusiasm for his "miracle," so she snuggled against him and took the hands of the little boy in hers. "If anybody ever earned his happiness, it's you, Walter. I'm so glad for you I could cry." And she did. But some of her tears were for Jack Nash. She couldn't help thinking what he was missing out on and she wished with all her heart that he could feel some of that pride and love for his little girl that Walter was feeling for this boy who wasn't even his own flesh and blood..

They went for their usual Sunday excursion then, as if there hadn't been a three month hiatus—into those towns where Jack might have been living. Only this time, Rose took Cynthia from Viola's watchful eyes and brought her along to be with little John Christopher, or JC, as Walter chose to call him. JC was a month shy of 3 and small for his age, probably from lack of proper food. He was also very quiet and reserved. Although he didn't turn down any love or attention that was offered him. Rose never saw him smile that first day, but he watched her with those Jack Nash eyes and an expression that seemed to bear the wisdom of the ages. After that ride ended she could hardly believe there was a three-year-old-baby mind behind those eyes. It was more likely the mind of some whimsical creature locked by a magic spell into his small boy-body. She didn't voice that opinion to Walter though, for he saw only the boy child and she didn't want to create any kind of enchantment around them other than the pride and love and joy that already existed in the new father's heart.

Her own daughter seemed captivated by her new cousin too. She smiled and jabbered at him the whole trip but for the most part she was rudely ignored. Not that she noticed. The boy spent most of the afternoon studying Rose's face and the back of her head when she turned toward the windshield and because he looked so much like Jack, that surveillance gave her a really eerie feeling. It also attached her so strongly to him that she didn't want to let him leave with Walter when the time came for them to go back to their big house on Grace Street. It was a really wrenching experience to watch him ride away from her. But she hugged her own little girl, who *really was* Jack Nash's baby, to her bosom and thanked God that as far-fetched as it seemed, as far beyond anything she could ever have imagined, she would have that boy of Walter's to watch mature and grow and become another Jack Nash. Just in case the original never did come back.

After that, the years passed without anything much changing for Rose, other than Cynthia Jackleen getting older and prettier. The only thing disappointing about the girl was that except for her mouth and her lopsided grin, she didn't look a thing like Jack Nash. Her hair turned out to be dark brown with a hint of Rose's coppery-red in it and her eyes turned from the bright blue at birth to a sort of amber brown. She seemed pretty well adjusted and happy even though she never got to see her daddy. Rose guessed if you'd never had one you couldn't miss him. Leo and Walter and the young man whose legal name was Ernest Scott but everybody called "Scotty," gave her lots of attention and did whatever a daddy could have done for her anyway, except sleep with her Mama at night.

Scotty had a shoeshine stand and he set it up sometimes outside Leo's Grocery, and sometimes a couple of blocks down the street between Barney's Newsstand and Santino's Funeral Parlor. Cynthia liked to sit beside him while he slapped his polishing rag back and forth and made up songs to entertain her and his customers. He kept good watch and seemed to enjoy her company and because Cynthia was so very obedient, Rose wasn't afraid to let her be as far away as the newsstand which was almost three blocks.

April 1937

Jack had been gone a little more than three years and Cynthia was two and a half, when Mr. and Mrs. Walter Bradley received a letter from Mississippi with the stunning message, "Mama is dead." Just two months before her 52nd birthday.

The details were brief and to the point; "Your mother passed away on Monday, the 12th of April in her own bed at home from a massive apoplexy on the 6th after suffering several minor attacks earlier in the year. We will be burying her in the Dobbin Cemetery on Friday the 16th of April." Because the letter arrived on Friday the 16th, neither of her Illinois daughters would be able to attend, but Claire Louise and Walter, with JC, went ahead and made their yearly spring visit to the Saylor family anyway. Rose politely declined the invitation to join them. When they returned two weeks later, she received the entire story.

Their unmarried sister Grace had been keeping house in her ailing mother's stead most all winter after a series of what were thought to be minor strokes. But a week before her passing, something a lot more serious struck that left Olly bedridden. On the morning of the 12th, Papa was summoned from the field by his frantic daughter. Brother sped back to the house ahead of Papa to find their mother suffering a seizure. He was saddling the mule to ride for the doctor when his sister called to him from the porch that it was already too late. A little later, he did get a doctor to come out but she was dead long before he got there.

She'd been feeling extra poorly for almost a year, so it hadn't been as much of a surprise for them as it was for Claire Louise and Rose, who had never been apprised of her situation and were unprepared for her dying. They cried in each other's arms, and Rose remembered that day Mama had talked Papa into using a horsewhip on Jack Nash instead of a shotgun, and the day Jack had sweet-talked Olly into blessing their marriage, and the very last time she was ever to lay eyes on her mama, when Rose lay bloodied and battered in the wagon in Mama's arms while Brother drove her back to the Nash farmhouse.

"O Sweet Jesus," she grieved. All the memories of Mama conjured up memories of Jack Nash and the torture of losing them both was more than Rose could handle. Finally she was weeping hysterically and Viola went to Doctor Miller and got her something to calm her down and put her to sleep. And Rose was grateful for that sweet oblivion.

It was several days later before she heard the rest of Claire Louise's report. That Papa had already got himself another woman and moved her right into Mama's house. She was a fairly young widow from the local rural area, who had three small children of her own. Grace, who had never married, who stayed on the farm to help care for Flora, was struck dumb when the woman showed up out of the blue with her suitcases and her children. It was less than two weeks after Ollie's passing, and Claire and Walter were still guests there.

Grace considered the embarrassingly hasty remarriage to be a betrayal of both her mother and herself, and she was packed up and gone before he could blink three times. She took with her everything she owned and most of what had belonged to her Mama and a bitterness Claire Louise would never have thought her capable of. She was living at least temporarily in a nearby town with Ida Belle and her husband. Ida Belle had married before Rose and had two children of her own. But Brother was staying, as was Cyrus William, who was only 17. Both sets of twins had set out on their own adventures in their mid or late teens

Claire Louise had tried to talk Papa into letting her have Flora since she feared that the widow might not treat her well. But Papa was violently opposed to that notion. He got so incensed that after some hours of confrontation on the subject, he ordered Claire Louise, Walter, and JC off the farm forever. That didn't surprise Rose a bit, but Claire Louise was devastated over it and felt the widow lady had put some terrible poison about her in her Papa's mind. Rose just shook her head and wondered how Claire could have known Papa all her life and still believe there had ever been anything other than *poison* in his mind.

After Mama's dying, something began to happen to Rose. She became obsessed with her own mortality and the quick and unexpected way death comes. Her talks with Walter became so morbid at times, he began to worry about her sanity.

July 1938

It was a sunny July morning when they took a drive to a Forest Preserve with JC and Cynthia. While the children picked wildflowers and played running games among the trees, Rose sat on a blanket spread on the grass with Walter lying on his stomach beside her. He was raised up on his elbows and his chin rested in his cupped hands and he wasn't thinking about anything, just enjoying the fresh air and the clean scent of the forest.

Rose seemed unusually preoccupied though, so after a while he decided he should make an effort to cheer her up. She smiled absently at his silliness but there was no real mirth in her. Finally he reached for her hand which lay limply in her lap and as he squeezed it she turned her head down to look at him.

"A penny for your thoughts, Rose?" he offered gently.

She shrugged and gave him another wistful little smile but made no reply. Looking directly into her eyes like he was, Walter could see the depth of her sadness and that she was holding back a whole lot of tears. So he urged her to unburden herself. "You've always been our rock, Rose Sharon. Our little optimist. The girl who never gives up. You know I depend on you to keep me going, and now you're letting me down."

Her eyes were meeting his but by then they were almost empty. He felt she was shutting him out. That she intended to keep all her bad feelings hidden away and share no more of herself with him or anybody. The bitter taste of fear slid down his throat into the pit of his stomach and he couldn't speak for a minute, so they just looked at each other in silence.

Finally, Walter couldn't stand it any longer and he sat up and grabbed both her hands while he continued to stare into her peculiarly vacant eyes. "Talk to me, Rose Sharon!" He demanded. "Talk to me!"

But she turned her face away from him.

When he didn't press her further, she looked at him again and shrugged, "I don't know what to say." Her voice was small and trembling. "I'm just so scared, Walter."

His voice caught on a barb of the fear that was filling his throat. "Of what, Rose? What are you afraid of?"

She breathed a long sobbing sigh. "Oooooooooh! Of living, I guess. Of being alone. Of going to waste. Of dying." Then there was a long pause but before Walter could think of anything to comfort her, she added, "Of not dying." And with a feeble shrug, concluded. "Of everything."

Because he was speechless, he pressed her hands together and started rubbing them between his own as if they were in danger of frostbite and he had to make them warm again. "And I don't know how to help you," he said in a soft sorrowful voice. Then he rose to his knees and pulled her up in front of him. He drew her close and held her like that through several deep and thoughtful breaths. "I love you, Rose Sharon! You and JC and Cynthia mean more to me than my own life."

He was saying more, but Rose stopped listening after he said he loved her more than his own life. She'd heard that before. Truth be told, it was one of the very last lies Jack Nash had laid on her and now she pulled loose from Walter's arms and snorted scornfully.

"More than your life?" she asked and her expression was hard as stone while through narrowed eyes she scrutinized his face. "Don't say things like that, Walter. I've heard things like that from better liars than you."

Then she scrambled away from him and got to her feet.

"I always knew he'd come back to me and as long as I knew that, I could stand being alone. As long as I knew it wasn't forever. But now I know he's never coming back." She was looking off into the trees and he couldn't see if she was crying or still stony-faced. "He's not ever coming back." Walter saw her hug herself and shrivel up like a dead leaf right in front of his eyes. *"He hated babies!* He just plain hated babies and because I didn't see how much and I didn't get rid of her he's never going to forgive me!"

Her searching eyes finally spotted the two children among the trees and she glanced down at Walter again. "And Jack Nash never forgives anybody. Not one time in his whole life did he ever forgive anybody! Oh! how that man could hold onto hate! And I knew he did that. I just didn't know he could ever hate me." She sighed again and it came from so deep within her soul that Walter felt ashamed to have heard it. "And now I'm just *wasted.* I had all that love to give him. All that joy to share with him. I had so much to give him and now, it's all wasted. And the most hurtful thing is, Walter, I know everything *he's got* is not being wasted! I know he's got somebody else. I know he's giving everything that rightfully belongs to me to some other woman!"

She started walking away then, very quickly, and Walter jumped up and grabbed her arm. "You're not wasted, Rose. You've given more joy to more people!" He started his speech with no thought and so he had to wait a minute for his brain to catch up to his mouth. In the meantime, she was trying to get her arm away from him. "Listen to me, Rose Sharon! You are just feeling sorry for yourself and that's nothing to be ashamed of after all you've been through, but you have to be honest with yourself, too. Nothing you've got to give to others is wasted. You've got more love in your heart than anybody I ever knew and you give it all the time. Every time you breathe out you are sending love to somebody. I can feel it! Claire feels it. Everybody who knows you feels the love that pours out of you and everybody is a better person for it. You are one of the *light-bearers*, Rose! You are one of those who bring God's light to the rest of us who blunder around in the dark."

Rose giggled, "If you see me like that, Walter, then I thank you, but that's not the kind of love I was talking about." She stopped giggling and looked at him with bitter eyes. "The kind of love I bore for Jack Nash I had to let die in me. I had to just let it shrivel up and die in me. I couldn't... I can't give that love to anybody else. Not to *anybody* else, Walter, and now it's dead and wasted and I'm dead and wasted, too, or anyway ...." She stopped talking all of a sudden and for a minute she was smiling. *"Anyways,* that was how Jack always said that word. He had a whole lot better way of talkin' than me, but he always said that word wrong." She finally got Walter's hand off her arm and gave him a smug smirk, and then she went on talking. "Anyway, I'm the same as dead and I'm tired of pretending otherwise. How old am I, Walter? What year is this?"

"It's … it's 1938, Rose. Don't you know what year it is?" He sounded so concerned she let him take hold of her arms again.

She shrugged. "I don't know much of anything anymore, Walter. I don't *want* to know much of anything either. I want to be dead. I want to be *really* dead and in my grave and not just this kind of dead!"

Then she realized she was caught again and started pounding with both fists on his hands which were holding her. "Let me alone, Walter. Don't try to be nice to me. I can't stand it when you're nice to me."

A sudden and desperate notion reared up in his mind. "Rose let me make love to you. You could *pretend* I was Jack if I made love to you. I could prove to you that you aren't dead! Rose, I know you've still got that kind of love in you. You just hid it away because you weren't using it. But I can make it come back. If you'll let me. Please let me, Rose. Let me be Jack for you."

She stopped struggling and looked up at him. He was so tall, she thought, and such a big man. Jack was nowhere near as big.

Walter waited a long time for her to say something. And when she did it was a disappointment to him.

"Dear, dear Walter," she sighed tenderly. "You are sure an extraordinary man! I wish I could let you make love to me." She snorted. "But those days are long gone for me. I can't be a woman anymore. Even if I was laying here naked and you were staring at me, I couldn't feel like a woman. I'd just feel disgusting and ugly." She swayed toward him and pressed her face against his chest. "I'm all wasted and dried up *and dead*. That's just the way it is…" she paused for a moment. "And I wouldn't want to pretend you're Jack, anyway. I've come to despise Jack Nash for he's the one that killed me!" She sighed another of those deep soulful sighs and Walter was struck dumb for a time. But she'd become passive again, so he led her back to the blanket.

"Let's just sit here and be quiet then, Rose. And after a while when you feel like it, you can talk to me about all these feelings you're having. I want you to talk everything out. I think you need to get it all out in the open so you can look at it and separate what's true from what isn't. But I promise I'll just sit here and listen. I won't say anything and I won't make you listen to my opinion about anything."

Several times the children ran up to sit beside them for a while until they got bored with the inactivity and darted away again. They were so animated and having such fun, Walter expected Rose to respond to their presence. But she didn't beyond a half-hearted smile or a nod of her head.

Eventually though, Rose looked over at him with affection in her eyes and laid her hand over his. "I ain't talked about him for such a long time." She said and then, to his relief her cold empty eyes started to get misty and pretty soon tears were pouring down her cheeks. "Maybe it would feel good to talk to somebody about him." But she didn't say any more and for a while she just sat there rubbing away her tears with the back of her hands and thinking. Walter had almost given up on her when she set her eyes on something way off in the distance and started to talk.

"That time Mama tried to save me from Papa—she told me he hated me because I loved Jack Nash more than I loved him. Well, if that's what he thought, he was sure right about that. I hated my Papa! Probably a lot more than he ever hated me." She snickered. "Did you ever hate anyone, Walter? I bet you didn't. You're too good! You have to be bad in order to hate. But then you have to be bad in order to love, too. Or at least to love Jack Nash. If I'd a been good, I'd never have chased after him like I did, and I'd never have laid in the hay shed with him and let him touch me like he did." Her voice twisted that word and she grimaced. "He sure knew how to "pleasure" me all right. He had mighty sweet hands. But I always made him swear he'd keep his zipper shut. And he always did, except that one time. And then papa caught him and thought sure we'd been up to something and Jack got himself horsewhipped. But we hadn't really. Probably just because I got scared and hit him where it hurts!" She snickered again and Walter thought he saw just a smidgen of a real smile in it.

Rose hugged her knees up under her chin. "Ain't this awful *ugly* stuff for you to be hearin' Walter?"

Walter shook his head. "Say whatever you feel like saying, Rose."

She stared off into the past again. "Well, Jack Nash left me after that too, but I knew he'd be back. And that time he did come back and he married me too. Even though Papa wanted to kill him."

Suddenly her voice changed. "Oh, but it's silly to dwell on all that, much less to talk about it. I was a fool to chase after him and I was a fool to marry him, and I'm just bein' a fool again sittin' here thinkin' about him. Worse yet, I'm still chasin' after him like a fool and you're aidin' me by drivin' me around every other Sunday hopin' I'll run into him someplace. Now, be honest with me Walter, ain't that bein' an extraordinarily ignorant dang fool?" She was rubbing off her tears again and Walter spoke softly to her.

"Why don't you just stop trying to be so brave? Just let yourself cry, Rose. Just let all that heartbreak pour out."

Their eyes held on to one another's and she nodded finally. "I want to." And then the tears began in earnest and Walter hoped they were cleansing tears this time so he let her weep undisturbed until her lamentation became peppered with giggles and then she couldn't stop laughing.

"Oh! Walter. You are so good to me. You always know how to help me." She got to her feet and bent over him to press a light kiss on his cheek. "But I think we are both doomed, Brother-in-Law. I got Jack Nash and you got Claire Louise. Jack's the worst sinner that ever lived and Claire Louise is the worst saint. May we all rest in peace, Amen!"

After expelling a relieved breath, Walter managed a grin and Rose sat on the grass beside him again. "You know what? I feel like I can see way off. Way off like in the future or somethin'." Her eyes widened suddenly and then she turned and looked at him with an anxious expression. "I think maybe I won't live too much longer."

Walter bristled. "Don't, Rose. Don't talk like that anymore!"

"No. No, Walter. It's all right. It's not scary. It's just like a, like a premonition, you know." She shrugged. "I feel like I should start putting my life in order. Go to church more, like

Sister Claire does. Maybe get Cynthia Jackleen baptized. Get my mind off Jack Nash and those old sad things. All those old—hopeless things."

Walter didn't like hearing her talk that way but he guessed it was better than some of the stuff she'd been saying up to then. So he let her talk and he listened without judging her words anymore. And at the end of it, there was a real sense of peace—for both of them.

That July morning in the forest preserve proved to be the last time Walter and Rose were able to spend a lengthy period of time alone together. But it had turned into such a good day for both of them that when Rose got back to her apartment she was her old optimistic self again. Full of hope and confident there would be good days ahead. Walter was so truly grateful to God for that, that he accompanied Claire to church the next Sunday and even went so far as to promise God he'd go every Sunday thereafter, if only Rose's life would get straightened out and Jack would come back into it.

For her part, Rose went straight to Leo and Viola and told them she wanted to join their church. "You are two of the best people I ever knew. I'd bet my last dollar that neither one of you has ever done a mean or unkind thing in your whole life."

Viola sought to convince her that everybody has sinned and so had they, but Rose disdained that opinion and interrupted her discourse. "I know how much time you spend prayin' and goin' to church and just thinkin' on God and being grateful and such and I feel like I need to do them things too. And I want to learn to do them like you do. The two of you. I want to join your church and be a Catholic just like you are. And I want Cynthia Jackleen to be baptized, too."

And that was why Rose Nash spent two evenings a week at the Rectory of St. Mary's with the Father, learning about the faith of her two dearest friends.

Although she wasn't positive she understood all the things he taught her and feared there were parts of it she might never comprehend, she was captivated by the Father's gentle manner and the genuine love and respect he showed her. And she had no problem understanding and accepting his Jesus, who was the same Jesus she'd grown up loving and trusting, and all his truths which she'd already come to trust in and believe from those nightly Bible studies with her Papa when she was a little girl.

One of the things she loved most about her new religion was the old church itself. The mystery and beauty of St. Mary's, dimly lit as it was at night with the red sacristy lamp hanging on its gold chain above the main altar and the hundreds of flickering votive candles in their little red glasses pulsating like the heart of Jesus and inviting her to drop to her knees and pray.

There was always somebody there worshipping God, and that gave Rose a particular thrill. Never had she entered the church without finding at least one woman already there on her knees in a pew at the front of the church near the big altar, wearing her babushka and saying her rosary in a soft whispery voice. Or a man still wearing his work clothes taking a few minutes on the way home to visit with the Lord. It was such a holy place. Rose loved the smell of the candles and the incense and the antiquity. She could almost *feel* her heart swell—it was beginning to overflow with love again.

She insisted Cynthia Jackleen be baptized right away. She herself had to complete the instructions but Cynthia was too young for that. The Father consented, so with Leo and Viola acting as godparents, the little girl was baptized on her fourth birthday that September in 1938.

Rose felt like that was her real birthday because from that moment on she was truly born into God's kingdom and belonged forever and always to Jesus.

Rose held her in a close embrace that day before they left the church. "This is the best thing I could ever do for you, Cynthia Jackleen. This is the best thing I have ever *done* for you!"

Rose, herself had been baptized in the river back home during a tent revival when she was eight years old. Preacher Kilgore had dunked her in the name of the Father and the Son and the Holy Ghost, so it was not absolutely necessary that the Father do it now. But it was her most ardent wish and so he was going to go ahead on condition that the first time might not have been valid.

And Rose found herself growing more and more anxious with the passage of time. She and Cynthia were walking to the old stone church at least once every day by then. Sometimes in the morning for an early Mass, sometimes in the evening for some devotion or other; there were so many different ones she had an awful time remembering which night the various ones took place. But a lot of times they just went to sit and look at Jesus on the altar and the beautiful smiling plaster saints scattered on pedestals at the front and back of the church and here and there along the walls. For Rose had found the greatest peace she had known in years. When she knelt in that place and felt the comfort of her Heavenly Father's love she could forget entirely the pain of losing Jack Nash.

As far as the rest of her life was concerned, she continued working at the grocery store, spending five or more hours there every day except Sunday. And now Claire Louise and Walter visited more or less regularly. Rose developed a closer attachment to Walter's boy-child, who continued to look like Jack Nash in spite of Claire's stern disapproval.

JC had attached himself to Rose as well, and he loved to spend time talking with her. He was now only a few weeks from his sixth birthday and growing more darkly beautiful by the moment. He proved to be highly intelligent and eager to learn. Now that he felt safe and secure with Walter's love, he was blossoming in every way. Claire Louise did her best to discourage Rose's desire to become a Catholic. She suggested she come with her to her church instead, but Rose felt Jesus was holding her hand and leading her the way he would have her go. So she resisted her sister's entreaties with a loving but firm "No!"

On a Sunday afternoon in early October, she was standing before a mirror in Mary Jean's bedroom fussing with her hair. She'd been hurrying to get dressed and prettied up because Leo and Viola were taking her out to a restaurant for dinner in honor of Viola's 50th birthday and Mary Jean had offered to watch Cynthia while she was gone.

While Rose struggled to get a curl just right at her temple, Mary Jean sat on the bed watching her with a solemn expression. When Rose met her gaze in the mirror, she cocked a quizzical eyebrow, causing her friend to shrug her shoulders.

"I was just thinking how pretty you are. You are really a beautiful young woman, Rose." She scowled at Rose's indifferent shaking of her head, and added. "You are, Rose! And at your age you should have boyfriends lined up all the way from here to Lake Michigan … all sorts of handsome young men fighting for your attention. You shouldn't be spending your Sunday evenings going out with a couple of old fogies like Leo and Viola. Not that I'm saying they aren't fine people, but, Rose, you ought to be going out dancing with some disreputable young stud who might just keep you out all night necking in the back seat of his Cadillac."

Rose grinned at her through the mirror and giggled. "Well, I feel kind of embarrassed by you suggestin' that, Mary Jean, 'cause I will be much more comfortable with Leo and Viola than I would be with some *'disrespectable stud'.*" Her eyes returned to her own image to see an embarrassed red blush spreading across her cheeks, so she turned away from the mirror and twisted to look down and make sure the seams of her stockings were straight.

Mary Jean snickered. "I didn't mean *disrespectable.* I had something a little more *risqué* in mind."

"I do think you're right about one thing, though—I really am a knock-out!" Straightening up, she grinned and threw Mary Jean a saucy kiss before turning away from the vanity and walking into the small parlor. "Walter and Claire Louise got me this dress."

Mary Jean followed behind her nodding her approval. "Well, they sure know your style. It looks perfect on you."

The dress was made of a soft, silky body-hugging material with a pattern of smeared colors—shades of peach and ecru and burnt orange, and it was perfect with Rose's coppery red hair and peachy gold skin. She took a seat on the divan to wait for Leo and Viola and noticed right away that Mary Jean was staring at her again with a serious look on her face.

"When are you going to let somebody take Jack's place in your life, Rose? It isn't natural for a healthy young woman like you to be alone so long. Even old as I am, I need a man every now and then—just to remind me I'm a woman."

Rose's jaw tightened and she turned away. "I don't think about that, Mary Jean, and please don't you talk about it."

The older woman glanced into the kitchen where Cynthia sat alone at a small dining table sipping from a glass of milk and eating a piece of chocolate cake and then she turned back toward Rose.

"You're letting the fact that one louse treated you bad ruin your whole life. Are you going to sit around and get old like me and never have a man hold onto you again? That isn't right, Rose. You need to be close to a man. You need to have more babies. You're wasting your life!"

That was when Rose turned on her with fire in her eyes. "You better not say any more, Mary Jean. You're a good friend and I don't want to be mean to you, but Jack is the only man I'll ever want. His lovin' was all I ever wanted but he killed that in me and I don't ever want to go through that again." She was on her feet by then and she took a menacing step in Mary Jean's direction. "Lovin' Jack hurt me more than you could ever know and I *will not* let myself get hurt like that again."

But Mary Jean wasn't intimidated. She shook her head, "Dammit, Rose. You shouldn't have put him up on a pedestal like you did. He was just a man. He was bound to let you down."

"Mary Jean, please don't say any more."

"Dammit, Rose! Listen to what I'm telling you! Jack was just a plain, ordinary, selfish, stupid man! He wasn't God, Rose! You tried to make him be God!"

Rose stared at her in silence, but you could see the wheels in her head were turning. Before she could speak though, there was a knock at the door. It opened just wide enough that Leo's head was able to peer around it. He nodded at Mary Jean and spoke to Rose. "Ready to go, Liepchen?" He seemed oblivious to the tension in the room as Rose turned toward him and nodded. Then she looked one last time at Mary Jean before she joined him in the hall.

"I made him be God?" she said in a querulous tone—and let Leo shut the door behind her.

1938 October

Tuesday, the 11th of October, which actually *was* Viola's birthday, dawned crisp and sunny, a sparkling autumn day and Rose thanked God and gave him all the glory when she rose up that morning and saw the sunshine pouring through her bedroom windows. She flung up the sash and leaned as far out over the street as she dared, raising her voice in song and praising the morning, for a heady sense of adventure had engulfed her—another premonition? *Something* was telling her this day would bring her some wonderful surprises.

Scotty, the shoeshine man, heard her singing and looked up from his place beside Leo's door. He waved and grinned at her.

"Good mornin', Scotty," she waved back and his grin got wider. "Sure is, Miss Rose, and you sure sound happy this mornin'."

She smiled down at him, "I do declare I am that," she told him and then drew back inside and closed the window. She dressed quickly and fixed breakfast for herself and Cynthia, who was up and dressed before it was ready. By the time she got down to Leo's and started her day's work, she could contain herself no longer.

"Do you s'pose it's just 'cause it's Viola's birthday?" she giggled. "Maybe it's just that this day is so pretty."

Leo and Viola and all the customers who came in contact with her that morning were charmed by her joyful optimism.

In a few weeks she'd be finished with her religious instruction and be formally admitted into the church. She mentioned this to Mrs. Pulaski in jubilant tones, and Mrs. Pulaski couldn't resist a broad smile as she insisted that Rose accept, as a special gift, her very own ruby-colored rosary that had been blessed by the Pope in person.

The entire forenoon passed like that and more than a few customers and deliverymen observed that the building itself, inside and out, absolutely glowed with some kind of supernatural light and goodwill that day. Not one sour face remained sour after encountering Rose Nash and little Cynthia in the Wesslemans' Grocery that morning.

After lunch Scotty stepped inside long enough to ask Rose if he could take Cynthia with him down to Barney's Magazine Stand for an hour or so that afternoon. She concurred and gave the little girl a kiss, reminding her to behave for Scotty or she wouldn't get her afternoon treat. It had become a tradition of sorts for each of them to choose an ice cream cone or candy bar from the store's delights every afternoon when Rose quit work for the day, and then, during a leisurely neighborhood walk, enjoy their treats together. Cynthia, with a most serious shake of her head, promised her obedience and then dashed outside, forcing Scotty to run to catch up with her. Rose watched her skip to the curb where she waited for Scotty to cross the street, and then she turned to find Viola standing near the counter and smiling at her.

"My birthday must surely be blessed because God has given me the best of all gifts." Viola moved closer and slid her arm around Rose's waist. "He's brought *the old Rose Sharon* back to me and Leo. Our girl with the irrepressible joyful heart!"

"Is that the one who looks about 16 and has that *Merry Christmas spirit* all year long?" Leo walked up from the back of the store and patted her shoulder as he passed by. "It's you all right, Rosy, and you are lit up like Christmas!"

Rose found herself giggling again—that feeling that some kind of miracle was imminent overwhelmed her and she fancied she had wandered into some kind of fairy tale world and that all her wishes were about to come true.

Thirty minutes later, Leo had finished boxing up some groceries for the delivery boy and was waiting for him to carry them out to the truck. As soon as he saw the boy drive up, he went to hold the door open so Bobby could come and go quickly.

The sun was almost blinding him, but he was pretty sure it was Mary Jean in the next block, tearing up the sidewalk as though demons from hell were chasing her and she was heading straight for him. He was about to call Rose to come have a look and confirm it was her, when he heard her shouting his name.

Leo stepped out far enough that she could see him and hollered back at her. "Mary Jean, I hear you! What's the matter?"

By that time she was on the corner and about to cross the street onto his block so he could finally understand what she was shouting.

"Tell Rose to come down to Santini's," she yelled and that time Rose heard her too. Leo turned frightened eyes from her to Viola, and Rose's heart sank into her stomach. She feared she might faint, "Something has happened to my baby!" And she shot out the door under Leo's arm and almost crashed into Mary Jean who had just that moment reached the store.

"Dear God, what is it, Mary Jean? Has somethin' happened to Cynthia?"

Viola came out behind her and stood clutching her husband's arm and praying out loud to Jesus and Mary and all the Saints and Poor Souls. Her voice sounded like the angels themselves to Rose, and she closed her eyes and nodded "amen" while she waited frantically for Mary Jean to tell her the worst.

But Mary Jean couldn't say anything. She was panting so hard she couldn't even breathe and she was trying to wave Rose's worry away by shaking her head "no" hoping to make her understand without words.

Rose had given up and was about to dart off to see for herself, when Mary Jean caught her breath and said, "Not Cynthia." "She's fine." "Jack" "It's Jack Nash!"

For some queer reason, the name didn't mean anything to Rose, or to Leo either. They both continued to stare blankly at the woman All Rose had comprehended were the words that said her daughter was okay. She wanted to lie down somewhere and faint. "Nothing is worse" she thought "than having your child hurt." And the relief she felt knowing Cynthia was all right left her no strength at all to cope with whatever really was the matter.

Viola was the only one who heard and understood what Mary Jean said. But the statement had left her stunned and she wasn't able to communicate her knowledge to her husband or to Rose either. And Mary Jean had hollered out "Santini's." That was the funeral parlor. Did that mean Jack Nash was dead?

Mary Jean's eyes darted from one to the other of them, still not understanding their lack of comprehension.

"I said it's Jack Nash! He's down at Santini's Funeral Parlor!"

That time comprehension came all at once to all of them. Rose sank back against the window of the store, suddenly her legs were too weak to hold her up. She put her hand over her mouth and Leo feared she was going into some kind of catatonic state. She looked as dazed as if somebody had hit her with a baseball bat.

"Is he dead?" she asked finally, in a stricken voice.

"Dead?" And then Mary Jean was laughing like a crazy woman. "No, he's not dead! He's just out there on the sidewalk, big as you please, leaning on his car and smoking one cigarette after the other!"

Leo and Viola both reached out to Rose then, but before they could touch her she had crossed the street and was racing down the sidewalk toward Santini's.

All three of them were yelling at her to stop and the delivery boy who was young and strong ran after her, caught up with her, and held onto her until Leo and Mary Jean could catch up. She threw a wild-eyed look at Leo and he saw tears washing down her cheeks but she was laughing.

"Leo, Leo! This is what was so special about today. God has given Jack back to me. Just like that other time. Only on Viola's birthday instead of mine." She could see he didn't understand the meaning of what had happened so she grabbed his arm and squeezed it to her body. "When he came back to marry me, it was my birthday. Now it's Viola's birthday!"

Leo looked anxiously from her to Mary Jean. "Wait, Rose. Before we jump to any conclusions,—let's hear what Mary Jean has to say."

They both looked expectantly at her and Mary Jean shrugged and shook her head. "What's to say? I don't know. I just saw Jack Nash and another guy park this car in the street in front of the funeral parlor and after the other guy went inside, Jack got out on the passenger side, lit a cigarette and leaned up against the car and that's where I left him. Big as life, and even better lookin' than I remembered. Rose," she grinned, and thumped Rose's arm with her forefinger, "I started to go up to him and ask the big dope where he's been keepin' himself, but I thought I better go tell Rosy first and so here I am." She looked from one to the other of them. "Well? You better hurry! Knowing Jack, he might not hang around long." She winked at Rose and started back toward the store. "I'll watch the store with Viola. You better go with Rose, Leo."

Rose spent one second debating with herself, and then she was gone.

The funeral parlor was two and a half blocks away, just south of Barney's Magazine Stand which occupied the corner at this end of the third block. Rose outdistanced Leo immediately and she was already crossing the second street before he was down the first. There was no thought in her mind except Jack. She had no plan, no words in mind, only the thought that he was there and she was going to see him again. She was going to look into those beloved blue eyes and be charmed by that dazzling smile again. After all these years she was going to be in his arms again.

"O Sweet Jesus! Sweet Jesus! Sweet Jesus!" she whispered over and over.

Her heart pounded so loudly she couldn't hear anything else, and she feared it might just quit beating altogether before she got to the end of the last block. When she crossed the street to the final block, a car almost ran her down and blasted its horn at her, but she missed the seriousness of the incident because her mind wasn't conscious of anything going on around her anymore. Only that she had to get to Santini's before Jack drove away.

As she neared the end of the second block she started slowing her pace trying to catch her breath. She didn't want to be as breathless as Mary Jean had been when she finally got a chance to speak to him. She could just imagine herself standing there sputtering and gasping until his boss came out and demanded "Drive me home, Jack," and him leaving her stand there waving her arms and stamping her feet and watching her beloved and his car disappear down the street.

She was in the crosswalk when she heard somebody call out to her and turning toward the sound, she saw Scotty on his usual perch and Cynthia Jackleen sitting in one of the seats and bouncing up and down with excitement at the unexpected sight of her mother. Rose took a moment to walk over and give the little girl a hug and a kiss and thank Scotty for taking such good care of her. Then she told him quickly she was looking for *Jack* and would he keep Cynthia in the chair until she called for her. Rose was anxious to bring the child to her father, but she wasn't all that sure he'd want to see her. Scotty's eyes got wide and he grinned and assured her he would handle Cindy which was his pet name for Cynthia.

Then Rose turned back toward the street while her eyes studied the handsome young man alongside the automobile parked there.

And there was no way she could have prepared herself for the moment she saw him again. The sight of him leaning there against the car, hatless, and with the jacket of his suit unbuttoned and hanging open over a beige-colored shirt and a brown tie with an orange and beige pattern splashed across it … the tie caught her eye because it looked like one she had bought to cheer him in the middle of one of his down periods … quite literally took her breath away. So much for taking the time to get it back earlier. She was stopped in her tracks as completely as if somebody had reached out and grabbed her.

Jack wasn't looking in her direction. His attention was on the entrance to Santini's. She saw him raise his arm and look at a watch on his wrist that glittered in the sunshine. He was more beautiful than even she remembered and Rose's heart fluttered and danced, and the skin all over her body tingled and burned with the anticipation of being in his arms again.

Standing there on the sidewalk, halfway between her husband and her daughter, Rose felt herself transported into the past again. It was the day that Jack Nash stood before her in that dingy justice of the peace office in Maysfield, Mississippi, and looked deep into her soul with his bewitching blue eyes, while he listened to her promise to love and honor and obey him. "Until death do us part" she swore to him and God both, and while she was looking into his eyes, she could honestly feel him inside her, filling all the empty places, healing all the wounds. She had believed it then, that the two of them were made one, just like Jesus preached in the Word, and she believed it yet. Rose Nash wasn't a whole person without Jack Nash and neither was he without her. That was one of those *truths* nobody could understand but nobody could deny either.

When Rose came back to herself, she heard all the noises around her and she knew she had no more time to waste. Jack lit another cigarette and then he reached for the handle of the door. Just then, panic rising, Rose glanced at the funeral parlor entrance and saw the door was opening.

"Sweet Jesus!" She cried and took a tentative step or two in Jack's direction. "Jack!" she shouted. "Jack Nash!"

Jack turned at the sound of his name and to her relief recognition lit up his face and his eyes worked their way all over her, just the way they used to when he took his first look at her every morning of their life together. Then his lips spread in a big grin that made it plain he was happy to see her.

And after that, in Rose's mind, everything started happening in slow motion. She was looking into that wonderful face and he was smiling and revving up all his beguiling ways and seductive charm and pretty soon she was floating a couple of inches above the sidewalk on her way to his arms and that was when he finally called out her name and started moving in her direction. "I'll be damned! Rose Sharon? Hell's fire, if it ain't my Rosy."

Rose didn't pay any more attention to the funeral parlor door so she didn't see the dark-suited heavy-set man step out, pause to fit the slate-gray fedora he carried in his hand firmly atop his silver hair and start down the steps. But he looked at her to see what kind of girl his driver had shirked his duty to socialize with.

Rose was so close to Jack she could see beads of dew on his dark eyelashes and like a bolt of lightning the knowledge came that he was crying for her, and she stopped all forward movement to stare at him in wonder. The joy bubbling inside her then threatened to carry her up to the stars and her only thought was to reach out and hang onto Jack to make sure he went soaring with her.

Suddenly she was conscious of Leo's presence, and of Cynthia running toward her only to be jerked back into Scotty's brown arms. And then there came a strange sound. A popping noise like a whole bunch of firecrackers going off at once, only the noise kept going and Jack and the heavy-set man started doing some kind of eerie dance with their arms flapping and their heads bobbing and their bodies jerking and jumping like puppets. That was when Rose's mind went off somewhere and left her to stand there like a fencepost with Leo's arms wound round her like a morning glory vine.

She just couldn't make out what was going on, but she heard somebody scream her name and then a whole lot of other noises drowned that out and everything just got more confused. She saw Jack stagger back toward the car and try to cling to it but then he started slipping down, and she imagined she could hear his fingernails scraping the metal and then he was down on the sidewalk and his blood was pouring out into the gutter. Rose imagined she could hear his heart shutting down like the motor of a car.

Rose couldn't let him die like that. Leo and Scotty were grabbing at her, trying to keep her from going to him, but only God could have stopped her at that moment and he would have had to strike her dead to do it. The sense of slow motion still prevailed. She went down on her knees beside him and touched his dear face, brushing away bits of debris and blood. She was smiling at him but her eyes were pouring tears while her voice gently crooned as if she were talking to Cynthia. She tried to lose herself in his bright blue eyes. He seemed to know she was there and he was trying to talk. Then her arms were around his shoulders and she was lifting him to her, pressing his face to her throat, kissing him, loving him, begging him not to die. Although there was chaos all around her and sirens were closing in, Rose felt some kind of unearthly peace and she tried very hard to convey that to the man in her arms.

All of a sudden out of nowhere the Father from St. Mary's was on his knees beside her. He had something in his hands and he was touching Jack and bending close to his mouth and talking real soft but loud enough and slow enough that Jack could hear and understand him. She felt Jack's struggle to breathe in her own body and she held him tighter willing her own life into him but she could only feel him getting weaker and weaker. While the priest was still talking to him and while she was still murmuring her prayers for him, Jack opened his eyes wide and looked straight into hers.

And plainly, above the pounding in her ears she heard him speak to her—"Forgive me for what I did to you, Rosy?"

Rose's tears washed over him and she shook her head. "I love you, Jack Nash. I forgave you a long time ago."

"Good" he whispered through bubbles of watery blood while his pretty mouth tried smiling at her, "Then maybe I can forgive myself."

He sucked in some air and made a hideous rattling noise that scared Rose. She looked at the priest whose head was bowed and who was making a sign of the cross on Jack's chest and she knew there wasn't any more time.

She hugged him closer and kissed him again and again. Jack looked up at her one more time and sighed her name like a prayer and then she watched his bright blue eyes dim and glaze over.

And after that there was nothing left that would ever mean much of anything to Rose Nash.

Dazed and bewildered, she watched helplessly as ambulance attendants and policemen took him away from her, and heartlessly ignoring her pleas and tears pushed her out of their way. Nobody would listen and nobody cared that he belonged to her. She was on her feet at last and weeping and grabbing at uniformed arms but they all threw her aside and cursed and swore at her and finally flung her so harshly that she flew backwards into the side of Jack's car, lost her footing and fell. Then she realized it was his blood she had fallen into and she went completely to pieces. She was screaming and sliding in her struggle to get away from it.

In the confusion, Scotty got through the police line and lifted her up into his strong young arms and carried her out of that nightmare and with Cynthia in Leo's arms they ran back to the safety of the grocery store.

Rose lay her head on Scotty's shoulder and sobbed. She didn't have the strength to fight anymore.

Viola and Mary Jean were frantic. "What's going on? So many police cars and ambulances!"

Mary Jean was asking the questions, but Viola, seeing the state Rose was in, shushed her and together they cleared a path up to Mary Jean's apartment where Scotty laid her gently on the bed. But she didn't stay there. She struggled to her feet screaming, "I can't stay here. I can't lay down in bed. I have to move around … to walk … to run …. I have to run somewhere—anywhere. I have to move. I can't be still. Sweet Jesus! I'll go crazy. I'm not going to be able to stand this. Leo! I can't stand this. I can't bear this, Jesus. O Jesus. This is just too much to bear!"

Leo was doing his best to calm her. He had her hand in his and she, as if finding a rope to cling to, drew his hand to her mouth and pressed it there.

He had managed to get his other arm around her and he held her firmly against his chest.

The two women watched her sobbing escalate until her shuddering resembled an epileptic seizure and they knew whatever had happened at Santino's Funeral Parlor undoubtedly had no redress.

Cynthia cowered forgotten at the entrance to the bedroom, mirroring the horror she had witnessed in her terrified eyes. She had started running to her mother when Rose took those first uncertain steps toward Jack Nash, but Scotty held her back and she watched that dark car come to a halt in the street—she saw something thrust out the back window that glinted in the sunshine. She saw what looked like a flash of fire and a noise like the firecrackers Uncle Walter had lit on the 4th of July. Then there was a commotion on the sidewalk and she saw a big man in a dark suit falling down the steps of the funeral home— she saw him collapse there and lie still with puddles of blood all around. Then she heard her mama scream and turned her head to see Rose kneeling on the dirty sidewalk and there was blood all around her too and she was holding somebody in her arms and she was talking to him and crying so terribly. And the Father in his black dress knelt down, and then the policemen came and took the man out of her lap; she got up and her clothes were all bloody and there was blood all over her face and her hands. And then the policeman pushed Rose and she fell down again and she was screaming and crying and Cynthia was so scared she couldn't breathe—she was gasping for breath and she knew she was dying just like her Mama was and just like those two men were.

Scotty was the one who came to her rescue at last. He saw she was paralyzed with fright, and he jerked her up in his arms and talked calmly and quietly to her. He tried to carry her away, but she saw they were leaving Mama so she started to kick and bite and scream for her. That was when Scotty handed Cynthia to Leo and turned back and picked up Mama.

Viola finally turned her attention away from Rose long enough to see the condition Cynthia was in and tried to comfort her but without much success. So she led her to Rose's side and attempted to call the woman's attention to the child. But Rose just stared at her and went on weeping.

Meanwhile, Mary Jean and Scotty stood together in the kitchen and she was asking him what had happened. Scotty, who wasn't really sure, shrugged. "I don't rightly know, Ma'am. Miss Rose called out to this man leanin' ag'in his car in front of the funeral home. '*Jack, Jack,*' she hollered, and then he came runnin' over to meet her and somebody in another car stopped in the street for just a minute and stuck some kind o' gun out the window and killed him. The other man had just come out the funeral home door and he got killed too. It seemed kinda like he was the one the gun was aimin' at and that other poor fellah just kinda got in the way of the bullets. But it killed him just as dead anyway.

Then Miss Rose got down in the street and took that poor man onto her lap and held onto him till the po-lice come and grabbed him 'way from her. And when she was tryin' her best to talk to them, they just pushed her off and the poor little thing fell down again and was sittin' in his blood and nach'erly she just went crazy then." He was shaking his head, and his expression was one of bafflement and unbelief while his eyes pierced Mary Jean's, searching for something to calm his own panic and to explain the injustice of life. "The little one, poor little Cindy. She done seen all o' that too!"

Viola had just come out of the bedroom and was standing at the door listening. She and Mary Jean were both crying, and even Scotty had tears on his cheeks. His mouth dropped open in a hopeless moan. He looked at Viola and said, "I wonder who that fellah was that Miss Rose was so happy to see."

But Viola was too stricken to speak. Instead she sagged against the door jamb and hung there hiding her face against her arms. After she managed to compose herself a little, she cleared her throat and shook her head.

"That was Jack Nash, Scotty. That was Cynthia's daddy."

The young man gasped, then nodded thoughtfully while his expression grew even more forlorn—Scotty was close enough to these dear people to know the story of Rose's lost love. "Poor little Miss Rose!" he cried. "Oh Lordy, Lordy."

Viola wiped her eyes with her apron and said to nobody in particular. "Somebody has to get word of this to Walter and Claire. They may be able help." She looked from Mary Jean to Scotty and back again. Helplessness was overwhelming her. The scene took on an artificial look, like a snapshot or maybe even a child's drawing with little stick people all in a row, staring out at her with blank faces. Little stick people not having any reason for their existence except that they'd been penciled in there. Little blank faces staring straight forward, trusting that whoever had drawn them there knew what he was doing.

There was a sudden jolt back to reality when she heard somebody calling her name and Leo's from the grocery store downstairs. Viola stuck her head back into the bedroom and looked anxiously at Leo who motioned her to go take care of it. He was fearful of stirring Rose up again if he tried to leave her.

Viola vanished for a time, but shortly thereafter, she was back.

"You better come, Leo. It's Father Paul."

"Ask him to come up here," he suggested, and then nodded to Scotty and Mary Jean. "Father will be a blessing to Rose."

But Viola shook her head and her voice lowered several tones. "There's some policemen with him."

Leo bobbed his head in understanding but seemed perplexed as to their presence. "I see. Do they want to talk to me? Or to Rose?"

"The detective wants to talk to Rose and to anybody else who was there." Viola's usually soft and sweet voice was harsh and contentious. "Should we let them talk to Rose, do you think? I think she needs to talk to a doctor first. If I have anything to say about it."

Mary Jean was scowling and she spoke in a stage whisper. "I agree with Viola. Rose is in no condition to talk to anybody and besides, what on earth can she tell them about a murder? She doesn't know anything about that." She looked at Viola to back her up and then she turned back to Leo. "You go, Leo. And Scotty. You were both there and you know as much as she does. Just tell them Rose can't see anybody until she sees her doctor."

Leo disengaged his hand from Rose's and placed her hand in Mary Jean's. Her sobs had turned into a steady quiet weeping by then, and she got off the bed and began to follow Leo out of the room. But Mary Jean tugged her back to the bed. "It's the police, Rose, and you don't have to talk to them."

Rose didn't acknowledge her at all. She just pulled her hand free and walked out of the room. Mary Jean hurried after her and saw her disappear down the stairs that led to the grocery store. "Good grief, Viola, that girl must be out of her head. She mustn't try to talk to those men in the state she's in. They'll get her all confused and from what I've heard about how the homicide department works, she'll end up being the one they charge with the killings."

"Oh, good heavens no, Mary Jean! You don't really believe that, do you?' Officer Crimshaw is such a decent man."

"Crimshaw is just a cop on a beat, Viola." Mary Jean's expression was grim. "It's the detectives from downtown who don't care who they punch around. Just ask Scotty. He knows what I'm talking about."

But Scotty had already gone downstairs and Viola could only stand there staring at Mary Jean and wring her hands.

"One of us has to stay with Cynthia," Mary Jean was saying. "But I think one of us should be down there to protect Rose from those jerks." She could see Viola cringe at the thought, so she nodded. "You stay here. I want to hear the story of what really happened anyway." She patted Viola's back consolingly on her way out the door. "Cynthia needs to be cuddled and petted. Maybe you can get her to talk about it." And then she was gone, and Viola closed the door behind her and took a couple of deep breaths before she tackled her job as counselor.

At first she couldn't locate the child and feared she had slipped downstairs after her mother. But when she had given up the search and left the apartment—was at the top of the stairs—she heard a soft whimpering in the direction of Rose's apartment, and there sat Cynthia, huddled on the floor against the door, her big sad eyes shining wet in the stark light from the single bulb high in the ceiling that lit the stairs and hallway.

"My goodness, Sweetheart," she said in a shaky voice, relief bringing back the tears. "What are you doing out here all by yourself?" And despondently, Viola acknowledged that she was a poor choice to help that baby unburden herself of the terrible memories of that afternoon because she could barely stand the thought of even hearing about them.

"I want to go home." Cynthia whispered between sobs. "I want my mama and I want to go home."

Rose had walked into the middle of a police *grilling*. There were a half dozen uniformed officers milling about the store like a herd of nervous cattle and two men in suits, neither of whom had removed their hats, were standing near the front door talking to Leo. Scotty stood a little ways off with his head down and fiddled with a button on his shirt while he waited for somebody to ask him something.

At that particular moment Rose felt pretty good. For one thing, there was a kind of numbness moving along her spine and from there, down all her nerves, bringing with it a kind of forgetfulness. She thought she could probably forget any of this had ever happened. She thought she could wake up tomorrow believing that all of this was just a bad dream and if Mary Jean ever came running up the street with stories about Jack Nash, she would just walk away and pretend she had gone deaf and everything would go back to the way it was yesterday. She wouldn't ever see him again, but that was all right because she'd know he was around somewhere doing something and being happy, and that was all she really needed to know.

Rose turned back toward the exit door. If she never spoke the words, she thought, she could keep them from being true.

"Rose. Rose, my dear child." Father Paul, whom she hadn't even noticed, moved toward her from her left, and laid his hand gently on her shoulder. "Do you feel like talking to anyone yet?" His kind eyes were compassionate and she could see genuine love and concern in them. She smiled and touched his chest with the palm of her hand. He was such a good man and he had been such a blessing to her all during those religious instructions. If she could talk to anybody it would be him, but she had made up her mind not to make any of today's events real by saying it out loud. So she tried to let her eyes tell him how grateful she was and kept her mouth shut.

"I know how worried you've been about Jack's soul," he said in a quiet voice. "So I must tell you he repented his sins Rose, and he received absolution before he died. I know you were right there and probably heard him, but I want to assure you he was saved. Jesus came to meet him. I'm certain of that." Rose had begun to frown and that worried the priest. She ought to be pleased about what he was telling her. Perhaps she was not as resigned as she pretended. Perhaps she was on the verge of a breakdown. He'd seen that happen often enough and in situations a lot less traumatic than this one. "Rose my dear, Jack is with God. He asked forgiveness for his sins. Does that make his dying any easier for you to bear?"

He had said it. The priest had spoken those awful words. She knew he meant to be kind and they had talked many times about her fears for Jack's soul, so he was only trying to reassure her, but she didn't want to hear he had died. If only the priest hadn't said those words.

So there went all her plans. She looked at Father Paul but she didn't answer his question. Jack didn't even know what absolution was or that such a thing existed. How could he do it if he didn't know what it was? The priest's hand moved off her shoulder to rest on her forearm and she was staring into his eyes. They were blue like Jack's but color was the only thing they had in common. There was no laughter in these eyes. No teasing. There was no fire there. She sighed and gave up. This man wanted desperately to help her but he didn't know Jack Nash. Jack didn't believe *anything* was a sin. How could he be sorry when he didn't even know he did it! Rose suddenly saw the whole thing as a ridiculous joke. A ritual forgiveness of sin for a man who loved sin. A man who ignored God and who never forgave anybody in his whole life.

Rose flung the Father's hand away and bolted up the aisle until she bumped into a little knot of policemen. "He's dead, that's all." she told them, "and nothing is ever gonna make that easy."

She wondered why all the officers and the two gruff-talking detectives looked at her so strangely. They just stopped talking and stared at her. That was when she noticed Mary Jean standing close by. She hadn't said anything, but it was plain she was keeping watch. It occurred to Rose that maybe they thought she was crazy running around and hollering like she had about Jack being dead, but then she saw her reflection in the front window. It had darkened in the store once the sun slipped above mid-heaven, so Leo reached over and switched on the lights. She just happened to be standing near the window and turned in that direction to behold herself. There was something smeared all over her. Her face and her clothes. She looked down at her dress and picked at her skirt and realized the splotches were damp and sticky. That was when she saw her hands and was embarrassed to see they were so dirty and she wondered out loud "What in the world have I gotten into?"

Nobody said anything and she moved a little closer to the light earnestly studying all the smears and streaks. The pretty blue gingham dress she'd put on with such joyful expectation that morning was ruined. "This morning?" she wondered absently. Was it still October the 11th—still Tuesday? Surely not! Surely weeks had passed since that glorious sunlit morning when she leaned out the window and sang her song to Scotty. And now that dress was soaked with something. The stuff was everywhere. Why hadn't she noticed before what a mess she was? Why hadn't somebody said something? Then suddenly she knew.

"Jack's blood," she gasped.

She looked up to see Leo coming toward her with tears in his eyes and then the room started spinning and she felt the floor rise up and slam the breath right out of her.

Immediately, Doctor Miller was called to come have a look at her and he ordered something from the pharmacy to help her sleep. In the meantime, Claire Louise arrived to help her with her bath and wash her hair and put her to bed. Then she and Walter and JC stayed the night and soothed and comforted Cynthia until she fell asleep in Walter's arms.

Rose slept until after noon the next day and then one of the detectives returned and asked a lot of questions, but there wasn't anything she could tell them that they didn't already know. He treated her with respect though and even answered some of *her* questions. The one thing coming out of that conversation that disturbed her was something she picked up on her own. Detective Halverson mentioned that the consensus down at headquarters was that John Nash, they kept calling him John even though she corrected them a dozen times, had never been the intended victim. "I'm afraid he was just in the wrong place at the wrong time," the detective said. "Your husband just happened to get caught in the line of fire."

In some ways that made her feel better. Knowing he wasn't one of those killer gangsters did ease her mind but at the same time it suggested the possibility that Jack wouldn't have been in the line of fire if he had stayed down there by the car where he was when she called out to him. If he hadn't walked out to the middle of the sidewalk to meet her … if he hadn't put himself right there in front of the man they wanted to kill … the bullets would have gone right over his head or else farther up the street in front of him. Plainly, they wouldn't have shot the man on the steps through the automobile Jack leaned against. And that was a thought Rose knew she just couldn't live with … that her *undying* love for Jack Nash had been the cause of his dying. That she had abetted the murder of her beloved husband. O Sweet Jesus! What were the sins she had done to deserve such a terrible punishment?

Since that notion horrified her, she kept it to herself. It was too awful to think that those who loved her, like Leo and Viola and Mary Jean and Walter might believe as she was beginning to, that she had been the instrument of Jack's death. If they were to believe that, or even wonder about it, she could never look any of them in the eye again. And Cynthia! What if Cynthia were to find out!

Everybody was so concerned with her mental state and her physical well-being. They were so compassionate and solicitous to her every need, they were making her feel guilty. But Rose couldn't stop being helpless and weak. She was down in the bottom of a well and she didn't have the strength to hold her head above the water anymore. Nor the will. Except when she looked at her daughter's drawn little face. That was reason enough to fight her malaise, she decided. And for a little while she made the effort. Sooner or later, though, because the sound of Jack strangling on his own blood and the picture of his beautiful eyes fading to black had been ingrained on her mind like a scene from a movie playing over and over and over, and she was dragged down again to the bottom of the well where she jettisoned all her hope.

That first morning after she'd slept so soundly with the aid of the sleeping potion and Claire Louise sitting beside her bed all night holding her hand and offering up prayers for her, Rose hadn't felt too bad. She guessed her heart was still trying to pretend it had never happened and her brain was going along with the lie. Anyway, she thought everything was going to be okay. But then she was struck down with the truth of why Jack got shot. After that, she couldn't do anything but pace the apartment and cry. And poor little Cynthia was so scared. She wouldn't talk about what *she* had seen on the street that day. Not even to Walter or JC, whom she adored. "*If only I hadn't gone down there,*" Rose kept thinking. "*If only I had let well enough alone.*"

After supper that evening, Walter went back to the house on Grace Street but Claire and the boy stayed another night. Rose couldn't sleep again and was wandering the house long after Claire had fallen asleep beside her. JC was put to bed on the divan and Cynthia slept fitfully on her cot in Rose's bedroom. She whimpered and thrashed around but she didn't wake up.

The morning of the second day—

Eventually, Rose lay down in her bed and closed her eyes. It was the hardest thing just to be still. She just couldn't bear being still. But she must have fallen asleep because sometime in the wee hours before dawn, something awakened her. At first she thought Cynthia must have cried out but she appeared to be sleeping soundly. Rose turned from her daughter's bed while her eyes searched the pre-dawn gloom for some sign of what had roused her. Claire was lying on her side facing away from her and there was no sign she had moved from that position all night. There didn't seem to be anything out of place and yet something had broken into her sleep.

Suddenly she heard it again.

"Rose." "Rose Sharon."

It was her fantasy come true, and her delight was such that she forgot she had watched him die a little more than 24 hours earlier.

She flew across the bedroom and into the living room. The pre-dawn light was just bright enough to let her distinguish objects around her. JC, whom she had forgotten entirely, lay spread-eagled and uncovered on the couch with his blankets trailing onto the floor. She was on her way to cover him when a movement in front of the library table caught her eye and when she looked in that direction she saw him quite clearly. The first thing she noticed was that he was not dressed the same as he had been when she saw him in the street. Instead he was wearing a dark cotton work shirt with the sleeves rolled all the way up above his elbows to show his fine, hard-muscled arms. The sight of him like that, looking like he did when he'd ride Wild Honey down the field road to meet her on one of those sultry Mississippi summer evenings and then fly like the wind with her almost all the way to Dobbin and back again, made her knees weak and her heart pound. He wore his leather vest unbuttoned, as he did back then, and his work jeans and his boots. He was even holding his grandpa's old gray Stetson in his hand and he was grinning at her … just exactly the way he did in the days when he loved her. She couldn't see the color of his eyes in that gray gloom, but she could see the crinkles around them and the laugh lines at the edge of his pretty mouth.

He reached out to her and joy rose in her like a bird taking flight. She could feel its wings fluttering against her ribs— tickling her throat—lifting her from all her sorrows right on up into heaven.

"Jack," she sang out to him. "I *knew* you'd come back to me!"

She took those last few steps to his arms but when her arms closed around him … he vanished!

Rose was too shocked to even try to understand what had happened. *It was Jack and it wasn't a dream.* She heard his voice … loud enough to wake her from her sleep. She had *seen* him! *Really seen him.* And he was so solid he blocked the light from the window. She couldn't see through him. He was no ghost.

While Rose stood there bewildered, staring at the place Jack had been just seconds before, Claire Louise charged out the bedroom door seeking with dread her sister's whereabouts. Glancing around the room, she saw nothing except Rose's obvious confusion and so assumed she was suffering a nightmare. Tenderly and with a reassuring smile, Claire took her arm and tried to steer her back into the bedroom. Rose didn't resist at first, she was still struggling with the notion of Jack's presence and disappearance in so short a space of time. But in the middle of the doorway she put out her hands and held on to the jamb on either side refusing to be led any further.

Claire, with a perplexed look in her eyes, let go and waited for her sister to explain.

"Sister Claire?"

"Yes, Rose Sharon?"

"I just saw Jack Nash. He was standing right there in front of the window." She nodded her head in that direction. "Right there, Claire."

Rose turned her head and stared back at that spot and in her mind's eye she was seeing him again. "He was grinnin' that same ole ornery grin just the way he used to. With his eyes all crinkled up."

Claire's face sagged. It was evidently a lot worse than she'd thought, and she started shaking her head and tried again to ease Rose into the bedroom and back into bed. "Rose—oh, Rose." She sighed sadly. But Rose ignored her.

"He was his old self all right. Just so handsome it swelled my heart to look at him. And you know what else, Sister Claire? He wasn't wearin' those city clothes like he has to wear on that dumb ol' job of his. He was dressed just the way he did down in Mississippi. He looked just like he was ready to jump on Wild Honey's back and tear off down that ol' field road."

Then all of a sudden, she was crying again. "He wasn't wearing that nasty old suit with his blood all over it." Then she was weeping—great pulsing sobs that were drawn from the depth of her soul; Juliet mourning the loss of her lover.

Claire tried to comfort her, tried to hold her. But Rose darted away to the window where Jack had stood. Cynthia awakened and came to stand next to Claire Louise, half hidden behind her billowy flannel nightgown and clinging to her thin legs, which by their very frailty provided scant comfort. From there she watched her mother, clad in her thin cotton gown, crouch down in front of the window in the early morning chill and diligently study the linoleum. What was she looking for? Even Rose didn't know. Footprints in the dust, maybe? Something. Anything.

"Jack!" she moaned softly. "My dearest love! You cain't be gone forever. You mustn't have gone without me!" And then she slid all the way down and stretched out on the floor, all the while saying his name over and over, until Claire Louise thought she too would go crazy. What should she do? she wondered. It was plain enough to her that Rose had gone over the edge. And with that thought Claire's eyes took on a look of smug satisfaction and she snorted with a sanctimonious smile and said what she was thinking, out loud. "Well, Papa, our feelings for that man have been proved accurate. Jack Nash has committed his last and most foul sin. He has driven our little Rose Sharon out of her mind!"

Cynthia looked up at her aunt with a curious and fearful expression. She didn't understand the meaning of the words she was saying but the tone of her voice was just plain mean.

Claire reached down and loosed Cynthia's hold on her. "Get back to your bed," she told her in a cold voice. "I haven't got time to deal with you, too." And the little girl backed off but she didn't go to her bed. Instead she stuck her thumb in her mouth and sucked on it because she had already learned sucking her thumb was considered a sin by Aunt Claire and she wanted to do something to show her defiance. But at that moment Claire was not interested in childish defiance. All her attention was on Rose and what to do with her. If Walter was here, she thought, he could drive her to a hospital and have her committed. But then she decided that might be too drastic for the time being. That would leave Cynthia Jackleen an orphan and since she and Walter were Rose's only close relatives, they would be obligated to take her in. Claire Louise would not have spoken her thoughts on that subject out loud but she did not want to take on the responsibility of raising Jack Nash's daughter. *The apple never falls far from the tree* she assured herself and the notion that Cynthia would turn out to be a good God-fearing woman was about as far-fetched as one of those heathen fairy tales Rose used to love.

Claire Louise stood there at the doorway into the living room for a long time, just watching Rose writhe on the floor and suffer through her delusion. Eventually, when she had made up her mind what she must do, Claire resolutely returned to Rose's bed. After a while Cynthia, having received no response to her rebellious act, followed along behind her and climbed in on her Mama's side of the bed.

Then Claire slept right through sunrise, and a little later, JC had to rouse himself to answer the door and let Leo into the apartment. Rose was still on the floor, but now she was kneeling with her arms crossed on the window sill and her head resting on them. Leo and JC noticed her at the same time and while the boy kept his distance, Leo hurried over and bending down, touched her shoulder gently. "How long has she been kneeling here, JC?"

JC shook his head and shrugged.

Leo turned to look at him and asked the question again.

"I don't know" the boy said. "I was sleeping."

"Of course. But where is your Ma?"

JC shrugged again. "I don't know. In bed, I guess."

Leo was having some difficulty rousing Rose, who was mumbling something but seemed to be entranced or asleep and oblivious to her surroundings. He persisted though and after some anxious moments at last she raised her head and looked up at him. It was plain she was relieved to see him there.

"Leo! Oh but I'm happy you're here. Claire Louise won't believe me." Then as she let him help her to her feet, she started shivering. Up to that moment she hadn't been aware of the chill in the room.

"Are you all right, Child? What in the world are you doing kneeling on that cold floor? You're apt to catch pneumonia! How long have you been kneeling here?"

He motioned to JC "Bring one of those blankets over here, son."

When he had wrapped it around her, he noticed she was smiling at him. "Well, Rose, I'm glad to see that smile on your face, anyway. Have you spent the night in prayer? Have you made your peace with God?"

Rose nodded and let herself be led to the divan where she sat and curled her feet under her. Then Leo lowered himself into the chair across from her. His smile was hopeful, but what she said next floored him.

"Jack was here." She said it and then sat watching his face to see his reaction.

He was too stunned to say anything at first. He could only think that Rose was much more damaged than any of them had supposed. At last he found his tongue. "You mean you had a dream he was here."

"Not a dream, Leo. Jack was here. He was standing right there by the table, in front of that window and he was as solid as you are." After a little pause, she added, "I couldn't see through him, I mean. Like as if he was a ghost."

Leo cleared his throat a time or two and then nodded. "What did he do, Rose? Did he say anything?"

She shook her head. "He just grinned at me!" And then she giggled. "He just vanished when I went to put my arms around him."

Leo nodded and looked over at JC who was riding the arm of the sofa as if it were a horse. "Did you see him too, JC?"

The boy turned his head and flashed his Jack Nash eyes at him. "I guess I slept through the whole thing," was all he said.

"Uh-huh." Leo was still nodding his head, but Rose knew he didn't believe her any more than Claire Louise had.

"Leo," she said quietly, "do you think I've lost my mind?"

He looked at her and his face flushed with embarrassment. "No Rose, no! Not at all!" But then he looked down at his hands in his lap and discovered he had been twiddling his thumbs, which was his unconscious sign of agitation and everybody including Rose Sharon knew that. His flush spread down to the collar of his shirt and Rose smiled.

"Don't feel bad, Leo. I understand if you think that."

"But that's not what I think, Rose." Then he cleared his throat a couple more times. "I think you've just gone through a terrible experience and you need some time to deal with it." He took a handkerchief from his pocket and daubed at his eyes and for the first time Rose realized he had been crying. "I'm not going to be very much help to you though, Liebchen, I'm sorry to have to say so, but Old Leo is just a big dumb grocery man who don't know much of anything except which products the ladies in the neighborhood are apt to spend their nickels on. When it comes to important things like what ails the spirit of a person or her soul, I'm a dummkoph! And this lack of wisdom is a terrible burden to me now, when you are so in need of someone with *true* wisdom."

A look of genuine surprise came over Rose's face and she scooted forward to grab hold of Leo's hands. "How can you think that? You and Viola are the wisest and dearest people in the world. You are the ones who helped me get through all those awful lonesome times after Jack left. You are the ones who have showed me how to be a proper mother to my little girl. And you are the ones who led me to the true church and guided me all along the way. If it wasn't for you and Viola, I would have given up a long time ago and run off somewhere to turn into a *floozy* or something. Honest to goodness, Leo, without you takin' care of me and overpayin' me for the little work I do downstairs, I would have lost my soul and Cynthia

Jackleen a long time ago." After a moment or two looking into each other's eyes, Rose leapt up off the couch and started pacing the floor.

"Only now, I don't think there is any more help for me. I don't see how I can go on now. The thing that kept me goin' all these years, I mean besides you and Viola, was the notion that Jack would come back someday. I really believed that with all my heart." She stopped pacing for a minute to look down into JC's face and to squeeze his thin shoulders affectionately and sigh at him. "And now, I know that can never be. I saw his life go out of him while I held him in my arms." Then she was pacing again. "I know he cain't come back and love me in this world ever again. Even last night, when he stood there lookin' so beautiful and alive again, he wasn't really in this world or my arms would have held him and never let him go."

Then she was quiet for a while, thinking about the vision she had seen. "But he was in some other place and he just came to let me know that. God let him come to show me he was there. And safe ... but someplace else than this world." She'd stopped walking again and was bent over the back of Leo's chair with her arms on his shoulders and her head resting on top of his. "Jack Nash cain't live in *this* world anymore. But I could live in his."

It was a little while before Leo understood what she was saying, and when he did his heart just about stopped. He bounded to his feet and stepped behind her, jerked her up and to his own horror as well as hers and JC's, raised his big square hand and slapped her across the face.

Her look was one of stunned amazement, and little JC was so horrified he jumped off the arm of the couch and started to pinch and bite and kick and create whatever mayhem he had to, to rescue his beloved from the clutches of that wicked abuser who up to that moment had been a kind, if boisterous, gentleman in his eyes.

It took some time for Rose and Leo, whose remorse was immediate and who would apologize without ceasing for the rest of his life, to convince JC there was no malice in the slap and that Leo had only struck out at her because of his fear that she might be thinking of harming herself. That was not an easy thing to explain to a 6-year-old boy who saw sin the way his adoptive mother did, in black and white with no excuse accepted. And with the stress of the explanation, the cause was forgotten and never did get the airing it probably should have.

Shortly after that, Claire Louise awoke and called out to the boy to come close the bedroom door so she could get dressed in private. When she walked out into the living room a while later, she was the Claire Louise whom Rose remembered from her youth. That skinny, orange-haired shrew whose tight mouth constantly proclaimed her interpretation of the Almighty's Wrath and who considered herself the embodiment of his punishing angels. Gone entirely was that penitent creature she had portrayed to everyone the day Walter brought her to Jack and Rose's apartment to bow down her proud head and ask their forgiveness. The woman who had sat and prayed while Cynthia was being born, the generous sister who had insisted on buying new curtains and all those pretty presents of fine clothes and candy had just deflated and floated away somewhere, leaving Jack's *"saggy-assed old hypocrite"* in her place.

Without any pleasantries, and without even looking at them she scurried to the cooking stove while her hands busied themselves readjusting some pins in her hair. "Rose has a lot to see to today, Leo. I hope you don't mind if we ask you to leave us alone for a while." And then as an afterthought she said. "And if it's not too much trouble, could you stop by Mary Jean's on your way downstairs and ask her to come get Cynthia? It would be a big help to us not to have her underfoot this morning."

Leo looked at Rose, who shrugged and seemed undisturbed by her sister's demands. So he nodded his head and tromped to the door. "Good morning, *Missus* Bradley" he said grumpily on his way out. "Good morning and good day!" and though she looked across her shoulder at him, she gave no reply, seemingly unruffled by his denouncement of her rude manners. He grumbled all the way downstairs. That woman was exactly what Jack always said she was. For a while, Leo had figured that Jack just didn't want to share Rose with her family and portrayed them as ogres to prove his point. But all

Sister Claire's charitable ways after Jack left must have been put-on. She couldn't have turned into the witch she was this morning overnight, could she? And what was she planning for Rose and Cynthia that needed all that privacy? Rose was terribly confused right now and maybe she was even capable of doing harm to herself if she thought she could find Jack again. Didn't that woman see the state she was in? Didn't she have any sense at all?

He didn't intend to ask Mary Jean *anything*. In the first place, he thought Rose needed Cynthia right now and he knew Cynthia needed her mother. Why was that woman trying to separate them? The longer he thought, the madder he got. By the time he walked through the grocery store door, he was almost foaming at the mouth. And Mary Jean just happened to be there helping Viola stock some shelves and discussing Rose's future. Neither of them had seen the side of Walter Bradley's wife he had just witnessed, and they didn't take his worries all that seriously.

"She's probably just as distraught as the rest of us," Viola said. "It's probably a mistake to judge her by the way she's behaving today. None of us are ourselves after what we've seen Rose go through."

But Leo, who was usually the one defending somebody's quirky actions to the two women, was not at all impressed with his wife's reasoning. "I guess you'll just have to see for yourself." He said with a superior look on his face. "But you'd best look in on Rose now and then. I have a feeling that woman is plotting something and that it's not for our Rosy's good." And then, out of spite, he decided to give Claire's message to Mary Jean. "Claire wants you to come take Cynthia off her hands. She says she doesn't need her underfoot today."

Mary Jean looked at Viola who returned the look and then they both looked at Leo. "She wants me to take Cynthia off her hands?"

"That's what she said."

Viola was shaking her head and her eyes had a worried look. "I think Cynthia needs to be with her mother," she said. "After all she's gone through."

Leo snorted and mumbled something under his breath as he walked to the front of the store.

But Mary Jean started for the back door. "I agree with you, Viola, but I think I need to look in on her anyway. I'll tell you what I think after I talk to Rose."

When Leo heard the door close behind her, he called to Viola. "Come up to the counter, Viola." And when she got there he leaned his hands on the counter and blew out a long breath. "I didn't want to say anything in front of Mary Jean, but I'm really a lot more worried about Rose than I was yesterday."

"Why Leo?—what's happened?" Viola stared at him across the counter but because he was looking down, she couldn't see his eyes. "Look at me, Leo and tell me what's worrying you?"

Then Leo told his wife about Rose's vision in the night and what she said about going where Jack was because since he vanished in her arms she knew he couldn't come back to her in this world.

"Oh dear God!" Viola gasped. "Do you think she's lost her mind?"

"Oh, no, no," Leo frowned and shook his head. "No. She's sane as any of us. But she's lost the will to live, Viola. Even poor little Cynthia can't take the place of that man and now that he's dead and she knows he's never coming back, she doesn't want to live anymore either." Viola thought he looked angry and she asked him why.

"I can understand how Rose feels," he said softly, "I know she and Jack had a very special relationship when there was just the two of them. Lord knows we all had good times together and we loved Jack just about as much as she did. And I know how lonely she's been for him these past 4 or 5 years. She's handled it very well, I think, considering how lonely she's been for him."

Viola was nodding her agreement to every word.

"But I am angry with her too. She's forgetting her little girl needs her as much as she needed Jack Nash. And now I'm afraid she's really thinking about leaving all of us to go with him." He sighed a couple of times and then he blew out another long breath. "We are just going to have to make her see how important she is to all of us. And to Cynthia especially. And I don't know what to think of that sister of hers. She could be a real troublemaker. She's an altogether different woman this morning, Viola. Hard as stone. And domineering! You had to be there I guess, to believe it. I swear she's up to something. I just wish I knew what it was." And then he slapped his hand against the counter. "And I'm mad at God too. He's a pretty harsh God who would take Jack Nash so violently away from Rose after all those years of patient prayers and trust!"

"Oh, Leo!" Viola cringed at his outburst against God.

"I know, Viola, and I'll be properly contrite tomorrow, but right now, all I can feel is Rosy's pain and it just makes me boil!"

Mary Jean knocked on Rose's door and JC came to let her in. She gave him a pat on the head and a smile and then saw Claire at the gas range stirring something in a pan. The coffee pot was percolating and Cynthia was at the table drinking from a glass of milk. JC went back to his seat across from her and watched Mary Jean warily.

"Are you going to take Cynthy away?"

Claire turned and gave him a warning glance. "What Mrs. Turner is going to do or not do is none of your business, Son." And then she nodded to Mary Jean. "Take a seat at the table. Cynthia's just about to have her breakfast."

Mary Jean did as she was told then noticed JC's attention was still on her and that his expression was somber. She smiled at him again but his eyes didn't get any friendlier. So she reached over the table to pat Cynthia's hand and asked her where Rose was.

The child started to answer but Claire interrupted, "Rose is getting dressed, I believe," and sat a bowl of hot cereal in front of Cynthia. "Hurry and eat now, so you can go with Mrs. Turner."

Mary Jean pulled a cigarette from a squashed-up package she took out of her skirt pocket, lit it, and then glanced around for an ash tray. "I know she's got some, Jack smoked like a chimney." JC was glaring at her by then and Claire was turning around in an exasperated circle while her eyes sought the vile receptacle. "Are you sure she hasn't thrown all that sort of thing out? That man's been gone such a long time."

"Rose hasn't ever thrown *anything* out as far as I know," she chuckled ominously, "but she could change all that this morning,"

Cynthia jumped down from her chair and disappeared behind her. Pretty soon she was back and sat a brown glass ashtray on the table beside Mary Jean.

Mary Jean caught her in her arms and gave her a big hug. "Thanks, honey." Then, with a satisfied smile, Cynthia climbed back onto her chair.

"Eat your cereal! Claire ordered. Her sour expression showed how little she appreciated cigarettes at the table, but she didn't put her opinion into words at that moment.

"Rose!" Mary Jean called out and almost instantly Rose came out of the bedroom. She was all dressed and her hair was combed. Mary Jean thought she looked much better than she had the day before. "Well, look at you! You look like you had a good night's sleep."

"Actually, she slept hardly at all." Claire said in a peeved voice, and Mary Jean figured Rose's restless night must have disrupted Claire's sleep as well.

Then Claire handed her a cup of coffee and pulled out a chair for Rose. Mary Jean watched her scrutinize her young sister's face. "She spent the night having *visions.*"

Rose sat down and smiled at Mary Jean. "Did Leo tell you I saw Jack last night?"

Mary Jean cocked her head at Rose and her brow furrowed, "Leo didn't mention that."

"That's because he thinks I'm crazy. They all think I'm crazy, Mary Jean. But I don't care what they think. I know what I saw."

Mary Jean sucked on her Chesterfield for a while and studied Rose's face. Claire snorted and dug her fingernails into the back of Cynthia's chair and the two children stared at each other.

"Well," Mary Jean said thoughtfully, and then she just sat there for want of something to add to that.

Claire snorted again and admonished Cynthia one more time to finish eating. "Mrs. Turner has better things to do than sit here waiting for you."

"Oh, well," said Mary Jean again. "I'm not sure I should take Cynthia away from her Mama today. Rose? What do you think about that?"

"Rose needs her rest." Claire was quick to give her opinion but Mary Jean waited for Rose to speak her piece.

Rose looked up at her sister. "What will JC do all day if Cynthia isn't here?"

"Walter will be here any minute, and he can take JC with him. I think you need your rest and that means you shouldn't have to worry about anything or anybody."

"But maybe Cynthia needs her mama today." Mary Jean stuck her 2 cents in again. "Maybe the little girl needs the security her mama's presence can give her."

Claire snorted and tossed her head. "Cynthia is just a child. Children do as they are told. Children haven't any business questioning what adults decide."

Rose smiled and reached for her daughter, and Cynthia slipped off her chair to go to her mother. But Claire Louise put out her hand and stopped her. "Obviously, anybody having hallucinations isn't fit to make decisions about anything. I have decided Cynthia is to go with Mrs. Turner." And then she turned to face Mary Jean. "If that doesn't suit you, I will ask Viola to come get her. This is not a matter I intend to argue about. The only question is *who* she is going to stay with."

Cynthia was beginning to get scared and Rose, in spite of her lack of determination, was starting to get upset. JC, who sensed Cynthia's fear, was also all tensed up but he wasn't sure who he ought to be angry with. Mary Jean did seem to be concerned about Rose, whom he adored, and that made points for her. Of course, he owed his Ma loyalty and that gave her some points. In the end he was saved the decision when Walter walked into the room and got everything straightened out.

Walter had a newspaper rolled up in his hand and he tapped JC and Cynthia on the head with it while he walked around the table to where Rose was sitting and stood there for a minute looking her over.

"You want some breakfast?" Claire asked.

He shook his head. "I had something at the diner." Then he bent and kissed Rose on the forehead. "You look a million times better this morning. I hope that means you're *feeling* better."

Rose shrugged. "I don't know. I wish I could talk to you about something."

"Well, you know you can talk to me about anything, Rose Sharon. What's the problem?"

Mary Jean got up then, smashed her cigarette into the ash tray, and announced, "I have to be someplace. Come on Cynthia, we're gonna go down to Viola's and get ourselves a candy bar," and she gave a warning glance to Claire Louise, "and we don't care if we didn't finish our breakfast." Then having caught a look of desperation in the boy's eyes, she tilted her head in his direction and spoke to Cynthia. "How about we ask JC to come along? I bet he'll be just plain bored all by himself with nothing but old people to talk to."

Walter grinned at JC and nodded his assent, so with a big smile, the boy left his seat and danced across the room to the door. Cynthia wasn't all that thrilled about leaving Rose and it took some time to convince her it was safe to go away and that her Mama would still be there when they got back.

Once the door had closed behind them, and Claire was pouring Walter a cup of hot coffee, she looked down the table at Rose and suggested in a cloying manner that she tell Walter everything that happened to her the night before. Rose smiled graciously at her sister and then, as if she wasn't aware of Claire Louise's devious intentions, looked deeply into Walter's eyes and shook her head.

"No, Sister Claire. Why don't you tell him?" And Walter watched her smile turn into a smirk as he took his seat on the chair JC had just vacated.

Claire was so surprised at Rose's unexpected sass that she wasn't sure how to handle herself. After a moment of sputtering and glaring, she stomped off in the direction of the bedroom. "I'll do no such thing," she snapped and shut the door firmly behind her.

Rose chuckled, "She has something wicked in mind for me, but I'm not sure what it is and I have to be on guard against her. But Walter! I know you are not one of those superstitious backward people who think everything they don't understand is of the devil." Her face leaned closer to his and her eyes poked even further into his, seeking his soul. "You aren't, are you? We've spent so much time together over the years I think I know how your mind works ... but maybe I'm kiddin' myself?"

Walter returned her stare with bewildered eyes. "What in the world are you getting at, Rose? I feel like I came in at the last scene of the play and I don't have a clue to what the plot is. Have you and Claire had some kind of serious falling out again?"

"I guess you might say that, Walter. But it's not exactly a *falling out* ... it's more like a regurgitation of all the same old crud she's been keepin' in her craw all these years. She never has got it out of her system, I guess. And now that Jack's back..."

"Wait a minute, Rose ... that last remark. What exactly is going on here?"

That was when her expression got serious and she sighed. "I feel like I can tell you anything and you'll not sit in judgment of it, that you'll understand and you'll know that I'm tellin' the truth. I hope I'm right about that, Walter, because if I'm not, then there's nobody I can trust to understand."

"You know that's all true, Rose. I would never doubt what you tell me as truth!"

Rose sighed again and nodded her head a couple of times and then she told him about being awakened in the night to find Jack Nash standing in the living room and the feelings she'd experienced afterwards. When she was finished she just sat there watching his eyes, which hadn't left her face for an instant. And she really did trust him to believe her.

Finally Walter broke his silence with a question. "He didn't speak at all?"

She shook her head. "He just grinned at me. But he did reach out his arms." Then her eyes got wide and her mouth made a pretty little "O". She grabbed Walter's hand and squeezed his fingers. "'Course he talked," she said jubilantly. "He called my name! 'Rose, Rose Sharon,' he said and that was what woke me in the first place!"

Walter was smiling at her. "Of course I believe you, Rose Sharon. There are any number of things in this world that I don't pretend to understand, but I know they happen so I can't doubt them. I don't doubt your experience either. But I can see how Claire would take it. She either thinks you've lost your mind or been visited by the devil. It's not meanness that drives her though, Rose Sharon. It's real fear and concern for you."

But Rose's smile was scornful. "You might not know her the same way Jack and I do, 'cause I am pretty sure it's meanness all right. I was thinkin' she had changed like she said, and she seemed to really care what happened to me and Cynthia for a while, but after I told her about seein' Jack last night, she just changed right back to the old Claire Louise. Just like that. And now I want to ask you a big favor."

He tilted his head at her in a gesture of sincerity. "Anything, Rose."

"I want you to take her home today. I don't want her to stay here anymore."

Walter looked stunned and he cleared his throat a couple of times, but he nodded his head "*yes.*"

"I just don't want to have to deal with her meanness right now. I've got lots to think about and her worryin' over me and bossin' Cynthia around just messes me up. This ain't nothin' personal against her. I mean, she's my sister and I know she wants to do what's best for me. She just don't always know what's best, and I don't want to have to argue with her about how I feel. You see what I mean, don't you?"

Walter got up from the table and stood looking at the bedroom door. "I understand, but I don't think Claire will. Still, I'll get her out of your way, if you're certain that's what you want. Just remember, you'll be alone then Rose, with all the responsibility of taking care of Cynthia on your shoulders. Are you sure you're ready to handle all that?"

"Mary Jean's down the hall. And Viola and Leo are downstairs in the store every day."

"But you'll be alone in these rooms every night."

"I'm not afraid, Walter. I've been here by myself every night for almost five years already!"

"Of course you have, Rose. I just want to be certain you'll be okay."

"I will." She said kind of peevishly and then she reached for the rolled-up newspaper he had carried in with him. She unrolled it and looked at the front page.

"Maybe you ought to wait a few weeks before you read that," Walter suggested hopefully as he reached over to touch her hand. But she was already looking at the picture. It was a shot of the sidewalk and steps in front of the funeral parlor and there were still policemen around and dark puddles of blood smeared on the cement—but the bodies were already gone. The picture made her shudder nonetheless and Walter laid his hand on top of hers. "I can put this up for you until you've had some time to heal, Rose."

"I just want to read what they said really happened." And so he removed his hand and rose to stand behind her, resting both hands on her shoulders. He could feel her body tensing up as she read the story though, and he was wishing he hadn't brought the paper up with him. Actually, he'd done it quite absent-mindedly, having read it in the car just before he came upstairs to her apartment.

"They say the man who got killed was a *mobster.* Is that the same thing as a *gangster*? Like they called that man Dillinger?"

"I guess so."

She went on reading quietly but then she rolled it back up and pushed it toward the center of the table. "They said his name was John Nash. That policeman kept sayin' that too. Jack was never called anything but Jack. I don't know where they got that John thing." She patted Walter's hands that still rested on her shoulders. "But I guess that's a good thing. At least nobody but us will ever know it wasn't some guy named *John Nash* who got shot to pieces on the street and died alongside that big-time crook. Truth be told, nobody else will ever know it was really my Jack."

"Yes," Walter agreed and walked around the table to pick up the paper. "I guess I'll tell Claire now that I want her to come home with me and JC. I'm sure she'll put up a fuss, so we have to hang together in this." Then halfway to the door, he bowed his head, sighed and asked her again. "If you're really sure you want it this way?"

Rose took a deep breath and gazed across the living room and out one of the windows there. There was a faraway look in her eyes as if she was seeing something besides the cloudless blue sky. Walter waited for her to reassure him of her decision and when she remained silent he turned around and searched her face. He saw her rub her eyes with the back of her hand. "I don't want to cry anymore. I think what I want is to go away somewhere. I don't mean forever … I just mean for an hour or two … just a long walk maybe … or a run. I feel like I need to run down our old dirt lane back home, like I used to do when I was a little kid. And I could feel the dust under my feet, and the wind pushin' against me and blowin' my hair around." Then she made a little moaning sound and sagged against the table. Walter took a couple of steps toward her.

"Rose? Are you all right?"

"I cain't be brave, Walter. I cain't be strong. I wish dyin' could come just because you wanted it to."

Then all of a sudden she was on her feet and shouting, "Damn you, Jack Nash! How could you do this to me? All I ever did was love you! You *wasted* all these years … you wasted *me*! And now you're dead! *Dead!* Walter, can you help me get through this? Please, please, please."

And that was when Claire Louise burst through the bedroom door and bounded to her, sideswiping Walter along the way. "See?" she was crying. "See what I mean? She's lost her mind. She's out of her head. We have no choice but to put her in a hospital." She tried to subdue her sister and get her down in a chair, but her efforts to calm Rose were having the opposite effect—she was driving Rose into an hysterical fit. In the end, panting and her chest heaving, Claire cursed the man she detested most in the world. "And every bit of the blame for this lies at the feet of that heathen sinner, Jack Nash!"

Shocking everybody, including himself, Walter came cursing and raging against his wife, leaving no room to doubt with whom his sympathies and interest lay. And that was not lost on Claire Louise, who had the first inkling *ever* that something greater than family ties linked her husband and her sister. Her mouth opened to protest his interference, but she said nothing. Instead, the air went out of her like a spent balloon and she staggered backwards to slump onto one of the kitchen chairs.

It was Walter who managed to calm Rose and to lead her to a more comfortable seat on the sofa in the living room. Then, because he did not yet realize his wife had finally seen through all those years of feigned marital fidelity, he ordered her to run down to Leo's and get a can of soup to heat for Rose Sharon. "She needs something nourishing, some kind of cream soup."

But Rose started retching at the mention of food and ran off to the bathroom. "Don't fix me anything, Sister Claire," she called from there after a few minutes. "I cain't eat anything right now."

And then Walter walked back to the kitchen table and spoke very quietly to Claire. "I think we should take Rose and Cynthia home with us tonight. It's much more comfortable there, and there aren't any memories to plague her so she can get some sleep. And during the day she can go outside and walk in the garden, or sit on the porch and not be bothered by anybody. She can rest and get well there."

Claire Louise stared at her hands on the table in front of her. She turned them over and studied her palms and then she turned them back and studied her short neatly manicured nails. But she didn't say anything.

Walter scowled at her. "Well, Claire? What do you think about my suggestion?"

Claire looked up finally and stared into his eyes but still she waited awhile before she spoke. Rose had come out of the bathroom by then and was at the sink getting herself a glass of water.

At long last, Claire spoke wearily, "I want you to take me and the boy home now." And without waiting for an answer, she stood up and walked into the bedroom leaving Walter to stare dumbfounded at her empty chair.

So Walter approached Rose with his suggestion and she shook her head. "I really appreciate what you and Claire Louise have done for me ... takin' care of me like you are. But I don't want you to put your own life aside for me and Cynthia. We'll be fine. Really!" She spoke through dry, cracked lips that split every time she spoke so she tried not to talk any more than she had too.

"Rose, but you're not taking care of yourself. You're not eating at all. Have you eaten since ....?"

She shrugged. "I haven't been hungry. But I *will* eat."

"You're going to get sick and then who will take care of Cynthia? You have to pull yourself together, Rose Sharon."

And Rose nodded agreeably. "I know, Walter. I will. It's just hard, that's all." Then as an afterthought she added softly. "Jack Nash was a big man. He left a big hole in my heart. It's gonna take some time to fill that up, is all."

"We want to help you, honey. Please let us do this for you. Let us take you into our home and pamper you for a while. That's all. Surely you can't object to that."

"You have helped me. You've helped me every day since it happened. How long have I been like this? How many days has it been?"

"Two. Only two."

Rose's eyes widened and her mouth fell open. "Just two days? O Sweet Jesus! It seems like a week! Are you sure it's only two days?"

Walter nodded.

"What did they do with Jack's body? Have they buried him already? If they haven't—can I have him so we can bury him like a Christian? Where is he? What did they do with him?"

She was starting to get stirred up again and Walter didn't know the answers to any of her questions. "Just calm down, Rose. I'll have Leo call that detective who came out here to talk to you. Leo knows the man and he can get all the information and let us know right away."

"Can you do it now? Can you find out right now?"

At that moment she looked up to see Claire Louise standing by the door with her hat and coat on and her purse in one hand and her valise in the other. "I'm ready to go now, Walter," she said stiffly. "We can pick JC up on the way downstairs, and you can stop and ask Leo whatever Rose wants to know on our way out."

"You're goin' home?" Rose asked incredulously.

"I told Walter I was." She answered tersely.

Rose didn't say anything else, though her thoughts were flitting around like a cloud of gnats. Here was the answer to her prayers and seemingly without any ultimatums from her. How had it happened? Had Claire overheard her tell Walter to take her home? It really didn't matter, she reasoned. Just the fact that she would be alone to carry out her plan was all that was important. Suddenly Rose felt as light as a feather. Everything was going to be fine. And she smiled at her sister who stared grimly back at her.

"I've learned the hard way to mind my own business, Rose Sharon. If you need any help in the future, you'd best go to your friends, the Wesselmans or Mrs. Turner. I don't think you and I will be crossing paths anymore. I must say I am not sorry that Jack Nash is gone for good out of your life. If it had not been for him, you and I would never have been alienated. I loved you so very much when you were a child ... before you got yourself mixed up with the likes of him. May God forgive him. I just can't."

Walter told her to hold her tongue, but she snorted and reached for the door knob. Rose stood staring at her back, feeling knives in her heart at the wickedness of her sister's bitterness toward poor Jack even after he was dead.

"Rose, I feel like this is wrong leaving you alone here. I wish you'd reconsider and let us take you home with us!" Claire Louise was already out in the hall but Walter didn't really understand what had happened. "Please, Rose."

"Do you really think I'd go to Claire Louise's house with her talkin' like that about my Jack? Walter, I'd rather starve in the streets!" And Rose walked around the table to stand in front of him. "You have been a wonderful friend to me and Jack both, and I love you for it. And I love JC like he was my own. But I'd be dishonorin' my husband if I went into that house after she wouldn't even let him set foot in it. And what she just said shows me she wasn't ever really sorry at all."

Then she hugged him and kissed him and he held her for a while, feeling like he'd lost the one true love of his life and his only chance at happiness. "Goodbye then, Rose Sharon. I won't argue with you anymore. But I'll be back tomorrow and we'll do whatever we have to, to get Jack back so we can have a Christian burial the way you want. Whatever you want, Dearest." And then he squeezed her tighter. "You don't know how much I love you. I wish ...." But he didn't tell her what he wished. He just took a deep breath and turned to the door, letting her hand slip slowly out of his along the way.

Leo's inquiry was made that very afternoon and it was learned that Jack Nash was still in the city morgue but would be released immediately to whatever funeral home Rose chose. Leo and Walter made all the arrangements the next morning and on the fourth day Father Paul held a prayer service for them at the mortuary and afterwards presided at the burial in a cemetery not far from St. Mary's Church. Father Paul couldn't give him a Catholic funeral, but he did manage a service that was Christian. He said some comforting prayers to lay him to rest and to soothe Rose Nash's broken heart. The day was misty and gray, as it should have been, with a cold wind out of the northeast across the lake that grabbed Rose's headscarf and almost tore it away. The misty rain turned to sleet even before they left the cemetery, and by the time they were safely back at Leo's Grocery there were patches of ice on the sidewalk.

Walter reluctantly returned to his own home at Rose's insistence, and she and Cynthia went upstairs alone to her shadowy apartment after promising to call him if she needed anything at all.

Apparently she had convinced all of them that she was ready to move on with her life. Even Leo, who had feared at first that she would kill herself or at least hasten a natural death by starving herself, seemed to think she was no longer in danger and was willing to trust her to go it alone.

But there in the dusky chill of her rooms, Rose Sharon Nash began to carry out the plan she had pieced together so single-mindedly once the reality of a life without hope had sunk in.

She found the second of those old yellowed suitcases she and Jack had packed with all their earthly belongings to carry to Chicago back in 1931. Jack had taken its twin with him when he moved out almost five years ago. Now as she caressed it absent-mindedly with her fingers, she wondered where that other suitcase was. Jack had probably burned it. He's such a well-off man now … and Rose bit her lip … or was, anyway. He'd have been embarrassed to keep such an old worn out piece of trash. She struck it angrily with her fist. "You and me, Suitcase! Two old worn-out pieces a' trash!" And she sank down to her knees on the floor beside the bed, overcome with tears of despair. She would have cried a lot longer but all of a sudden Cynthia Jackleen was standing beside her.

"Mama? What's wrong?"

So Rose dried her eyes and smiled as best she could. "Nothin' at all, Buttercup. I was just thinkin' I'd let you go stay at Uncle Walter's for a while. Wouldn't that be fun?" She raised up to sit on the bed and lifted the little girl onto her lap, hugging her close to her chest. "Then you and JC can play together as much as you like!" After a while she leaned away a little—took her daughter's precious little face between her hands and studied her intently. "Truth be told, you sure ain't got much of your Daddy's looks about you, nor mine neither. I guess you're an original all right. But that's good. That's very good! That's the very best thing to be, Cynthia Jackleen. Your own special self. *Your very own special self!"* Then she hugged her close again. "Though I always wished you'd be the image of your Daddy. Oh! He was such a handsome man. A beautiful man! Run get the picture, Sugar."

Reassured, Cynthia kissed her lips and jumped down off her lap. She took the wedding photograph off its nail by the bed where Rose had been keeping it since Jack moved out and brought it to her mother. With their heads together they looked at the handsome young couple and Rose, as she had a thousand times before, pressed her lips to her husband's face and then waited until Cynthia had done the same.

"You go play now, Sugar. I'll be busy in here for a while."

While Cynthia played with her baby dolls in the living room, Rose packed all her clothes … there really weren't many … neatly into the suitcase and then she carefully, lovingly, almost sacramentally lifted the oval framed picture that still lay on the table beside the bed and looked one last time at the image of her husband. "O Sweet Jesus! How pretty we were. How young … just a couple a' babies. And how happy! So much in love we couldn't keep our hands off each other."

She couldn't help smiling, but at the same time she couldn't keep the tears from filling her eyes. She kissed his face tenderly one more time and then pressed the photograph to her heart letting the heat of the love she still felt for him warm her. Finally, she laid the picture, frame and all, on top of her daughter's clothes in the suitcase. Kissing the tips of her fingers, she touched it one last time sending her spirit into it for eternity, and closed the lid of the suitcase.

Then she went into the living room and from a drawer in the library table she removed a writing tablet, some envelopes, and a pencil. In the kitchen again she sharpened the pencil to a fine point with a paring knife and then sat down at the table and started to write the first of three letters. One to Walter and Claire Louise, one to Leo and Viola, and a final one to Cynthia Jackleen, who was still playing house behind her in the living room.

"Sweetie pie, you can go in the bedroom and play with your babies now. I'm finished in there."

"Margie is visiting with Gladys in the parlor, now, Mama." Cynthia explained. But a little while later she disappeared into the bedroom where she kept her own little house in the corner with a bunch of cardboard boxes set up as pieces of furniture.

Rose was well into her first letter and took no conscious notice of her going.

"Dear Leo and Viola, my very dearest friends,
This is the hardest thing I have ever done …" she wrote with her face screwed up with intense concentration *"…saying good-bye to the two of you."*

She stared awhile at that first line and then swallowed hard and continued.

This thing I'm doing you would never approve, I know, and I myself don't really approve of it. I just have to do it anyway because I'm dead inside already and the outside is just taking too long to die. You see, I know Jack is waiting for me somewhere, and this is the only way I can get to him. This letter is just so I can tell you how much I love you both. How much I appreciate all the wonderful things you've done for Cynthia and me and even for Jack when he still lived with me. You mean more to me than my own mama and papa. Truth be told, you are Mama and Papa to my spirit too. You took me to church and helped me learn about God and got my baby girl baptized and got my Jack buried proper. I know you'll see to my burying too. At least I hope you will. I hope the Father isn't too upset about it. It's not how I wanted my life to be. It just happened and I can't seem to fix it. I never seem to be able to get in control of my life. It just runs on by itself like a ball of yarn somebody dropped that just keeps rolling and unraveling and rolling and unraveling without any purpose or order. Now it's just a big tangled mess and I ain't got the heart to struggle with it anymore. A thought just came to me how much the letter like this Mr. and Mrs. Nash left for Jack and his sisters hurt them. I sure never thought I'd be writing that kind of letter. Please forgive me for hurting you. You've been so kind to me and I love you so. Please don't stop loving me and please see Cynthia Jackleen gets to church every Sunday!

Your friend and spiritual daughter, Rose Sharon Nash.

Rose folded the letter and slipped it into one of the envelopes. Then she wrote *Leo and Viola Wesselman* on the front and placed it face down on the table in case somebody entered the room before she was ready.

For a few minutes then, she listened to Cynthia sing to her baby dolls in the bedroom and she smiled contentedly. At least Cynthia didn't miss Jack … would never miss him. But that was sad too. He could have been such a fine daddy. If only he had cared to be.

Then she began to write a second letter.

To Walter and Claire Louise,

Please don't be sad when you get this letter. I'm real sorry to hurt everybody like this, but I can't see no other way out. I've done a lot of thinking and it looks like the only way Cynthia Jackleen will have a normal raising is if you two people do it for me. I'm not able to think of anything anymore but Jack Nash laying in my arms with his lifeblood seeping away and his scared eyes going dead on me. I can't live another day with that going on in my head all the time. I'm giving Cynthia Jackleen to you, Walter and Claire Louise. I love her more than anybody alive and you all being family I think you'll raise her the way I'd want her raised. I give her religious teaching to Leo and Viola because I want her reared in their Faith, which is my Faith now, but I give her to you as your own daughter in everything else. I know you love her as much as I do and Walter, I know you're as fine a man as I ever knew and you will be the best Daddy my little girl could ever want. I've packed her clothes into the valise and I set it on this table and I've put in the wedding picture of her Daddy and me. I want her to have that. Please see she gets it when she's old enough. Also if there's any little trinkets or jewelry or whatnots of mine that she wants, please see she gets it. I ask that you tell her about me and about how much I love her. Remember all the good times to her and if you can think of nice things to tell about me please do that. Keep me in her mind in good ways if you can. And please try to say good words about Jack Nash to her. She needs to know what a fine man he was. How he worked so hard to give me nice things and how everybody loved him and how he could make you laugh no matter how bad things got and how handsome he was. Try not to let her know why he left us though. Maybe you could lie about that if you have to. I know I'm laying a heavy burden on you and I am really sorry about that. If I could think of any other way ... I'd do it different. But I cannot. I guess I should say the whole truth. I think I'm starting to lose my mind, Walter. I do not want anyone to know that, but I guess I should be honest so you know the real reason I cannot raise my baby girl. Of late, I been seeing Jack Nash. He calls out to me and then there he is and when I go to touch him he is gone. I know everybody thinks this cannot be but it seems so real that I think I am no longer in my right mind. Please try to be understanding and please forgive me. I do not want anyone to be hurting like I am hurting so please don't be sad. Walter, you always understood how I felt about Jack. Thank you for that. Please love and care for my little girl.

Your loving sister, Rose Sharon Nash.

Rose folded the second letter into its envelope and wrote *Walter and Claire Louise Bradley* on the face of it. She turned it over on top of the first envelope. As she took the last sheet of paper and made ready to write she noticed the pencil was dull, so she sharpened it again the same as before. When she had finished and was putting the knife away in the drawer, the door to the hallway opened and Leo peeked in.

"Rose, are you all right?"

She was taken by surprise and fear was in her eyes that he might see the letters and question her. "I'm okay," she said, though not very convincingly.

But Leo smiled with relief. "I don't know why, but I just had a peculiar feeling like one of your omens or something. I can't say exactly what I felt, but it was just a notion that something had happened to you. I don't mind telling you, it scared me. Look here," he said and stepped inside. "Look how my hands are shaking!"

Rose nodded nervously, "My goodness, Leo. How awful for you." Then to disguise her own trembling, she stood up and looked toward the sink. "Would you like a glass of water to settle your nerves?"

"Oh no, Liebchen. I don't want to disturb your writing. I just wanted to make certain you were okay." Then he looked around the room. "But how is Cynthia?"

Rose stood there with one knee on the chair and fiddled nervously with the pencil. "She's playing with her dolls in the bedroom."

Leo smiled, "Oh yes, I can hear her singing now." He seemed torn between staying and going. "You feel better now that the funeral is over, Rosy?"

Rose closed her eyes and shrugged and then she felt herself swaying and her eyes popped open as she struggled to restore her balance. "I feel numb, Leo, like when your arm falls asleep at night sometimes and you can't feel it anymore. Only it's my whole body that feels like that. "

Leo's big square face melted like a marshmallow in a flame and the sadness conveyed in his expression almost destroyed Rose's resolve. "Leo, dear Leo!" she crooned and her voice cracked on the verge of tears and then her eyes started streaming. "Please don't hurt for me. I can barely stand my own tears."

"You want to talk about it, Rose Sharon? I can stay and listen as long as you need me."

"It's too late to talk …. What I mean is it's too late to talk *today*." She was sure her nervous state would warn him of what she was planning and she strove desperately to reassure him of her well-being. "I was thinking I'd lay down for a while and try to sleep. I thought I'd take a drink of that wine you gave me before."

"Did that help you sleep?"

"Oh, yes. I slept like a baby," she lied.

"Well, all right, then. When you're ready to go to bed, why don't you send Cynthia downstairs for some candy? Viola and I will keep her occupied until it's her bedtime or until you decide to wake up. Whichever comes first."

"Sure, Leo. That would solve all my problems. Thank you."

"Well, then," he said and stepped out the door. "I'm so thankful you're okay. It's been a hard day, I know. But at least it's behind you now and you can start to move on with your life. Is there *anything* you need, Rose? *Anything* I can get you?"

"No. I cain't think of anything. But Leo, you might look in on us later, I mean before you close the store. Around dark, maybe? It would be nice if you'd come by then."

Leo nodded and just as he was pulling the door shut, Rose darted around the table and ran to him. She flung her arms around his neck and kissed his cheek. "Goodnight, Leo. I love you."

He was taken aback as he returned her embrace and kiss but not without giving her a curious once-over. "I love you too, Liebchen! Are you sure you don't want me to stay? Or Viola, maybe?"

She shook her head but she was not eager to let go of him. "I owe so much to you and Viola. You've been a papa and mama to me!"

"Don't be silly, Rose—you owe us nothing! You been a joy to us. You been the daughter we never had and you give us a granddaughter. Something we never dreamed God would bless us with. You don't owe us *nothing*. You mustn't think you owe us!" Then he seemed to remember something and hesitatingly, he held her at arm's length and looked at her. "Rose, I didn't know how to tell you this…or even if I should … but Viola and I … we both feel you've a right to know … now." He paused and took a deep breath. "You remember when you first started working in the store right after Jack left? And I told you I didn't think I could pay you enough and then right after that I give you more than double what we agreed on?"

Rose nodded—it was plain that whatever it was, it was really bothering him to talk of it. He searched her eyes and then plunged on.

"A month after he left you, Jack sent me a letter with money in it. Money for you. He asked if I would put you to work and let him pay your wages so he could support you and the baby and you would never know. I didn't want to deceive you, but he made it clear it had to be that way."

Rose started to protest and he shushed her. "There was never a return address and the postmark was Chicago. There wasn't any way to find out where he was, Rose. If there had been, I'd have let you know one way or another and after the first letter, there was never anything in the envelope but the money. And it was always cash. Always the same amount. I continued to pay you what I agreed to and just added his money to it. And so this whole five years, Jack Nash has been taking care of you Rose. He never stopped loving you. I couldn't tell you before because he didn't want you to know. But now you need to know, I think. Viola thinks so too. Were we wrong?"

Rose wasn't sure. Did that change anything? It made her feel less rejected but did it *change* anything? She smiled at Leo though, to reassure him. "I'm glad to know that, Leo. I kinda wish I knew it before. It might have made his goin' easier." She nodded her head, "Anyway, I'm glad to know it now. It means he cared and I'd about given up hopin' for that. Thank you, Leo."

Then she urged him back out the door without seeming too. It was so hard to keep this act up. She was not by nature a devious person and found it difficult to pretend to be something she wasn't. If he wasn't gone soon, she feared she'd give herself away. But he seemed to be convinced that everything was fine and so he patted her arm while he took her hand and put a folded piece of paper into her palm. Then he turned away and walked to the back stairway.

Rose closed the door behind him and went back to the kitchen table to conclude her letters. Before she sat down though she looked at the paper in her hand. Sure enough, it was the letter from Jack that Leo just told her about. She smiled. Who else, but the Wesselmans would hang onto that letter all these years, trusting that someday they could give it to her. She read it and crushed it to her lips and kissed it and then cried awhile. She would put it in with Cynthia's letter, she thought. One day that would mean something special to her, too.

Then she felt her firm resolve begin to break down. Tears were very near the surface and she wasn't at all sure she was doing the right thing anymore. So all those years Jack had been sending money. Taking care of her. Why couldn't he have come to see her? Didn't he ever wonder about his child? He didn't even know whether he had a son or a daughter. Wasn't he ever curious as to how she looked? *"Oh Jack! Jack! You made such a mess of everything!"* And then sadly, *"You sent me money because you were such a prideful man, weren't you,*

Jack Nash? You had to support us out of pride. It wasn't love or regret or anything else but your pride."

But it was a long time before she was at peace enough to write the third letter. This one was so special. It had to speak her heart and it had to speak it to Cynthia when she was old enough to read it and understand. Not to the Cynthia in the bedroom singing to her baby dolls but to a young girl Rose did not yet and never would know. "*O Sweet Jesus! Help me,*" she prayed.

"My dearest Daughter,

By the time you read this letter you'll have formed an opinion of me from the things you remember while we were together and the things your Uncle Walter and Aunt Claire Louise and your Granny and Grampa, Viola and Leo, have told you. I hope it's a realistic opinion and neither sees me as better or worse than I am. I wish I could have spent all these years with you but I am not able to do that. I don't imagine you'll ever really understand why, but it's the only thing I know to do considering the state of my life now. The reason I'm writing this letter is to tell you in a personal way how much I love you. How happy I was when I knew you were on the way and what a blessing it's been living with you and watching you grow up. You were the most beautiful baby ever born and are now the prettiest four-year-old girl God ever made. I know that by the time you read this you will be even more beautiful and so sweet and good that nobody can tell you from God's own angels. I hope you'll always listen to Leo and Viola when it comes to going to church and learning about God and being good and all that. They are your godparents. I chose them because they are such good people and they are as close to you and me as if they were my real Mama and Papa. You can ask Claire Louise about our blood relation. I've got hard feelings about them and shouldn't pass that on to you. You've got more aunts and uncles in Dobbin, Mississippi, and Claire Louise will tell about them too. The only thing in my life till you came was your Daddy, Jack Nash. I loved him since I

194

was a child of five and I never even looked at another man my whole life before or since he left me. He was the most handsome, the most exciting, the most manly man that ever drew a breath. There wasn't a woman or girl who ever laid eyes on him didn't want him for her own, and yet he loved me and wanted me and married me and left all those other ladies to mourn after him. I don't know how I won him, except that God blessed me with him. I need you to know what a fine man he was. He was a hard worker, and he did the meanest kind of jobs when we first come to Chicago just so I could have a house to live in and food to eat and when he finally got a job that paid good he bought me all kinds of lovely things and took me to fancy places. Peculiar as it sounds, your papa thought I was something special and he liked to show me off. Even after he left us, he sent money to Leo every month to see we were well taken care of, though he kept that a secret from me till he died. When Jack Nash finally came back to us, Cynthia Jackleen, he was in the wrong place at the wrong time and some crazy person shot him down in the street. That crazy person was being paid to kill the man who was standing near your Daddy. That's the worst thing that ever happened in my life and with him gone I am no longer a living person. I am dead inside, Cynthia and that's why I'm not able to stay here anymore with you. I just can't live anymore without your Daddy. Please be good for Uncle Walter and Aunt Claire Louise. They love you so much and they are so good to us. But remember you are a Catholic and the only one in our family, ever, so while you may go to church with Sister Claire please go to your own church with Leo and Viola, too. I ask you to keep God always Number 1 in your life. I didn't do that, Cynthia. I put Jack Nash first and that may be why I'm in such trouble now. I tried to make him be God I guess, and no man can live up to that. Please don't forget me and please don't think bad of me. I'm leaving you the only Kodak picture I've ever had of Jack Nash and me. It's our wedding picture in the oval frame that I been showing you every night of your life. Please don't ever lose it. It's all you have to remember us by. I guess that's all there is to tell. I haven't given you

much worthwhile in your life except to love you. That's
about all I had to give anyone. Don't forget Scotty and
Mary Jean. They always loved you too. And Cynthia, if
anybody ever asks you about your Mama, you can tell them
... though your Mama never did much of anything
worthwhile in her whole life, she sure did love your Daddy.
She sure did love Jack Nash! I hope you will love him too,
and I hope you will forgive us both.

Your loving mama, Rose Sharon Nash.

And then, last of all, Rose wrote on the back of the letter she had written to Cynthia, the words of a song that had come to her the night before in a dream—maybe to remind her, when she finally was old enough to open and read it, that on this terrible night, Rose had gone joyfully with her husband Jack, the love of her life, to be together in a better place for eternity.

Rose touched the letter to her lips, breathing her spirit into it, and then folding it, inserted it into the third and last envelope. She remembered to put the letter from Jack that Leo had just given her, inside with it, before sealing it, then she wrote Cynthia's name on the outside and added the words, "When she is old enough to read and understand". Then she sat very still for a while with her hands folded on the table before her, her mind slowly unwinding from the tension and stress of the letter-writing. Across from where she sat was a row of wooden hooks on which hung outdoor clothing, coats, hats, sweaters, scarves and beneath all of that sat a neat row of galoshes. They hung and sat there all year long ... winter and summer ... and now she noticed, for the very first time, Jack's wool cap with the ear flaps down. It was red plaid and he never wore it again after he got his good-paying job. It must have hung there undisturbed these whole five years. How had she ever missed it? She guessed it just got covered up with something over the years. Now it made her sad again and she was so weary of feeling sad.

She stared at it for a while thinking about the last time she remembered him wearing it. The day he told her to get dressed up in her beautiful blue silk honeymoon dress so they could go out that night and celebrate his first real job in more than two years. The job that in the end had killed him. That morning though, he had gone to load and unload trucks all day in the bitter cold with that big, orange-haired man … Jess somebody. She guessed she'd never known his family name in all the time he'd worked with Jack. And for a minute she sat there wondering what had ever become of him. For that matter, whatever had become of Rosy and whatever became of Jack? The times had been hard but the joy of sharing them made them good times … days and nights full of love and hope. Nobody could have told her on that day that she and Jack wouldn't be together forever, loving and laughing and teasing and giving pleasure to one another. Nobody! She'd have laughed in the face of anyone who tried to tell her that, on the last day she saw Jack Nash wearing that red plaid cap with the ear flaps down.

Without being aware she was doing it, she had started singing softly in her sweet, thin soprano voice, giving vent to the sorrow and loneliness she was feeling. It was a love song in a minor key with a sweetly beautiful melody that brought tears to her eyes and a smile to her lips. The song, in its entirety, had come to her just last night in a dream, when she'd finally fallen asleep after lying awake for hours dreading the morning and Jack's funeral and now the words to it were written on the back of her letter to Cynthia. As she sang, she started to sway right where she sat at the table and then, because the spirit moved her, she rose from the chair to circle the room, her body moving like an autumn leaf swirling through the air and drifting to earth on the cadence of her song. Never in her life had she felt so light, so weightless, so at one with the rhythm and the melody. For a time Rose Nash sang and whirled round the dusky old parlor and kitchen of her apartment forgetting entirely all the bad feelings that had only moments before assailed her. Cynthia Jackleen heard the consoling music of her mother's voice and came into the kitchen to stand with her back against the door jamb and stare; her eyes full of admiration and wonder, at her pretty young mother dancing so beautifully, so gracefully with such a happy and serene smile on her face. The song went on and on and the room, lit now only by the reflection of the city's lights on the mist outside the windows began to brighten with a cozy saffron-colored glow. It was so peaceful and so pretty that Cynthia slid down the door jamb to sit on the floor where she was soon lulled into a wonderfully contented nap.

"In the night I hear you call me
Your song comes across the meadow,
Daring me to follow, to follow, to leave this world
The world I know behind me and wander,
And wander among the stars with you…
Then I see you in the moonshine, the starshine
The silver mist that drifts across the high hills and valleys
And with the dawn it settles on the river
And beckons, and beckons me,
Rise and follow you ….
What must I do?
My heart says follow you
Don't count the cost ….
My heart says follow you,
My heart is lost.
So tonight I won't resist you
Your song is too strong for me to turn aside
I love you so madly
My heart is yours I must abide
Beside you, within you,
My heart and soul are yours
My eternity is yours
My life, my love—
I am yours!"

How long Rose danced and sang her song would never be known by anyone. Afterwards, she went to her bedroom, lifted the suitcase off the bed and carried it to the kitchen table where she placed it and arranged the three letters in a neat row alongside, only this time she placed them so the names written on them were topside. She prayed God's blessing upon each of them to ease whatever pain they might bring to the readers. Then she went to the table in the living room, picked up a little music box that Jack had bought her with money from his first big paycheck. She placed it beside the letters and tore a piece of writing paper in half.

"This is for you, Viola. I want you to keep it to remember me and Jack by." And she slipped it under the corner of the lid.

Then she walked here and there through all the rooms of the apartment, searching out a special memory for each of her friends and family.

She took an ornate silver-backed hand mirror, which was also a gift from Jack, and laid it on the table with a note to Mary Jean.

The radio Jack bought her so she could hear and sing along with all the music she loved, was a special gift for Scotty, who loved music as much as she did, and she wrote that in a note giving it to him.

And that was about all she owned that had any monitory value. Then she noticed beside her bed on the table, the shimmering ruby beads of the rosary Mrs. Pulaski had given her when she learned Rose was a new convert on the very morning Jack came back to his old neighborhood. She picked it up and lovingly held it to her lips to kiss the cross. Then she carried it to the kitchen table and tore another piece of paper in two and wrote Leo's name on it, and added "Please use this every day to pray for Rose and Jack Nash who you took such good care of all these years and who really need your prayers now."

One last look around the room showed her everything was finished. There was nothing left to do … except for Cynthia.

Rose went to her then, where she sprawled sound asleep against the doorjamb. She knelt beside her and cradled the child in her arms, rocking her and crooning softly an old lullaby from her own childhood, until the little girl began to stir against her breast and opened her big brown eyes, which looked more contented at that moment than Rose had ever seen them. They smiled at one another and Rose snuggled her closer still singing and still completely at peace.

Finally she ended the song and brushed Cynthia's soft curls back from her forehead. "Sugar," she said as calmly as she was able considering the nervous racing of her heart,

"Grampa Leo made me promise to send you downstairs before it got too late so he and Gramma Vi could give you some candy and visit with you awhile before bedtime. You can tell him your Mama is gonna go to sleep now and you aren't ready to do that yet." She smiled at Cynthia's eagerness to be gone before she even finished her message. "Wait a minute, now. I'm not finished talkin' yet."

Cynthia nodded enthusiastically and danced around her. Rose got to her feet and walked the child to the door. "Ask him to bring you back up in about an hour." And then her expression changed and the strain of the smile she was smiling started to hurt the muscles in her cheeks and her smile became more like a grimace. Instantly her daughter reached up and clung to her waist. She no longer wanted to leave her mother. She had never felt as close to her as she did at that moment and she had no desire to lose that sense of attachment. The passion of her embrace tore at Rose's heart and she wondered if she could complete her plan. If she left Cynthia forever, would the little girl ever stop grieving? Would she ever forgive her?

Rose bent down to kiss her, held her in her arms and kissed her and the two of them clung to each other until Rose realized she was transferring her own fear to her child. She sighed deeply and with some effort was smiling again. She took the child's hand and led her to the sink, above which were several shelves, and she took down a little red enameled cup that stood there next to a stack of dinner plates. She bent down with it to Cynthia's eye level. "Here's 10 cents. You take this and tell Grampa Leo I said you can buy whatever treat you'd like from all the treats in the store. That way you can have your choice this time."

Then she took what was left of her note paper and wrote instructions to Leo. *"Dear Leo, please let Cynthia buy a treat for herself and let her visit with you and Viola for a while. I want to sleep and she still wants to play. You can bring her back up in about an hour if that's okay. I would really be grateful. Love, Rose Nash."*

And then, albeit reluctantly, with the dime clutched close to her chest and the note wrinkled in her fist, Cynthia kissed her mama goodbye and let herself be herded out of the room and down the stairs.

Rose stood at the top with her jaws aching from the effort of smiling and watched until she had reached the bottom and opened the door that led into the grocery store. After giving Rose one final look and catching the kiss Rose blew to her, Cynthia disappeared from view, and a moment later, Viola stuck her head out and looked up to wave at her. "You rest easy, Rose Sharon. Your baby's in good hands." And Rose nodded. "I know," she said, too softly to be heard and turned away quickly to hide the tears that had already started sliding down her cheeks.

But unflinchingly, Rose walked back to the apartment and went inside, closing the door behind her. Then she glanced one last time at the table laden with gifts and messages before turning away and going into the bedroom.

At the bed she lifted a pillow and stared down at the pearl-handled revolver that lay hidden there. It belonged to Mary Jean Turner. She'd kept it in a drawer beside her bed. One day a year ago she'd shown it to Rose after there had been a robbery across the street and she needed to reassure herself of her ability to protect herself and her property.

Rose had forgotten about it until this particular need arose. This need to get out of the world and she'd managed to steal it that very morning before Jack's funeral when, for a change, nobody was paying her any attention. She hadn't had time to check for bullets though, and now she was afraid it might be empty. What would she do then?

With trepidation, Rose opened the chamber and relief poured over her. It was full and she smiled ironically. Hopefully, she'd only need one. Then she hesitated for a moment because the room seemed so warm and pleasant suddenly. Cozy and full of sweet memories. Not at all a room to die in ... death itself seemed remote and out of the question as she let herself gently down onto the edge of the bed and then, on her back, stretched out upon it. She bunched the pillow up under her head and lay there like that for a little while, the gun lying beside her with her fingers wrapped loosely around it.

Her mind didn't seem to be with her body anymore. It seemed to have already begun its journey out of the world. Everything around her was so still, and the reflected light in the room ebbed and flowed and mesmerized her with its flickering as her memories began to play before her like a movie on a screen and she watched herself and Jack and their whole life together pass quickly and continuously up there on the ceiling. While she watched she was aware suddenly of another presence in the room.

"Rose Sharon!" He was really there—pushing her over a little so he could take a seat beside her on the bed, looking down at her with those wicked, teasing eyes as blue as cornflowers and with that rascally grin that bedazzled her. She was so surprised she couldn't speak and she feared reaching toward him lest he vanish again.

But this time he was talking to her. "You're ready to come with me, Rose Sharon?"

"Can I?" She asked studying his beloved face with anxious eyes.

He leaned down to her and there came the shocking realization that she could feel his mouth on hers. His sweet kiss pressing against her mouth and she thought she must already be dead since all the other times he'd come she couldn't touch him at all.

Then he raised up a little and reached across her, laying his hand on top of her hand that held the gun.

"Not with that though, Rose. You couldn't come where I am if you did that and it would leave too mean a memory for our little girl." Then he unwound her fingers from the weapon and took her hand in his pressing it against her breast between their bodies.

"You know about Cynthia?" She hardly dared believe her own ears.

Jack straightened up again and his fingers brushed a coppery colored curl back from her forehead. "I know everything now, Rose. I know that I sinned against you and against her." He took a deep breath. "I know that I wasted what God meant to be a beautiful life with you."

Rose reached up and touched his beloved mouth. Some of his raven-black hair fell forward then framing his face.

"I can't bear it here anymore without you, Jack. I want to be with you."

"Come then," he said and instantly they were gone.

Cynthia Jackleen had not given Mama's note to Grampa Leo. She used the dime to buy two candy bars and a box of crackerjacks from the counter and then after giving him and Gramma Vi each a polite thank you kiss and hug she had run back up the stairs and opened the door to the apartment.

The room was shadowy, lit by the misty light outside the windows and Cynthia hurried through the kitchen to the bedroom door. She called to her Mama but there was no response.

Then she saw the man sitting on Mama's bed and Mama lying there beside him. Cynthia ran around him to the head of the bed so she could see the man's face and be close enough to talk to Rose. Just as she reached that position Cynthia saw him bend down and kiss Rose. Mama looked so happy and more beautiful than she'd ever looked before. Then the man raised his head and Cynthia was looking into his eyes. They were bright blue and bottomless and they swallowed her up in their depth so she could only stare at him.

But she knew right away who he was. He was Jack Nash, the man in the picture. The man Mama always told her was her daddy.

Wildly excited by then, she tried to talk to them. Called out to Mama … even patted her arm and finally tugged on the man's vest that was hanging open, but neither of them would acknowledge her. Wouldn't even look at her. It was beginning to scare her and she started to whimper when suddenly without any warning at all, Jack Nash was gone and somehow, in some mysterious, unfathomable way, Mama was gone with him!

A short time later, when Leo opened the door from the hall, a fleeting sense of impending doom flickered across his brain. There was an eerie silence and in the midst of it, a faint whimpering that he couldn't identify. With dread, he called out to Rose but there was no answer. Only the whimpering became more persistent.

"O my God! Don't let it be true!" he prayed as he forced himself to look into the bedroom.

He couldn't be sure. Perhaps Rose was only asleep. He noticed than the whimpering came from a tiny form curled up on the cot across the room. He could see the blackness of her wide open eyes and the terror that filled them even in this dim light. Should he turn on the light? Or would it make bright a memory it would be better Cynthia not have?

He went to her and lifted her in his arms. "Let's go down and see Gramma Vi,"

Cynthia struggled against him. "Mama," she whimpered. "I want my Mama." And by then she was crying openly.

"Let's see Gramma Vi first. Then we'll see Mama." And although it wasn't easy, he managed to hold her long enough to get her out of the apartment and down the stairs. She slipped away from him at the door to the grocery but he caught her again and firmly carried her to Viola.

"Viola, there's some bad trouble. Please get Cynthia something to keep her occupied while I see what has to be done."

Viola took the little girl and from the stricken look on Leo's face discerned what he had seen upstairs. "No! Dear God!" she breathed trying not to let her growing panic disturb Cynthia further.

Leo nodded grimly and rushed back up the stairs. This time he turned on the kitchen light and saw the suitcase and the letters and the several items set neatly upon the table. His body sagged back against the door while his brain fought to deny the inevitable.

It was an endless time before he ventured again to her bedroom and he switched on the electric ceiling light as he entered and took in the scene before him. Rose lay pale and cold. It was obvious her spirit had taken flight from her body. Leo had never seen death so plain before. Beside her on the bed was a gun … small and pearl-handled … he thought he recognized it as something Mary Jean kept for protection. And he heard himself moan her name, rather than consciously speak it. Then he fell to his knees on the floor beside her. "How could you let this happen, God? How could this happen? Why didn't you let me know it was coming so I could have stopped it? Why didn't I see it coming? Why didn't I stop it?

His self-rebuke went on and on while he sought some sign of life in her. At last he had to reconcile himself to the facts as they lay before him and at the same time he saw the futility of self-blame and he closed his mouth and took her small hand and held it between his palms, praying that he might forgive himself … forgive her … forgive Jack Nash … forgive God!

"Well, my sweet little Rose Sharon. At last you are at peace." He looked into her face and saw that it was true. She looked serene and happy. So he kissed her cold hand, which already looked like pale marble, and replaced it tenderly upon her chest. Then with his face pressed against the cool chenille spread, he gave into his feelings and wept bitterly.

On the morning of Rose's funeral, the sun broke through the gloom that had settled on the city the day Jack was buried. It shone golden and warm and a gentle Indian summer breeze rustled the last of the colored leaves still clinging to the trees in the cemetery, while the leaves that had already fallen crunched underfoot. The sorrowful little band of mourners wound their way past granite tombstones of all sizes and shapes and ages until they stood almost in the same spot they had stood only days before. The earth that covered Jack's grave was still fresh and now there was a newly dug grave beside his, into which they lowered the coffin holding Rose's remains.

Then good Father Paul read from his Bible and spoke some comforting prayers, at least they were meant to comfort, while a youthful altar boy in his starched white blouse atop his long black gown, rhythmically swung the incense burner perfuming the air around them. Nobody who watched and listened felt much better after hearing the words anyway. They had each loved and cherished Rose in his or her own way, but each had cherished her so deeply that losing her … especially by her own hand … was beyond comforting. Eyes, red and swollen from days of weeping remained dry at this, the final contact they would ever have with her in this world. Someday, perhaps, they would remember her without such unbearable sorrow, but for now the sorrow hurt like an open wound … too raw to touch … to gross to look upon, and hearts were too broken to ever think they could be mended and whole again. Rose had stood there with them those few days earlier, her eyes swollen and streaming tears. And now they were leaving *her* there. Going home without her. Laying her finally and eternally in the cold dark earth beside her one and only love, Jack Nash.

Claire was trembling so uncontrollably she feared she might lose her ability to stand and grabbed Walter's arm which she discovered was trembling right along with her. "Walter, I don't want to leave her out here all alone. How can we just go away and leave her here?"

But nobody answered her and after a while, the mourners turned away and walked back to their cars. Leo and Viola stopped for a few moments to converse with Father Paul before he and the altar-boy were whisked away in the parish car driven by a parish member who regularly chauffeured the priest on church business. Mary Jean took Scotty's arm and he walked with her to Leo's car, where he helped her into the backseat and then left the cemetery on foot to walk home by himself—his three companions didn't know exactly how far away the apartment he shared with his grandmother was but he didn't give them an opportunity to suggest he ride with them anyway; he chose not to make them feel the need to do that. It was simpler just to walk away without any conversation.

Mary Jean rode with Leo and Viola, and all three of them spent that ride in silent contemplation. Following in their own car, Walter and Claire Louise each stared wordlessly forward and the only sound was an occasional sniffle that Claire wasn't able to stifle.

The objective of their mission now was to remove the rest of Rose's things from her apartment. They had already taken the suitcase and letters and gifts she'd left them. Claire Louise and Viola had packed up all her personal things and they were already down at the Bradleys' to be given either to Cynthia or to Claire's church. All the furniture belonged to Mary Jean, so this was just a sort of mop-up operation—one last look around to make sure nothing was left behind.

Never mind that a plethora of tears had already been shed, and their resolve was to be quick and unemotional: when they finally walked into the kitchen, they found themselves standing around awkwardly and without purpose, while their eyes took in, for the last time, the familiar room that seemed so painfully empty now and almost supernaturally quiet.

Claire Louise's tears began to flow with renewed vigor. "I'm going to have to get through this quickly," she pleaded. "I can't bear to be here with her gone."

Leo nodded his understanding. "Isn't it remarkable the way that girl lit up everything around her? Except for the heartbreak she suffered after Jack left, she always made us look on the bright side." He sighed, "This is a dark and dreary room without her—and lonesome."

Walter was rubbing his eyes with his handkerchief. "Right," he spoke in a husky, breaking voice. "Let's make this quick or else I won't want to leave at all. I may decide to move in and try to hold onto whatever of her spirit she may have left here."

Claire grimaced and turned away, hoping that nobody besides herself saw anything but a brother's love in his remark.

And then for a while, each of them wandered aimlessly through the rooms, unhappy being there but dreading the end of their mission.

Walter found a toothbrush in the bathroom, and Claire told him to drop it in the waste basket. There was a writing tablet with some pencils and envelopes in the drawer of the library table that Claire asked if Viola thought Scotty might like to have. Viola gave her a nod so Claire handed them over. The little red enameled cup was discovered with its treasure of nickels and dimes, and Walter took that for Cynthia as a keepsake.

They seemed to be finished then. Rose and Jack and Cynthia Jackleen Nash appeared to have been wiped off everything that remained in the little apartment. It was no longer anybody's home ... just an empty set of rooms with nothing to remind them that a man and his wife had lived and loved there ... begun a family there ... separated and cried ... suffered years of loneliness and patient waiting and finally died there. Nothing left to recall to mind that life had begun and ended for a family in those barren rooms. Rose and Jack Nash had been scrubbed away, dusted off, and swept out and all that remained were two lonely rooms and a bath and one used toothbrush in a wastebasket. Nothing left of them except some cherished memories in the hearts of their friends.

Those loving friends and family, who now avoid looking too closely at one another as they file out the door and down the stairs because they don't want to cry anymore.

Back downstairs in the grocery, the sadness lifted a bit when Claire Louise and Walter paused to embrace Mary Jean and bid her good-bye before Leo and Viola walked them to Walter's car and the Wesslemans and the Bradleys found themselves unable to do any more for a while than stare at one another without words.

Eventually, Walter broke the silence, "I can't think of anything more to say," he admitted in a soft voice, and turned to look at his wife with a shrug. Claire Louise shook her head. "Walter and I just want to thank you for all you've done for Rose and Cynthia. You've been very good to them—and—and," she was obviously overwhelmed, and both Viola and Leo came to her rescue. "Rose and Cynthia are our family." "And Jack too, and we didn't do anything for them that wasn't returned a hundred-fold." "They brought only joy and love into our lives." "We are the ones who were blessed." and finally, "Gott in Himmel!—nobody has to thank us for anything!"

They denied the importance of their generosity in turns until Claire sighed and reworded her remark.

"I'm sorry—I know I said that wrong. I just—I just" she gave them a look of frustration and then turned away. "I can't talk any more. I need to go home now." Walter rushed to open the car door for her, talking as he went, "But we'll be seeing both of you often." he promised. "Rose was very firm about Cynthia going to church with you and wanting her to stay close to her Gramma and Grampa." Claire crawled inside the car and Walter closed the door quickly. "We'll have lots of time to visit once we get—once we recover from this ..." he was struggling to find the word he wanted and he settled finally for "this god-awful tragedy."

The Wesselmans agreed.

"We will come to see Cynthia. And you know how to get to our place too," Leo reminded them, "So you come on over whenever you feel like it. Please don't think you have to wait for an invitation."

And Viola added, "We are all family now and we won't worry about formalities like invitations."

Walter smiled and walked up to them, embracing Viola and Leo in turn before going back to his side of the car. "You Wesselmans are good people," he spoke from his heart. "Rose and Jack were lucky to know you and so are Claire and I. We are going to be one big family starting right now. But we've got to get home to Cynthia and JC now so they know they haven't been deserted."

"Right!" said Leo, "And Viola and me got to get our minds on stocking shelves or something. We'll see you folks real soon." Then he took Viola's arm and the two of them turned away toward the store. But before Walter could take his seat and close the door, Viola shook off her husband's hand and hurried back to give Walter one last hug. Then she backed off and watched him pull away from the curb and disappear into the traffic down the street. "God bless you both and the babies too," she called though she knew he couldn't hear her and then with tears streaming down her cheeks again, she climbed the few concrete steps to catch up with Leo who stood waiting for her at the door. "Oh, Leo!" she sobbed and he slipped his arm around her and just held her awhile. "I know, Liebchen. We are never going to stop missing her. Rose was a true daughter to us. We will pray for strength to get through this, but it is going to be lonesome without her and Cynthia to light up our little grocery store." He kissed her cheek. "Come inside now, Viola, we have a lot of praying to do."

Mary Jean was waiting at the counter and she confronted Leo as soon as he stepped through the door by waving the Closed sign at him to show she'd already taken it out of the window.

"Did anybody ever tell you how she died, Leo?" She had been horrified to learn that Rose had stolen her gun as a suicide weapon but she had been assured that the gun hadn't been used after all. Now she was anxious to know how Rose Sharon had ended her life.

Leo shook his head and shrugged his shoulders, "Nobody could say for sure." He tried in vain to move away from her. He wanted to do something constructive. Empty crates ... stock shelves ... move something. But Mary Jean was determined; she pursued him like a hawk after a mouse. Eventually he found himself at the end of an aisle with no place to turn so he had to give up. He stared at the shelves around him, giving the impression this was what he'd been looking for all the time and to his relief found some cans of peas mixed in with the stewed tomato display. With a satisfied grunt, he busied himself restoring order while he considered how best to answer his landlady's question. It took him awhile. She waited.

"They told me the autopsy didn't come up with anything at all. Rose Sharon was just *dead*, they said." He looked Mary Jean straight in the eye then and she saw *his* eyes were still very sad and very wet. "They said it didn't appear to be suicide at all and except for the letters, they wouldn't have considered suicide—on the death report, they just called it 'undetermined.' All they could say from what their autopsy showed was that she died of natural causes." He shrugged again. "Apparently, her heart just stopped."

"But how could that be? Rose was so young and she was perfectly healthy," Mary Jean argued. "Wasn't she?"

Leo shrugged again. He finished sorting the canned goods before he turned to look at her, shaking his head. "She was before Jack Nash died in her arms. I think maybe her heart broke then. I think maybe she died of a broken heart."

The End